THE RAILWAY CONSPIRACY

ALSO BY THE AUTHORS

The Murder of Mr. Ma

THE

CONSPIRACY

JOHN SHEN YEN NEE

SJ ROZAN

Published by Soho Press, Inc.
227 W 17th Street
New York, NY 10011
www.sohopress.com

Library of Congress Cataloging-in-Publication Data

Names: Nee, John Shen Yen, author. | Rozan, S. J., author.
Title: The railway conspiracy / John Shen Yen Nee, SJ Rozan.
Description: New York, NY : Soho Crime, 2025.
Series: The Dee and Lao mysteries ; 2
Identifiers: LCCN 2024042631

ISBN 978-1-64129-792-9
eISBN 978-1-64129-661-8

Subjects: LCGFT: Detective and mystery fiction. | Historical fiction. | Novels.
Classification: LCC PS3614.E267 R35 2025 | DDC 813/.6—dc23/eng/20240923
LC record available at https://lccn.loc.gov/2024042631

Interior design by Janine Agro

Printed in the United States of America

10 9 8 7 6 5 4 3 2 1

EU Responsible Person (for authorities only)
eucomply OÜ
Pärnu mnt 139b-14
11317 Tallinn, Estonia
hello@eucompliancepartner.com
www.eucompliancepartner.com

John Shen Yen Nee dedicates this book to SJ Rozan.
SJ Rozan dedicates it to John Shen Yen Nee.
And that's that.

PROLOGUE

Beijing, 1966

It seems every tale of Dee Ren Jie begins with a fight.

Dee himself is the most patient and just of men; yet in some places and in some times, patience and justice are not the virtues most prized by some men. In those times and places, preparing oneself for the rigors of physical combat is the way of wisdom, and Dee is also wise.

In years to come, men looking back on China in our day, as I am looking back now on England in an earlier one, may conclude that was how things were with us. I cannot say.

But with certainty, I can say this: it was how things were in London in the late summer of 1924.

CHAPTER ONE

London, 1924

"I'm just telling yer, Mr. Dee, and with respect, o' course, I don't much like this place yer've brought us to. A mist so thick I can almost grab 'old of it, and trees way over me 'ead, with 'oo knows what's walking around in 'em. Monkeys and such, I'll warrant! And the smell in the air—it ain't natural, sir. With nary a streetlamp to be seen. Just shadows and the shadows o' shadows. And deer! Deer, Mr. Dee! With great sharp 'orns. Could we not do our business elsewhere, is all I'm asking."

"We could do our business anywhere, Jimmy." Judge Dee, unseen, answered the complaint of young Jimmy Fingers from deep in the darkness under a massive oak. "The men we've come to intercept, however, insist on doing theirs here. Don't worry. If all goes well, I'll have you back on the streets of London within the hour."

This promise was a touch superfluous, as we had not left London. To reach the streets, one would have had merely to stroll ten minutes from the Richmond Park clearing, in which we stood. Our errand had not brought us very far into that greensward, certainly not far enough to encounter the King's deer, with or without great sharp horns. The damp and loamy scent Jimmy protested was, in fact, that of man's original

Arcadian state, in contrast to the scents Jimmy preferred and that awaited us beyond the park's walls: the smoke of coal fires and the exhaust of buses and motorcars, the aromas of cooked meat and horse dung and whatever was floating at the moment in the Thames. As for monkeys, the nearest were twenty-five kilometers away, asleep in their cages at the Regent's Park Zoo.

"Jimmy," I said, speaking in English as Dee had, for admire Dee as he did, the lad had yet to learn a word of Chinese, "does an evening in the greenery not suit you?"

"That it don't, Mr. Lao. The dark is too . . . dark! And things is rustling—" He jumped as a thing rustled. "I 'aven't spent a great deal o' time in such places, see. Parks and trees and all don't 'ave much to offer a man engaged in my line o' work."

Although Jimmy had for a time been, and was now again, in the employ of Dee, Dee had lately been absent from London for some months. In April, he'd sailed for China, and none of us—myself, Jimmy, or Sergeant Hoong, who completed our foursome here in the clearing—had been sure he would return, and if he were to do so, when. Hoong had reverted to his shopkeeping, with which he claimed to be content. I could not say as much for my sentiments toward my own life lecturing in the basics of the Chinese language at the University of London. Classes, when I took them up again, I found no more stimulating than when I first began them upon my arrival in London the year previous. For his part, Jimmy Fingers asserted, whenever we three met for a bowl of noodles—to his credit, the young man had developed quite an appreciation for the cuisine of my homeland during his first stint in Dee's service—that he was *tiptoeing the straight and narrow, that I am, sirs*. However, according to Hoong's intelligence, Jimmy had happily resumed his career as a pickpocket. Pickpocketing, of course, requires pockets to pick, which are hard to come by amid tall trees and things that rustle.

"Lao," said Sergeant Hoong now, interrupting my reverie, "you are lollygagging. Do you intend to take advantage of our time here to learn this skill, or have you so quickly lost interest in improving your fighting technique?"

Jimmy laughed. "Lollygagging! Mr. 'Oong, sir, that's a fine bit o' English yer've picked up there!"

I was less amused. "I am not 'lollygagging,' nor anything like it. I've practiced your one-inch punch until my knuckles bleed, and all I have to show for it is a sore shoulder."

"And bleedin' knuckles, o' course," Jimmy put in helpfully.

"In fact," I said, "I'm beginning to question the value of this vaunted skill. How much force can actually be exerted by a blow of such a short distance?"

Jimmy tilted his head thoughtfully. "A fair question, that."

Hoong, with a disdainful glance at us both, walked through the mist to a small statue of Cupid that stood at the center of the clearing. It was a silly, frilly thing, all curly locks and flower garlands. Pulling his fist back an inch from the sculpture's round belly, Hoong marshalled the energy of his body from the bottoms of his feet up through his torso, focusing it all into his forearm—or so he instructed me every time I attempted this technique. With a low cry (we were, after all, waiting in this place to create an ambush) of "Chuen ging, inch power!" Hoong thrust his fist an inch forward and made contact with the stone.

Cupid toppled to the ground.

"Oh," I said, rather weakly.

"Oh!" marveled Jimmy Fingers, with more strength.

"Oh," snapped Dee. "Hoong, really." He stepped forward from the oak's inky shadow.

Any man unprepared would have been terrified into paralysis by seeing Dee, in this form, appear between ancient trees at midnight. The black of his tapered trousers and tunic was echoed in his leather gloves and tall boots and in the silk cape, scalloped like bat's wings, that billowed behind him. Short, sharp horns protruded from his head, and his face, with features somewhere between a devil's and a dream-fiend's, wore a fierce and evil leer.

However, we three had seen Judge Dee costumed as Springheel Jack, the Terror of London, on previous occasions, and thus—with the exception perhaps of a tiny step back taken by Jimmy—we were not alarmed.

Dee, from behind the monstrous mask, gazed at the prone statue. "I hope you've only dislodged the thing and not damaged it," he said. "What would your father say?" Sergeant Hoong's father had been tutor to Dee and his younger brothers back home in Yantai. "I recognize," Dee went on, "how exasperating it can be to deal with Lao. Still, you must control yourself better."

"Exasperating?" I said. "I must protest! I was in no way the cause of this insult to Eros."

"I've been given to understand," Dee said, walking over the soft grass toward the statue, "that you and the young Lord of Love have parted ways."

I sighed. "We are perhaps more distant than we once were," I conceded. "Women, I fear, continue to bewilder me."

"Ah, Lao, but that in itself may be the difficulty. Women are no different from men except in the obvious respects. If you assume that a woman will behave in an unpredictable manner for abstruse reasons, you may count yourself bewildered not by her but by your own expectations."

"You yourself are so abstruse in your commentary, Dee, that I might almost believe you are mocking me."

I could not see Dee's face behind the mask, but I was sure it wore an entirely false air of wounded innocence.

"I must protest also," Hoong said as he bent to the fallen Cupid. "A rebuke from you, Dee, is almost more than I can bear."

"Yes, I'm quite sure of that," Dee said drily, joining Hoong on Cupid's other side. "Yi! Er! San!" On Dee's count of three, the two men, working seamlessly together, righted the stone image of that most fickle of deities.

"Well!" said Jimmy Fingers. "I just seen something I never seen before—two men 'oisting a statue with neither rope nor chain. Mr. 'Oong, Mr. Dee, you gents are full o' surprises. You too, Mr. Lao," he added generously, if disingenuously. "But look 'ere now. If we find ourselves at the point o' knocking over angel statues, it's certain we've been in this place too long. Mr. Dee, your Russian and his pal 'ave likely changed their minds. 'Ow about we scarper and get ourselves a pint?" In the moonlight, Jimmy's face held a hopeful cast.

"I think not, Jimmy," said Dee. "I hear them now." He held up a hand.

Jimmy cupped his palm behind his ear. "I don't—"

Dee lifted a warning finger to him.

I listened intently, though I could hear no more than Jimmy.

Hoong stood perfectly still, then turned to Dee and nodded.

Dee motioned us forward, and as one, we crept to the line of trees separating this clearing from the next. My heart pounded, thoughts of the matter to come banishing the banter of a moment before.

Three days earlier, after Hoong, Jimmy, and I had welcomed Dee back to London with surprise and joy, Hoong, at Dee's request, had begun discreet inquiries among certain people of his acquaintance, requesting information about an impending transaction in which Dee had taken an interest. Reports had come back that the business was arranged to take place tonight, in Richmond Park, in the small clearing just beyond the larger one where Cupid dwelt.

It was this transaction we had come here to stop.

CHAPTER TWO

Dee and Hoong had both indicated that the men we sought were nearby. However, to my eye, peer though I did into the clearing, nothing appeared but crisscrossing shadows of trees, thrown by the moon onto the grass.

Jimmy must have seen the same as I; his skepticism could be read in his squint and the twist of his lips. Hoong and Dee, however, remained tightly focused on a pale stand of birch edging the far side of the clearing. Seeing their interest, I tapped Jimmy's hand and nodded in that direction. We leaned forward to peer through the oak and alder, and I saw a deeper shadow shift beyond the white trunks. As we watched, an enormous shape began lumbering through the tree border and onto the turf. Jimmy stiffened. "Mr. Lao!" he choked. "It's a gorilla! Run!"

I clasped his wrist as he turned to flee. "Don't be absurd!" I whispered fiercely. "Dee has given you a task. You cannot complete it if you're halfway across London."

Dee hissed a whispered, "Silence!" The shape stopped, cocking its head as if listening. We all four froze. Apparently, it found things acceptable, for it started shambling forward once more. Jimmy clearly remained unconvinced, and to myself I admitted I saw his argument. Not a gorilla, this, but perhaps a bear? It also, I was forced to recognize, evoked the yeren, a semihuman creature said to dwell in Hubei province and which, until that night, I had never deemed anything other than mythical. I was at the point of wondering whether it was worth considering the possibility it was real when my attention, and the attention of my companions, was drawn by a new shadow darting along the edge of the clearing.

If the large shape evoked a bear, this smaller one, although advancing on two legs rather than four, put me in mind of a fox. Sinuous and graceful, it made no unnecessary movements. It circled the clearing soundlessly, remaining in the shadows of the trees. Pressed, I would have said this form was waiting for the larger to achieve the clearing's center.

A moment later, I was pleased to see my assessment of the situation proven correct. Let Hoong say what he might, I was not entirely lacking in martial skill, which begins, as Dee had often instructed—repeating the words of Sun Tzu—with knowing one's enemy and oneself.

The larger shape, arriving in the center of the clearing, turned about, plainly searching for something. When its back was to the fox-shadow, that form danced silently forward, tapped the other on the arm, and leapt nimbly back. The large shape—now, it was clear to see, neither gorilla nor bear, and certainly no yeren, but a man—whirled, roaring.

The two stood facing each other. The fox-shadow, now that it had stopped moving, similarly resolved itself into a man: a small, thin one with a sardonic grin on his sharp, Asian features.

"You lucky I don't kill you, Isaki!" the bear-man growled, dropping his arms from the boxing stance he had assumed. His face was European and his rumbling English was heavily decorated with the accents of Mother Russia. "You try to scare me for joke?"

"Try?" the other repeated. "Voronoff-san, you don't even make it difficult." This voice was higher than the bear-man's. The faint accent in his otherwise excellent English and his mocking use of the Japanese honorific pinpointed his origins to the Land of the Rising Sun.

"Someday, I squash you," Voronoff, the Russian, grumbled. "Here, now you take this, go away." From his overcoat, he withdrew a parcel, perhaps a foot long, wrapped in butcher's paper, and tied with string. He handed it to the fox-man, Isaki, who took it and offered in return a scornful bow.

As soon as the exchange had been made, Springheel Jack sprang, as it were, into action.

Into his pocket Jack reached, grasping a handful of something and hurling it at the pair. As the small round objects hit their targets, smoke burst out of them with pops and hisses. These were gunpowder-packed ball bearings Dee had prepared earlier in the day. Voronoff swatted as if at bees, while Isaki crouched and whipped his head back and forth, searching for the source. Before he could locate it, Jack leapt between the men and attacked them both, using a right and a left double palm, striking the center of each man's chest. Isaki was sent flying across the lawn and Voronoff reeling backward.

"'Oong!" Jack cried. "Ye might take an interest in that big bear-like villain on me left!"

Hoong, not small in stature himself, advanced on Voronoff. Voronoff, recovering his balance, reared back and tried to pounce on Hoong. I watched Hoong shift his body from left to right, executing a triple combination of uppercuts to the body and jaw of this giant. Voronoff staggered but did not go down.

While Hoong was occupied with Voronoff, Isaki leapt up from the turf. Grinning and reaching beneath his own cloak, he drew a katana, the long single-edged sword of the samurai.

"Oi!" said Jack. "Yer a ronin, then! A killer for any man's 'ire. Selling yer services—that ain't no 'onorable way to act!" This taunting served to anger Isaki, which I could only imagine was the object, as Dee had often said that angry men could be counted upon to make mistakes. Pointing the finger at Isaki for being a ronin was redundant and, I thought, a touch unsporting. The samurai class having been abolished by edict in Japan more than a half-century earlier, all those who continued to follow the Bushido were, by definition, ronin, masterless. Those who chose to live by the sword had no choice now but to sell its services.

Isaki, in a fury, raised his katana to sweep at Jack. Jack spun around and, from another deep pocket, launched a group of larger, solid iron pellets at a high velocity. They flew through the smoke and mist. Isaki, with the skills of a trained warrior, easily deflected the first three. The fourth, however, cracked him squarely in the forehead. He leaned on his sword, muttering, "Ush, very good," to acknowledge Jack's skill, and then shook his head and jumped back into a ready stance. He and Jack circled one another, attacking and parrying, searching for an opening.

While watching Hoong and Jack skirmishing with Voronoff and Isaki respectively, I endeavored to fulfill my own charge: to summon the Metropolitan Police. I'd been given a bobby's whistle by Dee for the purpose, and now filled my lungs with air and emptied them into it as forcefully as I could.

The shriek of the whistle was earsplitting and unmistakable. I blew again, confident that any bobby within a quarter mile would hear me.

However, Isaki also heard me. The anticipation of a visit from the force apparently not being to his liking, he snatched up one of Jack's deflected pellets from the clearing and sent it sailing toward me. I saw it coming and ducked. In retrospect, this was not the proper response, for had I remained upright, the pellet would have bounced ineffectually off my waistcoat. Instead, it came crashing into my cheek. The impact caused an intake of breath, and with the breath came the bobby's whistle, which lodged in my throat, and then I could breathe no more.

CHAPTER THREE

I emitted a series of soft and admittedly unattractive choking chirps, sounding like nothing so much as the parakeets that Chinese gentlemen held in cages as they walked around town. My hands went uselessly to my throat, where the whistle was wedged tight. I could do nothing for myself, and as I felt my lungs demand I supply them with air immediately or suffer the consequences, I was sure that my companions, occupied as they were, could not be depended upon to do anything for me either. I began to fear my last sight would be the waving tree shadows of a small clearing in Richmond Park, London.

But Jack, with Dee's preternatural awareness of his surroundings in all circumstances, glanced in my direction. Abandoning the fight with Isaki, he somersaulted toward me and, upon landing, delivered to my midsection the very one-inch punch with which Hoong had toppled Cupid. The whistle flew from my throat. Through my suddenly clear airway, I pulled in as much sweet Arcadian air as my lungs could hold.

I was doing the same a second time when Voronoff, taking advantage of Jack's brief distraction, shoved Hoong to one side and, with a roar, threw himself upon Jack. The Russian knocked Jack to the ground, grasped his throat with one massive hand, and attempted to choke him into oblivion.

It was time, then, for me to return the favor of a rescue. I gathered the energy of my body from my feet to my forearm and thrust a one-inch punch into the Russian's side.

It had no effect.

No, that statement is inaccurate. It had the effect of turning Voronoff's attention to me. Releasing Jack, he whirled on me, and before I could stagger out of his reach, he growled and clutched my beleaguered throat in that same giant hand. He tightened his grip, lifting me off the ground. Once again, breath began to desert me. Among tiny pinpricks of light bursting in my vision, I fancied I saw two lithe shadows circling the clearing, speeding past. A forest creature foot race? I tried to turn my head to watch, but my head being attached to my neck, it was not under my control.

Once again, I worried for the length of my future. But beside us, Jack picked himself up off the ground. Stamping down into a low horse stance to drive his gravity downward, he reached over, grasped the Russian—and, by necessity, me—and applied a hip and shoulder throw. Voronoff crashed down to the sound of Jack's thunderous roar.

Unfortunately, I was beneath him.

I could find no way to rid myself of what seemed to be fifty stone of Russian, push and twist as I might, until, with a loud "Ow!" Voronoff grasped at his groin and rolled off me to curl up on his side like an overcooked shrimp.

I struggled to my knees from the indentation my body had made in the damp turf. The Russian also attempted to climb to his feet, but Jack was having none of it. He sent a palm-heel strike into Voronoff's nose. The bear-man fell sideways and ceased all movement.

• • •

AS USUAL WHEN Dee is at the center of events, that night in Richmond Park found much other activity revolving around him. Also as usual, when I have taken upon myself the responsibility of recounting these proceedings—for Dee has little interest in recording his endeavors, whilst I, contrariwise, feel it is of some importance that posterity have these episodes available—I am forced by circumstance to narrate events in which I had no part, events that were described to me after their completion. Fortunately, others involved have less reticence than Dee and are often only too glad to enlarge upon their own roles.

The narrative that follows is the first, in this tale, of these accounts.

AT THE MOMENT when, Jack having dislodged the bobby's whistle from my throat, Voronoff encircled Jack in his mighty grip, Isaki bolted. The Japanese man had got his butcher-paper-wrapped prize and clearly decided he had no reason to remain to watch a battle being fought among a giant Russian, a small and ineffectual Chinese—myself—and some kind of British forest fiend. It was a measure of his affection for Voronoff that he dashed across the small clearing and headed toward the woods.

In doing so, he bumped into young Jimmy Fingers, in the shadows at the edge of the trees. Jimmy had seen Isaki speeding toward the woods but failed to get out of the way in time to avoid a collision.

"I beg yer pardon, that I do," Jimmy said, helping Isaki to his feet. "Yer not 'urt, I 'ope, sir?"

Isaki snarled, pushed Jimmy aside, and ran off.

Jimmy, looking around, determined that his services in the clearing were no longer required. Hands in his pockets, he turned in the direction of the streets of London of which he was so fond.

He had barely taken a dozen steps when the Japanese man came racing back through the woods.

As opposed to his earlier approach, this time, Isaki was making no attempt at silence. In fact, he was howling. Jimmy spun about when he heard the sound. "'Ell's bells!" he exclaimed, shifting aside just in time to avoid the leaping Isaki, who, having missed—or been avoided by—his target, grasped a branch to slow his fall and swung lightly to the ground.

Seeing the look on Isaki's face, Jimmy Fingers took off running. His path out of the Richmond Park woods being blocked by his would-be attacker, he charged back into the clearing.

THUS IT WAS that, in the grip of Voronoff's great hand, I saw what appeared to be a forest creature footrace, but was, in fact, Jimmy Fingers racing by with Isaki in fierce pursuit. The former was shouting, "Mr. Jack! Mr. 'Oong! 'Elp me, sirs, 'elp me!"

The latter was gaining.

Jimmy, a light-fingered thief by trade, was fast, but Isaki was faster. Jimmy dodged, zigzagged, and reversed direction. Isaki could not be slipped. Closing the distance between them, Isaki reached a hand for young Jimmy's corduroy jacket.

His fingers, instead, found the durable cotton cloth of the merchant tunic of Sergeant Hoong.

Hoong had stepped in front of Isaki, giving Jimmy the chance to dash across the clearing to the place where Jack was standing, fists on hips, cape billowing, between my awakening woozy self and the unconscious Russian.

"Mr. Dee, or as 'tis, Mr. Jack!" Jimmy panted. "Mr. 'Oong needs yer 'elp, sir!"

"Oh, Oi don't think so, Jimmy," replied Jack. "'E'd account it a great nuisance if Oi was to interfere."

I shared Jimmy's opinion that Hoong could use assistance,

but as I had no breath to say so, I remained on my knees, watching with Jack and Jimmy as Hoong took on the masterless samurai.

Hoong stood where he was, waiting for his opponent to make the first move. Isaki, attempting to put distance between them, burst out with a palm strike to shove Hoong away. This elicited no reaction from Hoong but a smile that glowed in the mist and fog, recalling to my mind the Cheshire Cat.

Having failed to gain his distance by dislodging the larger, stronger Hoong, Isaki spun into a flying back kick. At first, he achieved his aim: Hoong took a step backward. But Hoong's size belied his speed. With Isaki in the air, it was an easy thing for Hoong to swat Isaki's leg aside and send him reeling to the ground.

Isaki rolled into the crouching posture of an iaijutsu stance. In one swift action, he drew his katana from its scabbard and swept a one-stroke killing slash. Hoong sidestepped the flashing sword; no sooner had he than Isaki, almost faster than I could follow, swung the blade a second time. Hoong bent back almost double to avoid this cut.

"Dee!" I said. "Shouldn't you—"

But I stopped my own words as I saw Hoong shift his legs, say, "Tong gi bai fut, young boy worships the Buddha," and catch the katana in mid-third-strike, flat between his massive palms. He twisted his body and his arms and, with a grunt, snapped the blade in two.

Isaki stood in shock and disbelief as the broken sword fell from his hand.

Hoong moved in with a short, fast step and executed a one-inch punch. The energy of this attack penetrated into Isaki like a dagger, collapsing his abdomen, effectively stealing his breath. Hoong picked him up and threw him to the ground, where he remained in a crumpled heap.

Hoong stood over his Japanese opponent, watching for signs of feigned unconsciouness. Isaki showed none as he remained stretched out on the grass. Softly, he began to snore, as though enjoying a night's sleep in Richmond Park under the misty moon was the very reason he'd come to London.

"Well done, brother 'Oong!" said Jack.

"Well," said Hoong, looking over at the place where Jack, Jimmy, and even I, now able to bear my weight on my own legs, stood by the prone Russian. "I thank you gentlemen for not intervening. It's been some time since I've found myself in combat with a highly skilled practitioner of iaido. It was extremely interesting, and I used the encounter to experiment with various combinations of techniques and skills." He looked directly at me. "In the end, I hope you noted, Lao, I brought him down with a one-inch punch."

"I . . . but . . ." I indicated the unconscious Russian, meaning to explain the dire consequences of my own attempt to employ that skill. My bruised throat, however, suggested I be grateful it was willing to let air pass through it at all, and declared my vocal cords off duty.

All heads turned—the exceptions being the two insensible gentlemen on the grass—as the clomp of heavy shoes running along the path could be heard, along with the shriek of a bobby's whistle. Jimmy Fingers extracted the butcher-paper parcel from his jacket and handed it to Dee. It had been his remit in our proceedings to keep his eye fixed upon the package and intercept it if an attempt was made to bear it away. His relieving Isaki of this item during their collision at the edge of the clearing had caused Isaki to rethink his retreat and return in a rage.

"I'll be off, then, gents. Bobbies ain't among me close mates. Ye'll know where to find me." Jimmy dashed into the trees again.

Hoong, with a nod, disappeared also, through the shadow under the massive oak and into the night.

It was thus that Dee, costumed as Springheel Jack, and I, disheveled and barely able to croak out a word, found ourselves alone in the clearing when a bobby dashed in.

CHAPTER FOUR

"Here! Wot's all this then?" the arriving officer demanded in the traditional bobby greeting. He stopped in the misty clearing, taking note of the two men unconscious—one an Asian, one a European—and the two men standing—one an Asian, one a costumed nightmare fiend—and he hesitated. The calculus in his brain was almost visible: the two Asians canceled each other out, leaving a European versus a fiend. The winner of that contest was not in doubt. With narrowed eyes and raised nightstick, the bobby advanced on Jack and myself. I expected to be challenged as to our right to be conscious when the men on the ground were not, but the constable stopped, cocked his head, and lowered his nightstick.

"Why, it's Mr. Lao. And Springheel Jack, or whoever you fancy yourself." The young man chuckled. "You gents don't know me? I'm McCorkle, Timmy McCorkle. We met this April past. You'd requested the presence of Inspector Fox to a certain alleyway. He brought me along as his constable. Those were some doings, those were."

"Ah!" said Springheel Jack. "Doings indeed! Jack remembers yer, Constable."

I peered at the pale freckled face, and after a moment, I matched it to the one in my memory from that night.

"Of course," I rasped. "A pleasure to see you again, Constable." By the final word, I couldn't even hear myself.

"Are you all right, sir?" McCorkle asked.

"Fine," I whispered. "Just a touch of the ague." I indicated my throat.

"So, young Timmy," Jack said. "Been keeping yerself well? And the missus? Jack's 'eard a 'appy event is on the way."

The constable's smile lit up the clearing. "Yes, sir, we're expecting our first come Michaelmas."

"Why, that's grand," said Jack, and I nodded to echo the sentiment.

Dee had been in London for a mere three days, most of which was spent renewing old acquaintances, making new ones, and investigating the disappearance of the item we'd recently retrieved; yet somehow, he had come by the knowledge that this young constable, a peripheral player in the events of last spring, had a wife in the family way. It was indicative of how well I'd gotten to know Dee during our previous association that I was only faintly surprised.

"Thank you, sirs. But here now, that big fellow's stirring. Would one of you care to describe to me what's happened here?"

"Oi'd be glad to! For such a thing might be beyond poor Mr. Lao at the moment. With 'is ague an' that. That big fellow," Jack said, pointing, "is a Russian as calls 'imself Vladimir Voronoff. The little gent snoring over there is a Japanese called Isaki, though Jack don't know 'is given name. This thing 'ere"—he produced from his cloak the package given him by Jimmy Fingers—"this fellow, Voronoff, stole it for the purpose of selling it to that fellow, Isaki, though it ain't 'is to sell. Now"—indicating me—"Jack's good friend 'ere, that'd be Mr. Lao She. 'E don't 'old with that kind of thing any more than old Jack do. So we took ourselves 'ere to stop this business."

"I see," said Constable McCorkle. "And what is that thing there, and who was it had it stolen from him?"

"Ah, ye may well ask." Carefully, Jack unwrapped the parcel. Laying the butcher paper aside, he displayed the item across the palms of his black leather gloves.

At its top, the foot-long rod wore an onyx sphere crowned by a finely figured gold dragon head, its ruby eyes glowing. A four-sided gold sleeve sat below the sphere, ending in a short crosspiece of purest basalt. On the remainder of its length, the square rosewood shaft was horizontally scored twelve times, with Chinese characters incised on each face between the grooves. The tip again was figured gold. Even in the haze of the moonlight, its beauty was unmistakable.

"Oh," I breathed. "D—Jack, what is it?"

Springheel Jack cackled, swinging the item above his head as though to bring it down on mine. McCorkle's eyes went wide and he gallantly lifted his nightstick, but Jack stopped midair and lowered the rod again. "Why, Lao," he said, "yer don't know this thing? 'Twas made more than a thousand years since, in China, at the start o' yer Tang dynasty. This is a dragon-taming mace, so it is."

Constable McCorkle snorted. "The hell you say. I don't hold with that mystical bosh. That thing don't look magic to me. It do look valuable, though. Would that be real gold?"

"Aye, that it would, me copper. And while Jack don't disagree with yer opinion o' mystical bosh, still, it's a fact that in all its years, this beauty ain't never been stolen without something terrible 'appening to whosoever stole it."

Jack flipped the mace high overhead. We all watched, mesmerized, as it spun end over end, its gold glinting in the moonlight. It reached its zenith, paused in the middle of the misty air, and slowly descended, arriving in Jack's outstretched hand. Jack laughed, pointing the dragon head first at the groggy but awakening Voronoff, and then at Isaki, still snoring. "These gents being the proof o' me pudding."

McCorkle looked at Jack with the lift of an eyebrow. "You're never telling me the thing is cursed?"

"Oh, Jack couldn't say as to curses, me copper. But 'tis a truth that couldn't be truer that 'e 'oo steals it, things don't go well for 'im, while 'e 'oo restores it to its proper owner can expect to be rewarded."

"Can he now? And who is this proper owner?"

"A Chinese merchant, Wu Ze Tian by name. It was Wu as asked Jack to find this missing treasure and bring it 'ome. Bad broken up over the loss o' the thing, Wu is. And," Jack added, "most grateful Wu will be, Jack's sure, for its return."

"And Jack just happened to know it could be found here in Richmond Park on this midnight? To return it?"

"Oh, me constable, but o' course not. Jack 'ad to search far and wide for information leading to the finding o' it."

"Yes, of course. Far and wide. You wouldn't care to share your sources of information, I suppose?"

"Jack can't 'ardly say no more, except 'e can see yer've got the makings o' a fine inspector one day, with all these questions that come to yer."

The constable's freckled cheeks bunched up in a smile.

"But poor Jack, 'e's out o' answers and must be off," Jack said. "The constabulary'll return this item to its proper owner, Jack 'as no doubt." Snatching up the butcher paper, Jack had the mace rewrapped in a flash. He placed it in the hands of the astonished Constable McCorkle. With a laugh, Springheel Jack ran across the clearing, used his momentum to carry him three steps up the trunk of a tree, and somersaulted onto a branch.

"Wait!" said the constable. "Where would this gentleman, this Wu Ze Tian, be found?"

"Wu Ze Tian may be found in Mayfair, at a fine brick 'ouse in Bruton Street. But Wu ain't no gentleman, me McCorkle! Wu's a woman of business from far Cathay. She's made 'er 'ome in London these past months while she carries on with some o' this and some o' that."

"Bringing such a valuable object with her?"

"Constable," said Jack, from high among the branches, "if ye was the owner o' a dragon-taming mace, would yer leave it behind?"

THE EVENTS THAT followed were simplicity itself. McCorkle blew his whistle to summon more of his fellows. Two arrived and put Voronoff and the awakening Isaki in restraints. Although Voronoff, when questioned, repeatedly insisted Wu Ze Tian had given him the package with instructions to convey it to Isaki, he was believed by none. Timmy McCorkle doffed his constable's helmet to me, wished me a good evening, and he and the other bobbies took the men off to the Roehampton Street Police Station, whence they had come.

Once alone in the clearing, I whispered, "Dee? Are you there?"

No answer was forthcoming. I asked again and waited but only saw the shadows of branches dancing on the turf. I became increasingly aware that, as Jimmy Fingers had pointed out, things rustled. My throat put up a sudden clamor for brandy, and I could not help but agree. I headed for home.

CHAPTER FIVE

At that stage of my time in London, "home" was a small flat in George Court in the neighborhood of Covent Garden. Issuing from Richmond Park onto Grove Road, I was overjoyed to find a taxicab, not a given at that hour. I sank onto its leather seat with relief, which lessened as the driver began a jovial commentary on everything and nothing. This review continued without pause, even after such phrases as, "What d'you think of that?" where one might have expected the conversational burden to fall, however temporarily, on me. Upon reflection, I realized that though unhoped for, this situation had a bright side. The drive was not a short one, and the cabbie's chatter served to keep me awake as we went on—also, at that hour and after such a night, not a given.

Nevertheless, I was grateful when we arrived at the building that housed my flat. I paid the garrulous cabbie and climbed the stairs to the first floor, where I extracted my key. When I walked in, I was not surprised to be greeted by Dee, occupying my upholstered chair.

Dee wore his nightshirt and robe. About his neck, on a gold chain, hung a jade bi given him at birth by his parents. Longevity bats decorated one side, and the reverse carried Dee's name and the words "first-born son." He never removed it, not even when he wore the Springheel Jack costume, which was right now draped across the back of a wooden kitchen chair.

Most importantly, however, I saw that on the table waited two glasses of brandy.

"My," I said. "How clever of you." I lowered myself into a kitchen chair, took up one of the glasses, and inquired, "How did you arrive here so fast? In that costume, you could not have managed a taxi."

"Jack 'as 'is ways, so 'e does." Dee smiled as he sipped. "Ye can go far, and fast, too, clinging to the back o' an omnibus late at night."

"And your clothing?"

"Hoong will have taken it with him," he answered, reverting to the Chinese we spoke between us. "As arranged."

"Ah! I'm glad to see that Dee has returned, and the Terror of London has gone back to his lair for the night."

"Oh, me professor, but yer never can tell when Springheel Jack'll strike! But yes," Dee said, changing languages and voices again, "I believe I won't have much employment for Jack in the immediate future."

I sipped my brandy, feeling a comforting warmth slide down my recently besieged throat. After some moments of silence, and feeling the warmth extend to my belly, I spoke aloud what I'd found myself thinking as I rode in the taxi: "I must say, Dee, it's been a pleasure having you in London again."

He peered over his glass. "Are you quite all right, Lao? I haven't been here seventy-two hours and already your life has been threatened, you're bruised, your suit is covered in mud, and your best brandy is in danger of becoming extinct. I fail to see the pleasure in any of that."

"Well, it happens that my days had grown dull."

"In summer? With roses, and late sunsets, and the circus in

town? Or," he said with a tiny smile, "are you still languishing after Miss Mary Wendell?"

"Certainly not that," I replied, with some dignity. "Miss Mary Wendell is now Mrs. Washington Jones, and preparing for an autumn voyage to China. There, she and her husband will take up missionary posts in an attempt to bring their vision of Christianity to our apparently benighted people."

I myself was a Christian, having made my conversion in Peking. Dee was not. We shared, however, a distaste for the European missionaries whose aspiration to conquer and colonize China was as palpable as that of the various nations' military gunboats standing off our shores to protect the trade of their merchants.

"Though I wish Mrs. Jones well," I continued, "I am in no way languishing after her. The dullness of my days comes rather from the fact that beyond my lecturing responsibilities and my friends, of whom, thank you, I have a growing number, I have little to engross my attention beyond my own writing. On that front, I have just completed a book and not yet begun the next. Thus, I am at a bit of a loose end." I drank more brandy and poured us each another.

"I'm sorry to hear that," Dee said, "though I must congratulate you on the completion of a new work. Can you tell me its name?"

"*Mr. Ma and Son*. It's a—"

"Lao, we'd agreed—"

"Highly fictionalized account"—I interrupted him, as he had me—"using, but by no means following faithfully, some of the events of last spring. You, for one example, play no part in it."

"Ah," he said.

"Nor does any man's murder. I've kept to our agreement, Dee, but I'm a writer, and material is material."

"Of course." He smiled. "I apologize and look forward to reading the book."

"Your apology is accepted." We sipped brandy in peace. "I was rather hoping," I confessed, "that your return to London would occasion activities that would provide a fresh font of material."

"You sound disappointed. Has tonight not lived up to your expectations, then?"

"No. Perhaps a novella could be made of what happened in Richmond Park, but I admit to regret that this situation has been resolved so fast. I imagine you'll be returning to Geneva now, to continue in your diplomatic duties there, and leave me to my dull days?"

"Actually," said Dee, "no."

"No? But Madam Wu's mace has been recovered. Was that not the reason you came to London?"

"It was not, though my being here was a convenient circumstance when the mace went missing. No, I was sent for a different reason." He rolled his brandy snifter between his palms. "Do you recall, Lao, that last time I was here, I was visited twice by Commissioner Lin? Well, I have spoken with him again."

I lowered my brandy and looked severely at my friend. "I do recall those visits, and I further recall that they were, in reality, hallucinations, Commissioner Lin having been dead these past seventy years. And that they occurred when you were in the grip of opium, the taking of which you promised to abjure. If you and Commissioner Lin are once again exchanging pleasantries, I hope I'm not to understand a return to this drug is the cause of this renewed acquaintance?"

"No," Dee said, smiling. "I vowed I'd abstain from its use, and I have. You have no worries on that score. Nevertheless,

Commissioner Lin appeared before me while I was in China and instructed me to return to London."

I considered this. "While I'm gratified to hear you have ceased your dependence on opium, Dee, I cannot profess to be untroubled by the fact that, in what should therefore be a clearheaded state, you continue to see ghosts."

"To see and to talk to," he replied. "Though, as on the previous occasions when we two interacted, Commissioner Lin was the more loquacious. He advised me to make plans to return here, not to Geneva, when I left China. I did so, traveling on the Trans-Siberian Railroad and thence by various train lines across Europe from Moscow."

"You took the railway route at Commissioner Lin's recommendation?"

Dee smiled. "No, he left that choice up to me, but he said 'as soon as possible.' The passage here from China by fast steamship takes six weeks. Overland by rail, Peking to London can be accomplished in nine days. It nearly leaves one breathless."

"Indeed, railroads are the future," I said. "I shall be glad when China develops a rail system comparable to England's, or to that now crossing the vastness of America—a system built by Chinese labor, I might add."

Dee nodded. "It would be of great benefit to China to have such railroads. Yet an advantage of that magnitude also entails risk."

I felt a welcome rush of relief to have someone with whom to discuss issues of immediate import to China. With the exception of Sergeant Hoong, my days in Britain were, unsurprisingly, spent largely among Britishers, whose concerns were almost entirely British.

"To what specific risks are you referring, Dee?"

"I fear the struggling government may not yet have enough strength to curb the forces that would vie for control of such an asset. Already we've seen conflict over the Eastern Railway through Manchuria."

"Beyond conflict, I believe. Are there not rumors of a conspiracy, some complex political machination involving the Eastern Railway?"

Dee gave me a sharp look. "These rumors have reached London, then?"

"You've heard them too?"

"I have. I was unable, in China, to either track them to their source or discern the object of the conspiracy—if it exists. It might be merely a manifestation of China's unease regarding the current push-pull with Russia and Japan over the Railway."

"I suppose it might. And the government as presently constituted may, as you say, be too weak to resolve that push-pull satisfactorily. However," I said tentatively, unsure of my friend's opinions on the subject I was about to broach, "perhaps a system in which all people felt they truly had a part and a voice, a system in which a man could account any sacrifice he made to be for the good of all, not solely for the benefit of his rulers—"

"Oh, Lao." Dee gave a long-suffering sigh. "Are you about to put forward the communist argument? I will be happy to debate the virtues of the communistic versus the nationalistic forms of government, but perhaps we can agree to take up the subject at a future time, when we are both more lively and have had less brandy."

"Very well," I said. "It is a debate I look forward to having. But before we retire, for if I don't know the answer to this question I shan't be able to sleep, I must ask: if the purpose of your return to London was not the recovery of the dragon-taming mace, what is it Commissioner Lin has sent you here to do?"

"That," said Dee, "we shall have to wait to discover."

His answer took me aback. "You mean you don't know?"

"I do not."

"Ah," I said, considering. "Still, I suppose it's wise to follow the instructions of as powerful a ghost as that of Commissioner Lin, even if one has no idea of the reasons behind them. Do you have, then, any inkling when your purpose here will be revealed?"

"None."

"In that case," I said, draining my brandy and standing, "I propose that we retire for the night before it any more closely resembles the morning. Thus, if Commissioner Lin calls upon you tomorrow, we'll be revitalized and ready."

Dee raised an eyebrow. "Am I to understand, then, Lao, that despite the difficulties of this midnight's proceedings, you're prepared to join me in whatever this upcoming enterprise might turn out to be?"

"Dee," I said, adopting a serious mien, "if you were to try to stop me, I'd be forced to fell you with a one-inch punch."

CHAPTER SIX

In the as-yet unsullied early August morning, Dee and I made our way across the city. Dee, as usual, insisted on walking, and at a pace that far outstripped that of normal men. Hoping to perhaps distract him, I asked him about his willingness to place the dragon-taming mace in the hands of the Metropolitan Police.

"Such a valuable object, Dee. I wouldn't want to impugn the honor of the constabulary, but any man would be tempted by an item so precious."

Dee smiled. "Perhaps. But though Constable McCorkle affected not to hold with any mystical bosh, the suggestion that the mace was cursed gave him a slight pause, as I'm sure you observed. The further promise of a reward for its return, he clearly found enticing. The fact that he has a child coming who, if McCorkle were to be caught in a misstep, would be left to be raised by its mother alone, was enough, I believe, to seal the mace's fate. But Lao, you're breathing heavily. I fear that in my absence, you've fallen a bit out of shape. Perhaps you've overindulged in British food, though I can scarcely credit that anyone would willingly do so."

"Your opinion of the cuisine of England is not unknown to me, Dee, although also not entirely shared. And as you gave no notice of your planned return to London, I have failed to engage in the sort of physical training needed to assure my ability to run a marathon race on the city streets."

"It is important to always remain prepared. That way, when the need presents itself, you will be ready."

I would have answered, but at that moment, Dee dashed into the street. A cart horse, frightened by the blare of a motorcar horn, was whinnying as it reared on its hind legs. The wagon driver, tugging on the reins, tried with little success to control his animal amid the bleating of additional horns pressed by drivers anxious to be on their way. The wagon was in danger of overturning. Pedestrians, fearful of being trampled, shrieked and scattered. Dee leapt to the noseband of the rearing horse and pulled the beast down. He spoke into the animal's ear and stroked its muzzle. The horse, though clearly still unhappy, calmed enough to enable Dee to lead it to the curb. Motorcars passed it and peace returned.

"I thank ye, sir," said the driver to Dee. "This beast is young yet and hasn't got the hang of working the city streets. That motor horn must've played a note that stirred her soul."

"The drivers of motorcars will have to learn to share the roads with barrows and horse-drawn wagons," I said, "or we will have nothing but chaos to look forward to."

"Oh, I think there'll be no sharing," the driver said. "This beauty will be my last horse. When she's ready for her pasture, I—or my sons—will turn to a lorry for our trade." He nodded to the side of his wagon, on which was painted "Feldman and Sons" and "Fine and Varied Goods" in black letters outlined in gold. "We deal in haberdashery, cooking wares, items of use."

"Well, then," said Dee, "we won't keep you." He whispered to the horse once more and stepped aside. The horse whinnied.

"She likes you, sir," said the driver. "Might you be a horse trainer by trade?"

Dee smiled. "No, nothing like it. I am a judge—my name is Dee Ren Jie. This is Lao She."

"Well, Mr. Judge Dee Ren Jie, if you ever decide horses is your true and proper calling, you come to Stepney and ask about for Feldman. Or"—he grinned—"if you're ever in the market for a bit of haberdashery." Feldman doffed his hat. He clicked his tongue and the cart moved on.

"What did you say to that horse, Dee?" I asked. "It calmed her right down."

"I recited from *Romance of the Three Kingdoms*," he said. Seeing the look on my face, he chuckled. "Often what's said is less important than how it's said. I spoke calmly to her. She was reassured."

Dee and I wove through the throngs of nannies, newsboys, buskers, and businessmen. From an old woman with a barrow, Dee purchased two plums. He handed one to me. The use of my pocket-handkerchief was required to clean my chin of its sweet juice. The August day was already hot and would grow hotter, just as the morning light, clear now, would become thick with kitchen smoke, motorcar exhaust, and the exhalations of untold hurrying humans. From the doorway of a tea shop came the alluring scent of fresh-baked pastries; from the alleyway beside it, the stink of rotting fish. Voices in conversation, the cries of peddlers, and the horns, brakes, and hissing tires of vehicles mingled with the shouts of bobbies at intersections trying, with varying degrees of success, to organize the disarray around us.

And yet, this chaos did not hold a candle to Peking's, where pedestrians were not confined to pavements but swarmed in the streets until nudged by a horse-cart, a rare lorry, or an even more rare luxury automobile; where the ever-present scent of cooking oil blended in the air with the fine mist of sand blown in from the Gobi desert; where more goods were sold off wagons and from stalls than out of storefronts; where laundry dried on lines overhead and underfed rickshaw runners raced the wealthy this way and that while shirtless farmers with baskets of greens on long poles across their shoulders moved grudgingly aside.

A wave of homesickness washed over me.

I was still contemplating the myriad ways the Peking of my youth differed from the London of my current life when Dee and I crossed into Mayfair. Immediately, the streets became wider and calmer and the tree canopy thickened, lindens and oaks shading us while we walked. The shouts of hawkers dropped off as though the same invisible barrier protecting these precincts from the peddlers themselves also forbade their cries from disturbing the peace of the well-to-do who lived within.

Not checking for the street names posted on the corners of the buildings, Dee led the way with a confidence bordering on familiarity. We soon found ourselves on Bruton Street and at the door of a handsome brick house. Dee pulled the bell.

After a moment, the door was opened to us not by a butler or the lady of the house but by a small young woman, stony of face and straight of back. Her dress was the loose black tunic and trousers and black cloth shoes of the traditional Chinese retainer, but over the tunic, she wore a silk qipao waistcoat in a deep forest green. Beside her, at the alert, stood a mahogany-colored Chuandong hound.

"Judge Dee Ren Jie," the unsmiling young woman said before Dee could speak. Her Mandarin, while clear, was oddly accented.

"Good morning, Feng," said Dee. "And Mei Qiang." At the sound of Dee pronouncing its name, the animal wagged its tail. The young woman gave it a hand signal, apparently granting permission to approach. It did, sniffing at me and then returning its attention to Dee. He gave it an affectionate scratch around the muzzle. "This is my friend Lao She."

He seemed to be introducing me to both the young woman and the dog, so I offered greetings to both. In return, I got a curt nod from Feng and a tail wag from Mei Qiang.

"Madam Wu expects you." The young woman's face did not change its demeanor as she stepped aside.

We were led through a large entry hall and shown into a sitting room, though Dee seemed to know the way perfectly well. The hall struck me as stark, with only a Chinese scroll painting of a tiger on one of its white walls and no carpet on the polished wooden floor.

In contrast, the sitting room was fully furnished, although in a most modern style. Angular white leather chairs and a similar sofa mingled comfortably with the graceful but severely plain cherry wood of Qing sideboards and a scholar's writing table. The walls here bore no more wallpaper than did the hall, and the artworks hanging on their ivory expanse, far from being ancient scrolls, consisted of large canvases bearing squares, circles, and triangles of bright color. Bookshelves held volumes in English and Chinese, many of them poetry. The curtains at the tall windows were a plain French blue, with neither pattern nor swag. The sideboards and cabinets, I was relieved to see, held the occasional Chinese treasure, though none of the overwrought work of the Ming. A lotus bowl from the Northern Song here, a dancer from the Western Han there—and on a low elmwood cabinet, an empty stand.

"Please, come in." The invitation was issued by a woman's voice, low-pitched and pleasing. I turned in the direction from which it had come.

In London, I had encountered a fair number of women of

business and seen many more hurrying to and from their places of work. As London was at the forefront of fashion trends in both politics and clothing, I had also noted more than a few young women walking—self-consciously, as it seemed to me—in trousers made of men's suiting and tailored to men's styles.

Never before this moment, though, had I seen a woman of wealth and power such as Madam Wu had been described to be, and such beauty and maturity as I could myself see that she possessed, wearing a man's pleated camel trousers, white shirt, and silk tie, complete with ruby tie clasp.

"Dee." The lady smiled warmly. Her glossy hair, cut in a blunt bob, swayed forward as she inclined her head. I estimated her age to be close to Dee's, fifteen or so years beyond my own two decades and a half. As she walked forward to greet us, I chanced a glance at her feet. Clad in brown sports brogues, they had clearly never been bound.

"Madam Wu." Dee bowed. "This is my friend Lao She."

"A pleasure to meet you, Teacher Lao," Madam Wu said in a Mandarin whose accents were those of my home city but not, like mine, of its streets. Rather, her elegant tones spoke of private tutors in walled gardens. A wealthy woman with an education and natural feet—quite a forward-looking family she must have come from. "I've read your articles and some of your stories," she continued, speaking to me. "I greatly admire your insistence on the Baihua style."

I was dumbfounded. Baihua, the plain form of written Chinese developed to allow writers to express ourselves in ways accessible to all and not solely to those classically educated, is, of course, the style used in the China of today. In 1924, however, to find an educated and powerful woman advocating its use was as unexpected to me as Madam Wu's style of dress.

"I'm honored, Madam Wu," I managed to stammer.

The lady smiled in a kindly way at my discomfiture and

invited us to sit. I chose an angular chair whose leather upholstery was surprisingly comfortable. Dee and Madam Wu sat together on the sofa. The young woman, Feng, entered, bearing a lacquer tray on which stood a pair of teapots, one in the British style and one in the Chinese. The tray also held two fine English teacups as well as two smaller cups without handles, out of which green Chinese tea is enjoyed. Dee smiled as, without asking, the young woman—whose hair, I noticed, was cut in exact imitation of her employer's—poured for him from the Chinese pot into a Chinese cup.

"For you, Teacher Lao?" she asked me, in that odd-sounding Chinese. I requested British tea, which she gravely poured for me, and she gave the same to Madam Wu.

"Thank you, Feng," the lady said.

"Shall I stay, madam?"

"You may if you like. You can learn much from these gentlemen. Teacher Lao, this is Gao Feng, a young woman of high intelligence and many talents."

The young woman, cheeks reddening at this praise, seated herself on a hassock. She frowned, as though preparing to listen intently. It occurred to me that Mandarin might not be her native dialect; perhaps she came from one of the fartherflung corners of our land. The dog, who had entered with her, sat down sphinxlike beside the hassock.

"Lao She," Dee said to Madam Wu, "enjoys British tea, English poetry, European religion, and the beauty of Occidental women."

Slightly irritated at Dee for these personal remarks, I put in, "Who would not? The tea is bracing, the poetry moving, and the religion profound."

"I agree on all counts, Teacher Lao"—the lady smiled—"but although I appreciate these things, I prefer their Chinese counterparts."

"I must add," I added, "that the beauty of European women, of course, cannot approach that of the women of our homeland." I lifted my teacup to Madam Wu, then also to Gao Feng. For some reason, this deepened the scowl on the young woman's features.

"Yet," Dee continued, speaking as before to Madam Wu, "as I discovered last night in a discussion about the railway, when it comes to his views on the proper form of government for China, he leans toward the untried communist system. He doesn't seem impressed by the nationalistic values that have built such powerful European states as France, or Germany, or indeed our hosts, the British Empire."

"Is that true, Teacher Lao?" asked the lady, the smile continuing to play about her lips. "Are you a Communist, eager to seize the fields and factories and assign their ownership to workers and peasants?"

"I wouldn't say that, madam. The communist system, as Dee has helpfully pointed out, is untried in China. What has worked in other places might not succeed for us. I think it inarguable, however, that if the wealth of our vast land continues to disappear into the pockets of foreigners and rich Chinese while workers and peasants starve, China will experience growing turmoil within and weakness in the face of threats from beyond our borders." If it is possible to drink one's tea emphatically, I proceeded to do so.

"I agree with you that the threats are real," Madam Wu said, with a slow, considered nod. "I remain unconvinced, however, that the wide distribution of power into the hands of those who are likely to have little vision beyond their own admittedly urgent needs is the way to meet them." She raised an eyebrow. "But this issue came up between you in a discussion of railroads?"

"It was the challenges China will face from foreign powers

as we attempt to build a rail system to match that of Europe or America that prompted it," Dee said. "The powers already tussling over the Chinese Eastern Railway will train their sights on every new attempt to lay tracks across our country."

"Yes, undoubtedly. For that, and for so many other tests to come, China must be ready."

CHAPTER SEVEN

As we sat in the stark but not unappealing front room at Madam Wu's residence, the lady sipped thoughtfully at her tea. "But come now, Dee," she said, eyes sparkling at the change of subject. "Tell me, how goes the investigation into the theft of my mace?"

"The investigation goes well," said Dee. "In fact, I expect it to bear fruit at any moment."

The ringing of the front doorbell just after Dee had spoken made me wonder, as I often had, whether Dee actually did possess some psychic sense unavailable to most. Gao Feng and the dog stood as one and strode together to the door, returning moments later with Constable Timmy McCorkle. In his arms, he bore a paper-wrapped package. Feng gave a hand gesture to the dog, who was growling. The growling stopped.

"Ah." Dee stood. "I believe this must be the emissary I was expecting. Dee Ren Jie," he said in English and bowed to the constable.

"Er—Constable Timothy McCorkle, Metropolitan Police Force." The young man made an awkward attempt to return Dee's bow while avoiding the mahogany hound, who had come near to sniff him. "Mr. Lao, I'm glad to see you here. It assures me I've found the right house. You'd be Madam Wu, then?"

"I would, and am." The lady's English was smooth and unaccented. "Would you care for tea, Constable?"

"That would be grand, thank you." McCorkle spoke almost with relief. I imagined the décor, the retainer and dog, and the company were not quite what he'd been expecting. "This place," he said, sitting on the edge of a curved and padded chair, looking around with wonder, "it ain't quite what I was expecting." Perhaps, I mused, I also had a psychic sense, heretofore untapped.

"Not all Chinese people can be found in darkly curtained and smokily incensed rooms, Constable," Madam Wu said. "Or in opium dens."

"Oh, no, missus—milady—madam—I never meant that! It's just . . . well, these white walls, and these chairs, and the books and the paintings and that . . . I mean, you'd be hard-pressed to know what they're about, the paintings, wouldn't you . . . Oh, thank you!" That was directed at Feng, who had, without asking his preference, given the young man a cup of British tea with milk and two spoons of sugar. He slurped at it. "I don't mean to give offense. I only . . . I mean . . ."

"No offense taken, Constable," said Madam Wu. After a few moments, she said, "I believe you've brought something for me?"

"Oh! Oh, yes, of course." McCorkle's teacup rattled in its saucer. Half-standing, he looked for a place to set it down.

"Sit, please, Constable, and finish your tea. Feng, will you bring me the package?"

McCorkle did as he was told, sitting as Feng rose, took up the paper-wrapped package, and handed it to Madam Wu.

I had a moment of trepidation as Madam Wu began to untie the string and peel back the paper. Notwithstanding Dee's faith in the stick-and-carrot situation the young constable found himself in, the mace was worth more than a constable could earn in a lifetime. It would be understandable, if not forgivable, to find temptation had overcome young Timmy McCorkle.

But the jubilant look on the face of Madam Wu allowed me to relax.

Madam Wu lifted the dragon-taming mace from the protective paper. Its beauty, evident last night by the glow of the moon, was even more apparent now in the bright light of day. The delicacy of the incised work, the confident gleam of the gold, and the inky blackness of the basalt and the onyx could almost make one believe the thing did possess the ability to channel forces from another world. This impression was only made more powerful by the dragon's flashing eyes, rubies the same shade as those in the tie clasp of Madam Wu.

"Oh, well done," Madam Wu said softly. "Very well done." After a moment, she looked up and handed the mace to Feng, who walked across the room and placed it upon the empty stand. It gleamed in the sunlight.

"Constable," said Madam Wu, "I'm in your debt. How did you find my lost treasure?"

"Well, I didn't, actually. It was given me by Springheel Jack."

The lady's brows knitted together. "Springheel Jack?"

"A British phantasm, a fairy-story specter employed to frighten children into good behavior," Dee said with a shrug. "Apparently, there is a man going about London in Jack's costume, taking upon himself various tasks. And you saw this man, Constable?"

"That I did, last night. Mr. Lao was there, he can tell you."

"Were you, Lao? And you saw him also, this spurious Springheel Jack? You didn't say." Dee's eyebrows raised.

"You didn't ask about my evening," I said. "In fact, as I

recall, when I returned to our lodgings, you were peacefully snoring." This was no truer than what Dee was saying, but neither was it any more false. "I was out for a stroll in Richmond Park and came upon the scene. Springheel Jack, or whoever the fellow really is, was engaged in a battle with two other men over possession of a wrapped package. I blew a police whistle I carry in my pocket. As I was wondering whether to join the fray—although I would have found it difficult to know which side to choose, as the two other gents seemed unsavory but that Jack fellow is hideously ugly—this gallant constable came running. Jack, having just laid the other two low, explained he had interrupted the exchange of stolen goods. He unwrapped the package, showed us this glorious piece, and told us who the real owner was. Placing it in the constable's care, he vanished."

"I see," said Madam Wu. "This—Springheel Jack? How did he come to be there, at just the right moment?"

"He claimed to have 'searched far and wide' for information regarding this exchange," said the constable.

"But that would imply he knew it was going to happen."

McCorkle nodded. "This Jack, he's a strange bird. He has the repute of a frightening fiend—and the face of one—but he's been known to assist the constabulary before this. I couldn't say why."

"Has he?" said Madam Wu. She appeared intrigued. "And the other men? The thieves?"

"They were placed in the care of the Metropolitan Police Force also," said McCorkle. "It's my understanding that the large one—he's a Russian by the name of Voronoff—was the one as stole it, and was selling it to the small one, a Japanese called Isaki. Voronoff claims he never stole it but was given it by you, madam. Don't you worry, no one believes him. They're both locked up now and likely will be for some time. Your testimony, madam, might be required in court, of course."

"Of course." The lady inclined her head. "I'd be happy to give evidence against men of such low character. As I said, Constable, I'm in your debt. Perhaps, Feng, as the constable takes his leave, you could offer him a small token of thanks?"

"Oh, madam, but I couldn't—" McCorkle began.

"Nonsense, Constable. Both he who steals it and he who restores it must get their just rewards. So legend says. Feng?"

Gao Feng rose, the dog rose, and McCorkle finished his tea and rose also. As they walked to the sitting room door, Feng paused at the same cabinet that now bore the mace on its stand. Sliding a drawer open, she removed a small silk purse and handed it to the constable. Eyebrows high, he took it, and they proceeded through the hall to the front door.

Madam Wu's eyes rested for a moment on the mace and then turned to Dee. "I can't help but think," she said to him, "that you're in some way responsible for the constable's lucky intrusion into the situation."

"If any information I uncovered was useful to Scotland Yard and to yourself, madam, I'm grateful for the privilege of being of service."

"Yes, of course." The lady's eyes met Dee's. "Now, at the risk of appearing unforgivably rude, I must attend to some pressing business. Lao She, I'm honored to have met you. I shall give a banquet to celebrate the return of the mace. I hope you'll consider attending. As Dee knows, I have a fine chef. Dee, shall I see you soon?"

"If you like, madam, I'll try to return later in the day."

Dee's eyes, I now noticed, had in them the same sparkle as Madam Wu's were continuing to display.

Madam Wu showed us to the door. Feng and the hound were nowhere in evidence. Madam Wu bowed to us each and, with a final smile, shut the door behind us.

"Well," I began. "Dee—"

"Lao, have you plans for the day?"

"I—plans? No. The university term having not yet started, I've been cast back on my own devices."

"Perhaps, then, you'd care to join me for a late breakfast? And after that, if you feel fortified, we might take in a show at the cinema."

CHAPTER EIGHT

"The cinema?" I said. "After breakfast? Yes, well, why not? While we wait for word from Commissioner Lin. Do you have in mind any particular picture show?"

"I have."

"I hope it's not the new Douglas Fairbanks film, *The Thief of Bagdad*. I've already seen it. It was enjoyable, but nothing in it demanded a second viewing."

"No," he said. "The film I'm interested in is one you will not have seen. Come, let us hurry to our congee."

Dee and I made our way, again on foot, to Limehouse, where we entered Wu's Garden, a dining establishment to which I'd introduced Dee on his previous trip to London. The Wu who owned the café was, of course, no relation of the Madam Wu whose home we'd just left. We five hundred million Chinese share among us just one hundred family names. If it were possible to trace ancestral lines back as far as the Xia dynasty—that is, four thousand years—it might be that common forebears would be unearthed. As it is, it is normal to come across unrelated people every day of the same name as oneself.

Once Dee had mentioned congee, my own appetite had turned in that direction also. We ordered two bowls, with dried fish and pickled vegetables to accompany them. Tea was delivered to our table immediately, and fat Proprietor Wu smiled and waved from behind his counter at the front of the café.

"Madam Wu is quite gracious," I said as I poured tea for Dee. "Though her taste in décor is perhaps a bit ahead of my own. Does her husband share this penchant for the modern?"

"Ah, Lao, your delicacy does you credit. Madam Wu is unmarried." Dee tapped his finger on the table to thank me for the tea.

"Unmarried? But—"

"She has chosen to be addressed as 'Madam' because, as a woman of business, she finds herself taken more seriously if it is assumed that a man is behind her demands and decisions."

"She doesn't object to having to perform this subterfuge?"

"She objects strenuously. But she's a woman who keeps her eye on her goal. To reach it, she will make use of whatever tools are available."

As Dee had said he himself would do the same when it was suggested I join his investigation soon after we met last spring, I understood him to be approving of the lady's approach.

"Still," I said, "I'm surprised she's not more interested in the communist system. One of the party's tenets is the equality of men and women."

"Madam Wu's concern is with China's strength in relation to the nations besieging us. Japan most especially, but Russia and the European powers—and even America—are watching our situation with greedy eyes. China's transition from imperial rule to a republic must be solidified and reinforced before the political composition of that republic is debated."

Small dishes of dried fish and others of pickled cabbage, mustard leaves, bitter melon, carrots, and chopped long beans arrived at our table, and soon after these, steaming bowls of congee. We added the fish and vegetables each to our own taste and began to enjoy our breakfast.

"Am I to understand, then," I asked Dee, continuing the conversation, "that once the current government's hold on power is, as you say, solidified, you would be willing to consider the merits of communism?"

"Just as it's not my way to put my faith in a path that's untried, it's also not my way to discount any promising one."

"I see. And this political analysis to which I was just treated," I said. "Are these solely your own thoughts, or also those of Madam Wu?"

"We largely agree."

"You are both Nationalists, then."

He gave me a severe look over his congee bowl. "I'm employed by the Nationalist government, Lao. I'd have refused the post if I didn't believe in the hopes of the republic."

"Of course. And Madam Wu?"

"Her foremost interest is the success of her business, which, because I feel you're about to ask, is real estate investments and the importing and exporting of textiles. Business can't function without a strong government to enforce the laws. That same strong government will coincidentally be able to maintain China's sovereignty in the face of threats from other powers."

"It seems that you and she have discussed the situation extensively, and yet you have only been in London three days now."

"We met in Peking," he said, finishing his congee, "and became good friends. Now, if your interrogation of me is complete, it is time we headed for the cinema."

HEAD FOR THE cinema we did, detouring through the narrow, cobbled Limehouse streets to the shop of Sergeant Hoong. Hoong, senior to Dee by the same decade and a half that Dee was senior to me, had settled in London after a military career to become an herbalist and a purveyor of the sort of items by which Europeans are mildly baffled but which Chinese workingmen find useful.

"Ah," Hoong said when, looking over from the foot of a ladder leaning against the shelves, he saw that it was we who had set the bell above the door to tinkling. "Dee, Lao. I see my attempts to earn my humble living are about to be interrupted again."

Jimmy Fingers waved jauntily from the ladder's top rung, where he was wrestling bolts of cotton cloth onto a shelf.

"Oh, come," said Dee. "You can't claim you didn't enjoy our outing last night."

"Any hour spent in the presence of you gentleman is enjoyable."

"Hoong," said Dee, "perhaps you have been in this country for too long. You speak as a perfect British politician, offering flattery and falsehood. I acknowledge that we have caused you a great deal of trouble—"

I raised my eyebrows at "we," but Dee continued on.

"—and we have come to make amends. As I see your shopkeeping duties are light at the moment, perhaps you would allow Lao and myself to take you to the cinema. You as well, of course, Jimmy."

"A picture show?" said Jimmy from above. "Why, that would be enjoyable, so it would."

"And you, Hoong?"

"I'll be glad to accompany you. Unless the picture you are offering is *The Thief of Bagdad*."

"You've already seen it also?" I said.

"I have not. However, twice since it opened, I've had Britishers in my shop requesting to be shown carpets that fly."

"But . . ."

"Precisely. Fortunately, I was able to tell them truthfully that this shop doesn't carry carpets and send them on to Agajanian's."

"For which that merchant no doubt thanked you," Dee said.

"Agajanian has a silver tongue and his shop sells fine wares. I wouldn't be surprised if he was able to persuade his customers that carpets do not, in fact, fly, but that in view of their disappointment with regard to that fact, he is prepared to offer a deep discount on his finest stock."

"And people will believe the price he's quoting is a low one?" I asked.

"Ah, Mr. Lao," said Jimmy, "but that's what people is best at. Believing what they want to believe."

Jimmy leapt off the ladder, landing at our feet. He staggered but remained upright. Laughing, he threw his arms wide and, in a broad imitation of his own accent, said, "Oi'm Spring'eel Jack, Oi am!"

"Very good, Jimmy," said Dee. "We'll have you running across rooftops in no time."

Hoong turned the bilingual door sign to the "closed" position, locked up the shop, and we four strolled—if any perambulation in Dee's company could be called a stroll—to Stepney.

"Oh! Is it the Palaseum we're making for, then?" said Jimmy. "Many's the 'appy 'our I've spent in its plush seats, leaving me cares behind me."

But to Jimmy's dismay, we bypassed the Palaseum and ended at the Majestic Kinema on Ben Jonson Road. "Oh," said he.

"This picture palace is not to your liking, Jimmy?" said Dee.

"Oh, it's all right, Mr. Dee. Just—you can see for yourself this Majestic Kinema place, it were born to be a warehouse. It ain't got the splendor of Mr. Ben 'Ur's Palaseum."

"Surely the name of the Palaseum proprietor cannot truly be Ben Hur," I interposed.

"Oh, but it is, Mr. Lao. Strongest man in the world, is Mr. Ben 'Ur."

"The name," said Hoong, "was changed by deed poll some years ago. Mr. Ben Hur was born Henry Ben Solomon."

That cleared up my confusion but was also not relevant to the current proceedings. Dee fetched the price of four tickets to the less splendid Majestic Kinema—tuppence each—from his purse. Jimmy pronounced the cost more reasonable than at the Palaseum, which raised the Kinema's standing in his eyes. Hoong peered at the playbill on the stand at the entrance. "Dee," he said, "I fear an ulterior motive has brought us here."

"A motive, yes, though nothing about it is hidden. My motive is, I want to see this picture."

He led us past the ticket-taker and into the dark of the hall while Hoong and I exchanged looks. Jimmy was all eagerness, but I was apprehensive about a film whose title was *Man of a Hundred Faces* when the one of those faces on the playbill—clearly meant to represent the evil genius of the picture—was very much like Dee's.

My misgivings turned out to be not without foundation. In fact, if anything, the film was more distasteful than I'd been prepared for. A Chinese man—portrayed by a European actor made up to look not only Asian but like Dee—went about London with a sneer and a leer. With an oily smile, he convinced trusting tradesmen and unsuspecting shopgirls that he was an inspector from the Metropolitan Police Force. From each tradesman, he stole an item of great value, storing his treasures in the sleeves of his ridiculous robe and later placing them, with a cackle very well illustrated by the theater organist, on the elaborately carved shelves of his dark, smoky den. From the shopgirls—all of them blond, large-eyed, and small-boned—he stole rather more. Using, as the title cards announced, "dark Chinese magics," he mesmerized each, led her, blank-eyed, back to this same smoky den, and after a gap of time during which the title cards assured us unspeakable things were occurring, threw her, weeping, her hair mussed and her white dress torn, into the gutter outside. The valiant Metropolitan Police Force made a number of efforts to apprehend the villain, but the titular hundred faces enabled him to evade capture. This wretched state of affairs continued until the hero of the piece leapt onto the scene.

Springheel Jack.

"Dee!" I whispered, but Dee only lifted his hand. So I held my tongue and watched the exploits of a Springheel Jack in a costume and mask considerably more hideous than those used by Dee in the same persona. Jack chased, caught, and challenged the evil hundred-faced villain, battled him, was defeated by him, chased him again, and battled him again, until the final confrontation, on the slates of a rooftop high above London. There, Jack was able to overcome the scoundrel and, with a kick, send him flying off the roof and splashing into the Thames. The malefactor struggled, cried out, and finally disappeared under the thick, black water.

When the lights came on, I was incensed. "Such anti-Chinese sentiment must be stopped!" I said. "It is beyond offensive to be portrayed thus. And you, Dee—surely that caricature was meant to be you! How dare they—in fact, why do—who—" I realized I was so angry I was sputtering, and so I stopped.

"I agree about the offensive nature of the portrayals," Dee said, "though I can scarcely credit that even the British could take seriously any moving picture this foolish. As to your observation about myself, however, didn't you notice who is responsible for this cinematic nonsense?"

After a moment, the lights in my head came on also. "Oh! It wouldn't be Mr. Ted Bolton? Of Princely Pictures?"

Dee nodded. "I think I can safely assume I made an impression on him when we two met last spring."

"An indelible one, I'd say."

Hoong spoke. "I wish someone would indelibly impress upon Mr. Bolton and his Princely Pictures that it would improve his next moving picture immeasurably to have the fighting look at least plausible. If his actors require instruction I can make myself available."

"These are not 'actors'!" I protested. "They're buffoons of the lowest order!"

Jimmy Fingers looked from one of us to another. "I warrant ye gents know better than I do, but if I may say it, I ain't sure yer taking this picture in the right spirit. 'Twas an 'owler and no mistake. Coppers tripping over each other, and Spring'eel Jack flying through the air on ropes so thick you could see 'em! And what Mr. 'Oong says about the fighting! It made me laugh every time one of 'em laid another low with a punch that never came near 'im. Larking about, that's all this was. And that Spring'eel Jack! Oh, Mr. Dee, 'e don't 'old a candle to—"

"Jimmy!" I said.

The lad clapped a hand over his mouth. Then, "To—to the fellow we've seen, 'ooever 'e may be!" he finished triumphantly.

Dee smiled. "I'm gratified to hear the fellow we've seen rates higher on your scale of derring-do than this *artiste*. Nevertheless, this portrayal may be of some use. Jack here is presented as a hero. The next time Londoners spot Jack on a rooftop, those who have seen this picture will be likely to cheer."

We made our way out of the theater, blinking as we came into the light of day.

"I think we now can understand why this picture isn't being shown at the Palaseum," Hoong said.

"Why's that, Mr. 'Oong?" Jimmy inquired.

"Mr. Ben Hur is a gentleman of the Hebrew faith. The insults to an entire race, such as this picture casually dispenses, would find no welcome from such a man."

"Do you know him, Hoong?" Dee asked.

"We've had tea on occasion, to discuss philosophy and compare fighting techniques. Mr. Ben Hur is a boxer. A most interesting fellow."

"I should like, one day, to meet him," Dee said. "Now, I must keep an appointment."

Thus we four parted ways. Jimmy went to his lodgings nearby, for he lived in Silver Street. Hoong went back to his shop. Dee headed to Mayfair once again, to visit Madam Wu, as he had promised.

As for myself, I had a meeting to attend.

CHAPTER NINE

The university was between terms, but that state was not to be confused with abandonment. Instructors sat in their offices, adjudicating one another's academic papers for various learned journals or writing their own. Many students had gone either home or on holiday, but a number had remained: artists with stubbornly incomplete canvases in their studios, scholars with theses still manifesting as unruly piles of paper; in short, those with work as yet unfinished. Add to those populations the category of students from abroad for whom the journey home and back again was too long to make between terms, and you would find stone buildings whose hallways still echoed with hurrying feet, albeit fewer, and campus walks whose turning trees still saw earnest groups of young people sitting in their shade, albeit in smaller number.

It was to one of these earnest groups I was hurrying, though they were meeting not under a tree but in a Latin classroom otherwise unused until the return of its scholars. I felt an unexpected relief immediately upon entering through the heavy wooden door, even though I sensed disapproval in the blind stone gazes from the busts of Pliny the Elder, Julius Caesar, and Gaius Marius on their plinths. My comfort came not from the place, nor the subject taught there, but from my first sight of my fellow meeting attendees. All were Chinese.

I had not been in a group consisting solely of my countrymen since coming to London, if you except the populations of Chinese eating establishments. I say country*men*, but I must amend myself, for of the approximately three dozen students in the room, fully a third were members of the fairer sex. The unexpected longing for home I'd felt earlier in the day was reinforced by the sight of faces thin or wide, plain or handsome, solemn or smiling, but all Chinese.

The meeting had not yet begun, and tea and biscuits were laid out on a table by the windows. The biscuits, as the exigency of availability demanded, were British, but the tea was the astringent green tea most Chinese favored. Since coming to London, I'd developed a fondness for black British tea, as Dee had noted, but what was on offer here was the tea of home, and I suddenly very much wanted some. I made my way to the table and poured a cup. As I sipped the sharp, hot liquid, I listened to the murmur of Mandarin around me. I looked across the room to the banner at the front announcing this as a meeting of the Chinese Youth Communist Party.

A thin, intense young man approached me. "Teacher Lao," he said in Mandarin with the accents of the north. He gave a brief bow. "I'm Ang Chun. I'm pleased to see a member of university staff here. All Chinese, no matter our stations, must be prepared to stand together and fight to correct China's course and rid our homeland of foreign powers and of corruption!"

"I can find no objection to anything you've said," I told him. "I look forward to hearing the discussion."

Ang bowed again and shot a glare at another student as he strode away. That young man, taller and more muscular than Ang, caught my eye, gave a half-smile, and started in my direction. He, like Ang, bowed when he stood before me.

"Teacher Lao," he greeted me as his compatriot had. "I'm delighted to see you here. My name is Peng Lian Liang. I'm the Communist Party secretary in London. I imagine Ang gave you a warm welcome also?" He glanced with some degree of amusement toward the intense Ang, in conversation with a bespectacled man who seemed slightly older than the rest, perhaps my own age, and whom I didn't recognize from the halls of the university.

"Beyond warm," I said. "He seems quite prepared to ignite the revolutionary flame."

"Ang wasn't happy when his father sent him abroad to study. He's convinced armed struggle will soon break out in China between the Communists and the Nationalists, and he wants to be there when it does."

"I regard that idea with some dismay," I said. "China must stand strong against enemies within and without, and a strong China will require unity, no matter our views. What you speak of is nothing short of civil war. Do you really think that's inevitable?"

"I hope not. But that," said Peng, smiling, "is what we've convened to discuss."

With that, Peng bowed and left my side. He crossed to the front of the room, where the lectern stood. "Comrades," he addressed the crowd, "please take your seats." Although his voice was not loud, it was commanding, and the hubbub of conversation was quickly replaced by the clatter of chairs, with the stranger being shown by Ang to the first row. Ang took the seat beside him.

"Welcome, comrades," said Peng, when everyone was seated. He introduced himself as he had to me, and went on, "I see some new faces, for which I'm glad. I hope you all take the opportunity after the discussion to greet those comrades you haven't met yet, including myself, and to talk about how you can be part of the important work we share—the work of shaping China's future. There's much to discuss today, and we have a special guest, so we'll begin immediately with committee reports."

There followed a period of accounts of progress made by committees on recruitment, pamphlet-writing, pamphlet distribution, and fundraising. Contact with the central communist organization in China was reported on, as well as with other communist student associations in Leeds and at Oxford.

I was fascinated. Not by the reports; they were predictably dull, the cost of pamphlet-printing multiplied by the number of pamphlets printed being unexciting no matter whether the pamphlet's subject was stomach potion or revolution. My interest was in the revolutionaries. Men and women both, all dressed, as I was, in the European style—the women in dresses or skirts just an inch or two below the knee, the men wearing trousers and tweed jackets—each offered his or her account in dedicated detail, clearly convinced that communist revolution in China would be an excellent thing and that the work of this particular committee would help to bring it about. I myself, leaning cautiously in the same direction, could not help but admire the sure conviction of these young Communists.

I also could not help but notice the growing agitation displayed by Ang Chun, the intense young man who had first greeted me, as the reports went on. When the stream of committee chairs flowing to the front finally trickled dry and Peng Lian Liang once again took the lectern, Ang sat forward.

"Thank you all for your hard work," said Peng. "The glorious edifice of revolution can only be built stone by stone."

Ang rolled his eyes.

Peng went on, "Today, as you know, we have a guest and we're quite anxious to hear from him. Please welcome Comrade

Zhou En Lai." Peng bowed to the spectacle-wearing stranger, who returned the bow as he stepped behind the lectern.

"Comrades," he said, "I've just come from Paris, where the movement to build an international Communist Party is proceeding well." This occasioned murmurs of approbation. Zhou went on to give an account of the development, as seen from Paris, of solidarity among workers across national lines. He was an effective speaker, and I felt myself stirred at the idea that workingmen—and women, I reminded myself—might indeed come together and fight for their rights everywhere.

"There's been much talk," Zhou continued, "concerning China in particular, as to whether the proper road forward to revolution is one of gradual reform, as is the British system, or will demand violent means, as happened in Russia. For myself, I do not have a preference for either the Russian or the British way. I would prefer something in between rather than one of these two extremes."

"Not possible!" Ang could hold himself back no longer. All eyes turned to him as he jumped to his feet. "What would you do, storm a reactionary stronghold and then hold polite discussions as to the possession of the territory involved? Once violence is invoked there can be no turning back—and violent revolution must begin in China immediately!"

Through the voices raised in agreement or argument, Peng spoke up. "The communist movement is not yet powerful enough to prevail through armed or military means. We must take the gradual approach and build ourselves up."

"The gradual approach gets us nothing! We'll never be powerful if we don't show strength! We must inspire the people through a willingness to put ourselves in danger. The time for talk is through!"

"There are many who feel the approach this comrade advocates is the correct one." Zhou En Lai addressed the muttering room. "And as many who feel the opposite. I think the debate—"

"Debate! Pah! Strength begets strength. A slow, steady plodding begets weakness. Violence is the only way to revolution!" With that, Ang Chun stalked out of the room.

Peng Lian Liang rose and addressed Zhou En Lai. "Allow me to apologize for the behavior of Comrade Ang. He is a devoted believer, but his fervor makes him impatient."

"Many believe as he does," said Zhou, looking to the door Ang had stormed out of, "that the struggle for reform in China must come to violence. I hope they're wrong. But I fear they may be right."

CHAPTER TEN

The following day, having not heard from Dee that any instructions from Commissioner Lin had been received, I went again to the university. I took to my desk at the School for Oriental Studies and began preparing my notes for the next term's classes. As I methodically worked, I considered the words of Ang Chun. If slow, steady plodding begat weakness, as he said, then by the end of the coming term of classes, I could count upon being incapable of lifting so much as a teaspoon.

My day brightened with a knock upon my door. I was hoping, of course, for a visit from Dee, or, failing that, Sergeant Hoong, but I was ready to welcome any sort of distraction. That which greeted me took the form of one of the young boys who served as general dogsbodies around the university, running errands for the porters and the professors.

"Mr. Lao, sir," the boy said, doffing his uniform cap and holding an envelope forward, "this 'ere came for you. Mr. Wilkins said I was to bring it up."

"Thank you, Peter." I exchanged a shilling for the envelope. Peter grinned, replaced his cap, and ran off.

I opened the envelope—of square, fine paper—and though the contents did not offer any hope of further distraction for this day, they held promise for the following one. Inside was an invitation to a banquet to be given the next evening at the home of Madam Wu Ze Tian, to celebrate the return of the dragon-taming mace.

I PRESENTED MYSELF at the fine brick home in Mayfair at the appointed hour of the appointed day. The stony-faced young woman, Feng, and the red hound, Mei Qiang, granted me entry. Neither greeted me as a friend, though neither growled, which I accounted a success. They led me to the same front room where I'd met Madam Wu two days earlier. There, I found a small group of men and women, some sitting, some standing, all with glasses in hand. The murmur of conversation was in English, which did not surprise me, many of the number in the room being Westerners. Dee, I spotted immediately. Standing by the fireplace, he was deep in conversation with the one other Asian man in the group, a gentleman with round glasses and a mustache. I saw that Dee had chosen, as I had, to pay tribute to the occasion by dressing in traditional Chinese scholar's robes. I also recognized the Honorable Bertrand Russell and his wife, Dora, whom I had met in connection with Dee's earlier visit to London. Dora Russell, to my surprise, wore a green silk qipao and trouser set. Her feet were clad in embroidered slippers, and an ivory comb adorned her hair. The Russells, I reminded myself, had spent considerable time in China. It was reasonable to suppose they had had clothes made during their stay. Bertrand Russell, like the other men in the room, with the exceptions of Dee and myself, was in European formalwear, but I wondered if he'd obtained a silk scholar's robe in China, and if so, if it suited him as well as the qipao suited his young wife.

"Ah, Teacher Lao. My house is honored." Madam Wu approached me with a bow and a greeting in Chinese. In contrast to Dee and myself—and Dora Russell—she was clothed in the latest British style: Her golden silk frock shimmered with beadwork, and a black fringe ran from her bare right shoulder diagonally across her body to the hemline on the left. Silk stockings and gold shoes with high heels and pointed toes completed her ensemble.

The Republic had been declared in 1912. China was no longer ruled by an emperor, and the sumptuary laws reserving yellow clothing to the imperial family had long since been repealed. Chinese were free to wear what we wanted, yet centuries of tradition made it difficult for many people to feel comfortable donning clothing of the shade Madam Wu wore this evening. I got the sense that not only did Madam Wu not share these qualms, but that with tonight's dress, as with the men's tailoring she wore in the daytime, she was sending a message to all who saw her.

"Please, come in," she said and then switched her language to English. "Will you have a cocktail before dinner? I can offer martinis, or perhaps you'd prefer a French 75?"

She led me to a table where a young, red-cheeked Englishman was dispensing clear drinks, and golden ones the precise shade of Madam Wu's dress. I was coming to the idea that this lady did nothing without intention.

Madam Wu left me in the care of the barman as she went to greet another guest. I had previously tasted a martini, an American concoction, and didn't care for it, so I opted for the other and found it pleasantly light. As I sipped, I looked about the room. I spotted Feng bowing to Dee and saying something. He apologized to the gentleman he was speaking with and started to follow her out of the room.

"Dee." I approached him and spoke in Chinese. "Is everything all right?"

"Lao! I'm glad to see you. Everything's fine. My presence is required in the kitchen. Though 'required' is inaccurate. Madam Wu has done me the honor of permitting me to prepare the roasted duck; however, her chef, Chung Kao Kun, is in no need of assistance from an amateur such as myself. Furthermore, if he were, in addition to her many other sterling qualities, Feng is possessed of knife techniques that put mine to shame."

Dee was an excellent chef. I'd tasted the products of his labor in the kitchen and seen his knives flash as he chopped and boned. I found it difficult to believe anyone could improve upon his methods. The young woman's countenance, however, warmed with a tiny smile, though she shook her head and kept her gaze downcast.

"Really, Lao," Dee continued, "if you ever get the opportunity to see Feng at work, you'll be much impressed. Now, however, I'd appreciate it if you'd take on the care of Yoshio Markino. I fear without protection he'll be crushed under the heavy weight of A. G. Stephen."

"That gentleman is Yoshio Markino?" I lifted my glass in the direction of the man Dee had just left, who was now inclining his head to converse with a young blond woman sitting in a chair beside him. "I'm an admirer of his work. I'd be delighted."

"Yes, and that one is Stephen. Director of the Hong Kong and Shanghai Bank. Referred to as 'the Lion.'" Dee nodded toward a portly European gentleman on one of the angular white chairs, looking a bit like a pudding on a platter. He was in conversation with another European, a man in his midthirties with an easy smile and keen blue eyes. Stephen kept casting glances, however, at the pretty blonde. "The gentleman with whom he's speaking is called Anthony Cartwright, and the lady by whom he's distracted is Marie Markino," Dee said. "Markino's French wife."

I was beginning to see the difficulty. "I'll unfurl my banner," said I, "and ride to the rescue."

Dee, Feng, and the hound left the room, and I crossed it to introduce myself to the well-known Japanese painter of fog.

CHAPTER ELEVEN

The evening passed quickly in a pleasant haze of interesting conversation and excellent food and wine. My cocktail discussion with Yoshio Markino and his wife was joined by the final guest, a man I hadn't yet met and whom I was delighted to find to be the poet Arthur Waley. We four conversed on the subject of the arts, modern and ancient, Asian and European. Our only interruption was the call to the dining room, A. G. Stephen having apparently decided that the acquaintance of the pretty, shy Marie Markino could be made over the dinner table.

The fairer sex making up the minority of the party, the seating could not, as is the European preference, alternate man and woman. Dee was seated to Madam Wu's right and Bertrand Russell to her left. To Russell's left sat the man with whom A. G. Stephen had been talking earlier, and I found myself beside him. He introduced himself with a firm handshake and a grin. "Anthony Cartwright."

I was shaking his hand and telling him my name when a voice came from my other side. "Tony was an apprentice to Sherlock Holmes."

I turned to my left to find Dora Russell, wearing, in addition to the green qipao, a teasing smile.

"Mrs. Russell," I said, aware that I was reddening. This was an effect this lady often had on me. Although my experience with the fairer sex was limited, it was not nonexistent, and in light of it, I was unable to interpret Dora Russell's behavior toward me as anything other than flirtatious. I was flattered but also confounded. The woman had a husband, for whom I had the greatest respect, and who seemed totally at ease with—even amused by—her comportment.

"I've told you to call me Dora," she rebuked me lightly. "Tony, Lao She is a scholar and a writer. He's an associate of Dee's."

"Ah, the celebrated Judge Dee. Yes, he and I briefly spoke just now. It's a pleasure to meet you, Mr. Lao. I must, however, correct the impression Dora may have given you about my relationship with Mr. Holmes." Cartwright's keen eyes now met mine with admirable frankness. "I have had, since a boy, a great reverence for the famous detective. I was lucky enough many years ago to be employed by him on some cases and to have been given instruction now and again on certain topics. But I would hardly, more's the pity, dare describe myself as his apprentice."

Yoshio Markino, who had held Dora Russell's chair for her, seated himself on her other side. "What is it, Mr. Cartwright, you do now?" he asked.

"I travel," Cartwright answered, as though traveling were a profession. "When I arrive, I find occupation. I'm just back from Manchuria."

"Are you indeed?" I said. "I'm Manchu myself, but from Peking. I've never been to the north."

"I'd have thought it dangerous," said Dora Russell. "Such a troubled region."

"All of China is troubled, Dora," Cartwright replied. "And not an inch of it isn't fascinating. Even the trains are extraordinary—the Chinese Eastern Railway is such an accomplishment."

From across the round table, Dee asked casually, "Can you enlighten us as to the meaning of the conspiracy rumors swirling around it?" I had not been aware he was listening to our discussion, but his joining it once the railroad was mentioned came as no surprise.

Cartwright laughed. "I've heard them, but I have no idea what they mean. Rumors in China are so thick on the ground, it's a shame they're not a crop. They could feed the nation."

The rotating tray in the center of the table, laden with the traditional first-course cold platters of jellyfish, bean curd, five-spice beef, and seaweed, pivoted and offered its bounty to each in turn.

Cartwright asked me, "Did you meet the Russells in Peking?"

"Oh, rather not." Bertrand Russell chuckled. "Lao, you might tell the story of our meeting. I think it will amuse the party."

Thus I found myself recounting for Cartwright and any who cared to hear it the tale of my introduction to Bertrand Russell and to Dee. I spoke because Cartwright appeared genuinely interested and also to distract my attention from Dora Russell.

"A brawl in the jails!" Cartwright laughed when I got to the high point of the tale. "I'm sad to have missed it."

Bertrand Russell leaned forward. "Stick with Dee," he said, "and he'll find you another."

Dee shook his head in mock dismay. "Russell, I must protest. As you well know, my days and nights are largely spent in peaceable pursuits." I noticed a small smile playing on Madam Wu's ruby lips. Dee continued, "Why, earlier this week, Lao and I could be found at the cinema."

"Did you see *The Thief of Bagdad*?" asked Dora Russell. "Douglas Fairbanks is splendid!"

"No, it was a picture called *The Man of a Hundred Faces*," I answered.

"An execrable piece of Yellow Peril trash!" exclaimed Cartwright. "I was appalled to find it even existed. Really, sometimes when I return from an extended trip abroad, I feel I must give my fellow Britons the same scrutiny I turn on the Jurchen and the Bushmen, because the actions of Englishmen can be equally unaccountable."

Before I could make an answer, Yoshio Markino smiled from Dora Russell's other side. "This idea, Cartwright-san, not a bad one. Most people think place of birth makes identity. Foolish. Thinking this way limits . . . limits thinking!" He laughed, and we all smiled, and conversation broke into smaller groupings as our plates were changed for clean ones, the cold foods removed, and platters of deep-fried balls of sweet crab meat placed on the rotating tray. We each received a bowl of fragrant jasmine rice. The tray was turned so the ladies could take the first pieces, reversing their silver chopsticks to reach onto the common platter. Madam Wu took a particularly crisp golden orb and placed it on Dee's plate, then did the same for Bertrand Russell. She took her own portion, and we all followed.

"May I ask, Mr. Cartwright," I said as I lifted a morsel of crab, "what you do in England between your trips abroad?"

"I dabble in the sciences. I learned from Mr. Holmes that nothing compares to the knowledge gained from testing one's own theories in one's own laboratory. I have a small workshop in Hazlitt Road."

"Tony," said Dora Russell, "makes things explode."

"Also bubble, fume, melt, and divide by both mitosis and meiosis. And, occasionally, just sit glaring at me and refusing to react at all," was Cartwright's rueful response.

"Ah, the frustrations of research work. Familiar to any academic, no matter the field," I said, raising my glass to him.

When the crab had been removed and replaced by a grayling in satiny sauce and we'd all taken our portions, Madam Wu offered a toast. "To China's future." She raised her wineglass.

"China's future," said we all, and drank.

"May I say, Madam Wu, how pleased I am to see your mace returned to its rightful place," Arthur Waley said. "A piece with such history."

"Such beauty," said Markino.

"Such value," A. G. Stephen growled.

"A piece," Dora Russell said, "that, unless I'm wrong, is reputed to be capable of cutting through illusions to see the truth underneath."

"You are quite right, Mrs. Russell," Madam Wu said. "The ancient tales credit it with that ability. They also say it contains the power to marshal unseen forces in support of he—or she—who wields it." The lady smiled. "I'm just grateful to have it back"—she lifted her glass in acknowledgment to Dee—"and I was quite disappointed to find that Vladimir Voronoff had stolen it. We'd become friends, or so I thought. He's a White Russian, one of the many who renounced Russian citizenship after the revolution and fled to Harbin. I believed I could trust him; after all, we have common cause against the Russian military enemy."

"I'm sorry, Madam Wu, to contradict you in your own home," I said, possibly given the courage to speak up by my earlier cocktail and my current glass of Riesling. "But common cause with the White Russians can only lead to tragedy in China. They, as gentry and landowners, are the aristocracy whose merciless oppression of the peasants was the very root of the revolution. Our own peasants are chafing under a similar weight right now. For China to be seen to be in league with the overthrown Russian aristocratic class could ignite a tinderbox of resentment among our people."

"Why, Lao," said Dora Russell with a smile, addressing me by my family name, as men addressed one another, and as Madam Wu also did, "I didn't know you had these leanings. Well said."

"Lao is convinced that unless we all embrace the communist cause, China will have no peace." Dee lined up his chopsticks on their rests while the staff collected our plates and replaced them with new ones so that we might enjoy the salty crisp chicken now being brought to the rotating tray.

"Judge Dee is exaggerating," I said, perhaps a little stiffly. "I will go so far as to say that I believe the just complaints of the people must be addressed or we can expect turmoil to continue and to increase."

"Strength is what China needs," said Madam Wu. "Strength is what will bring China peace."

"Strength is a treacherous commodity," Bertrand Russell responded. "Sometimes, it's needed, I agree. But those who rely too heavily on it to support their principles inevitably forget those principles and begin to wield strength for its own sake. They become dictators, despots, and warlords."

"Are you referring to Zhang Zuo Lin?" A. G. Stephen peered at Bertrand Russell. "If so, I think you can be confident the man had no principles to start with."

I found this an extraordinary statement, not that I doubted its veracity. Zhang was a ruthless military commander who switched loyalties as the political winds blew. But to hear a director of a bank that funded the opium trade to China speak of principles was galling. If I had not been a guest at a celebratory occasion in the home of Madam Wu, whom I'd already contradicted, I'd have challenged the man his right to this opinion. Instead, I lifted a chicken tidbit to my lips as Madam Wu said, "As I understand it, the principle on which Zhang operates is that only a united and strong China will be able to withstand pressures from without and within. His methods can be heavy-handed, even harsh, but one could wish the Nationalists understood power as he does."

The discussion continued on in this fashion as glasses were refilled, plates and platters removed and replaced. The chicken was supplanted by king trumpet mushrooms braised with mustard greens, redolent with the dark taste of black vinegar. Talk grew louder, conversations began to overlap one another.

Finally, new plates were exchanged for old, and Dee's roasted duck was brought in with its requisite pancakes, hoisin sauce, cucumber, and leeks. The butler placed it on the sideboard. Dee rose to make the first cuts, separating the skin from the flesh and laying it aside. Then, surprisingly, he turned and offered the knives to Feng. The young woman looked to Madam Wu, who smiled. Feng approached the sideboard, took the knives, drew in a breath, and began. I watched in astonishment as the blades flashed and chimed. She had the duck in slices and arranged on the platter almost before Dee had resumed his seat.

I resisted the urge to applaud.

"Thank you, Feng," said Madam Wu. The young woman bowed her head, and the duck was served. We rolled slices in pancakes with cucumber and leek and dipped the resulting cylinder in bowls of glossy sauce. I was in the midst of a stimulating discussion with Arthur Waley on the subject of Chinese poems about cats when I heard Dee offering yet another disparagement of communism as a threat to the future of China.

"Excuse me," I said to Waley. I turned to Dee. "Dee, you are far too sensible to believe all these things you are saying. If you're putting this nonsense forth to elicit reactions from members of this gathering, you have got one from me."

Before I could continue, however, A. G. Stephen spoke up. "The threat to China," he said, in his deep growl, "is neither in communism nor nationalism. Nor warlords. Nor national identity," he snapped, rather gratuitously, at Yoshio Markino. "The threat is much closer than that."

"I don't take your meaning," I said. "Could you elaborate?"

The question was mine, but in answer, Stephen looked straight at Dee. "Come see me at the bank Tuesday morning."

"Very well." Dee nodded.

"And now, I'm sorry, Madam Wu, but I must take my leave. Thank you for the evening." At this, A. G. Stephen stood from the table. Feng was dispatched to fetch his coat.

Madam Wu rose also and joined him at the door, where the two spoke. When he left, she returned to us. "Mr. Stephen extends his regrets to you all. He is not feeling at his best." She smiled. "I sincerely hope my feast has given him nothing to complain of!"

To a chorus of denials, the plates were once again exchanged, for bowls this time, and we finished off the banquet with sweet red bean soup.

"Madam Wu," said Dee, when all was devoured, "may we have the honor of congratulating your chef?"

Madam Wu sent Feng for Chung Kao Kun. When he appeared, it was clear he'd changed his kitchen jacket for a clean one and that he dwarfed every man in the room. Chung's shoulders strained his seams, and he could have hidden a roast squab in each giant hand. He placed hand over fist and bowed his closely cropped head at the company's applause and applauded back in thanks.

At the evening's end, we bid farewell to our hostess and to one another. Promises were exchanged to maintain the friendships that had begun or continued that night. Madam Wu stood silhouetted in her doorway until the last guest had reached the pavement. As she shut the door, leaving us in the yellow glow of streetlamps through a gathering fog, I stated positively to Dee that he could get back to my flat however he pleased, but that I, after so much food and drink, would be taking a taxicab.

"After so much food and drink is precisely the time one needs to walk," Dee said, but I maintained my position, and he, with a smile, gave in.

CHAPTER TWELVE

The following day passed without incident. Dee went about whatever business he had in London, and I ensconced myself in my university office to continue my project of despairing over my students.

The next morning, however, was decidedly different.

I emerged from my bedroom to find that Dee had both types of tea and *The Times* on the table. He was frowning.

"What's wrong?"

"Well, Lao, two things happened while we slept. For the first, I received the anticipated visit from Commissioner Lin."

"Did you indeed?" I stopped in the act of pouring my tea. "Was he . . . agreeable?"

I will mention here that both Dee and I knew full well that Commissioner Lin Tse Shu was dead and had been so for seventy years. This apparently did not stop him from communicating with Dee. Previously, he had—quite harshly—issued Dee instructions that had, when finally understood and followed, resulted in the successful resolution of our earlier investigation. The doctors in Vienna would hold, of course, that these instructions were coming from the very mind of Dee himself. They'd declare that he'd conjured Commissioner Lin as a way to explain things that needed, in fact, no explanation beyond the one they would discover if Dee were just to lie on their sofas and talk about his childhood.

Nevertheless, Dee was in London, not Vienna; the only sofa he had at his disposal was the one in my sitting room, which was serving as his bed; and it seemed, however the late Commissioner Lin had gotten here, that he was in London, too.

"He was stern," Dee said, "as he tends to be. Also, the meaning of his words was veiled. The king, he said, had presided over all but could not account for everything. I asked for further explication, but he vanished."

I sat with my tea. "He really is a most confounding fellow. I wonder if he was like this in life. Do you have any idea at all what he meant?"

"I didn't at the time. But now, to some degree, I do. *The Times* provided a clue this morning, announcing the second thing of relevance that happened while we slept." Dee unfolded the newspaper and laid it before me.

A large headline told us that, during the night, Hong Kong and Shanghai Bank director, A. G. Stephen, known as "the Lion," had died.

CHAPTER THIRTEEN

Shocked at the news, all I could do was pour more tea for Dee and myself. I read through the article. Then, at a bit of a loss, I offered to toast some bread on the rack over the gas flame. Dee, however, countered with a surprise: from the icebox, he fetched dumplings, a gift from Madam Wu, whom, as I knew, he had visited the previous day. Dee heated sesame oil in a cast iron pan and then added the crescent-shaped pockets. They began their sizzle toward golden doneness.

While the air filled with the pop of hot oil and the scents of pork and garlic, I sipped tea and thought. "Are you saying, Dee, that the king referred to by Commissioner Lin is the lion, king of the jungle? A. G. Stephen, then, metaphorically?"

"I think it's probable. Stephen, as the bank's managing director, did preside over all."

"If that's so, what do you suppose it is for which he could not account?"

"That I don't know. Or what, when we learn it, we're expected to do with that knowledge. It's worth remembering, however, that Stephen had invited me to see him at the bank this morning."

"That's right, he did! When I asked for an explanation of his cryptic remark on the nearness of the threat to China."

"Precisely. Did it not strike you as odd that it was your question, but me he wanted to see?" Dee lifted the dumplings into two bowls.

"It did." I rose to take from the cabinet the mixture of rice wine vinegar and soy sauce. I put the bottle on the table with pairs of chopsticks, and we began to eat. "I was of course going to insist upon coming with you," I said, swallowing a bite of pungent, salty pork.

"I was, of course, going to insist that you did." Dee chewed contemplatively. "However, I think we must change our plans. I shall go see the Lion, but I'd like to suggest a different task for you."

"Dee." I put down a dumpling and looked at him. "Go see the Lion? A. G. Stephen is dead."

"As is Commissioner Lin. And yet, dead men can still speak."

We finished our dumplings while Dee explained his plan.

THE STRATEGY INVOLVED Dee and myself separating, each to his own business. My part was simple enough, and I shall recount it first. It involved some disagreeable moments but no danger and resulted in nothing—until its very end.

After our excellent breakfast and the washing-up, Dee and I left my flat. He went to Limehouse to collect Sergeant Hoong, while I took myself to Belgravia to collect what I could.

The home of the late A. G. Stephen in the leafy precincts of Eaton Square was a fine limestone edifice. Black wreaths hung in the windows and a black ribbon covered the doorbell, so instead of pulling that, I lifted and rapped with the bronze lion door knocker. The heavy wooden door was eventually opened by a manservant wearing a black armband.

"Yes?" he said. His lips pursed in distaste as he gazed at me.

"I'm so sorry to bother you at this time," I said brightly. "But, of course, it's at this time that I felt I must come. To pay my respects, you understand, and—"

"The visitation will be tomorrow at the Linton Funeral Home and Chapel." The man made to close the door.

"Oh, but that's hardly what I mean. I'm writing a book, you see." I held up my pen and notebook. "On the remarkable life of Mr. Stephen. It's truly been my own life's work. Mr. Stephen spent so many years in my home city of Hong Kong. It was there I began my tome. When he came back here, I followed immediately. I've gathered vast amounts of material on his life—did I say I'm an instructor at the University of London?—but the opportunity to learn the exact circumstances of his death, any last words, to speak with those who were with him—why, it's extraordinary, really. I had to come while all these things were fresh. Now, may I ask you, my good man—"

"You may not. Such impertinence!"

"Oh, but surely—"

He looked down a nose no more patrician than my own but considerably more out of joint. "You Chinese! I was Mr. Stephen's butler at the Hong Kong household as well. It was like this day in and day out, Chinese endlessly importuning for one thing or another. I've shooed many Chinese from our door. Shoo!"

Since he was shooing me like a dog, I was tempted to bite him; but I was investigating. I thought, What would Dee do? I smiled. "As you were his butler, I'm confident you have insight into Mr. Stephen that no other can match. My book will present the *real* A. G. Stephen to the world. It will take the Lion and make him human—"

"I doubt it will, but whatever it does it will do without any contribution from me!" At which the man shut the door in my face.

I gazed at the bronze lion roaring two inches from my nose. That interview could not be accounted a success. Was there a new strategy I could employ? Again, how would Dee handle this situation? Perhaps I should go home, change my suit, and return as a different man on a different errand, for I was certain that this butler couldn't tell one Chinese person from another. As I was weighing this tactic, the door opened. Upon finding me still on his doorstep the butler glared. Then, "Oh, hello," said a new voice. A freckled young woman with a nurse's watch on her coat's lapel smiled at me as she stepped from the door. She turned to the butler. "Again, my condolences to the entire household, Mr. Thwaite."

"Thank you, Sister."

The young woman, making the assumption most would make upon seeing someone at the doorstep, moved aside so that I could enter the house.

"That, Sister, will not be necessary!" And Thwaite the butler shut the door in my face again.

The young woman gave me a puzzled tilt of the head.

"I'm afraid Mr. Thwaite doesn't care for me," I said. I extended my card, told her my name, and explained my invented mission.

"The story of Mr. Stephen's life! That will make a marvelous read." She tucked my card in her purse. "I'm sorry Mr. Thwaite was so icy. But how rude of me not to introduce myself! I'm Alice Green. I was Mr. Stephen's nurse."

I glanced at the emphatically closed door. A third encounter with the icy Mr. Thwaite seemed unpromising. Miss Green, however, provided a fresh opportunity—one that Dee, I was sure, would urge me to seize upon. "I didn't know Mr. Stephen required nursing care."

"Yes, he's not been well since he came back to England. I was surprised he chose to go out the night before last. But he said there were people he needed to talk to. He went to a Chinese banquet, oh, it sounded marvelous! I suppose you've been to many."

"Indeed." I turned with her to walk along the pavement.

"Perhaps I can find out for you the name of the host. You can talk to them."

Of course, that name was well known to me, but I felt it wouldn't benefit my investigation to admit I'd also been in attendance. It was a shame to deceive such a charming young woman; however, I'd come here on a mission. "That would be very kind. Miss Green, I apologize if my question is unseemly, but for my book, you see—were you with him when he died? Did he speak at all?"

Her smile grew. "I don't mind. I know you writers are always hoping for the dramatic. How exciting, to be a writer, always in the midst of a story! My own imagination is rather deficient, I'm afraid. We nurses are a practical lot." Her eyes sparkled, then saddened. "I'm sorry to have to tell you, though, that Mr. Stephen simply expired. There was no point in Mr. Thwaite's being so . . . emphatic. He could have just told you there was nothing to say."

I detected a note of sympathy in the young lady's voice and decided to make use of it. Shaking my head sadly, I said, "I fear Mr. Thwaite has no affection for Chinese people."

"No," she said, in that odd way the English language has of allowing a person to agree by pronouncing the negative. "I'm afraid you're right. I'm sorry your visit was wasted."

"A visit on which I meet such a charming person as yourself can never be called wasted," I said. "But is there nothing you can tell me? For my book?" I made my face hopeful.

"No, nothing." Suddenly she laid her hand on my arm.

"Oh, but one thing did happen. I'm sure it's meaningless, but it might add some color to your work."

"Color is exactly what I'm after!" I said, fearing her unexpected touch had made me color, myself.

"In that case, I can tell you that last night, rather late, Mr. Stephen had a visitor—one he did not seem pleased to see. The man stayed a short time, and they talked in the parlor. When he left, I took Mr. Stephen up to bed, as he was already very tired to the point of being groggy. The visitor"—here, she smiled conspiratorially—"spoke with an accent. Polish, or Hungarian, some such thing. Between ourselves, although he was dressed plainly, I'm quite sure he was a count or a duke. I imagine he was hoping to invest a sum with the bank and visited Mr. Stephen's home at night to avoid attracting attention on the streets of London." She frowned in puzzlement. "Though if he wanted to invest, why would Mr. Stephen not be pleased to see him?" This difficulty had evidently just occurred to her.

"You didn't happen to learn the gentleman's name?"

"No, I'm sorry." She appeared abashed. "I can tell you he was a glowering sort of person, thin and dark, with a mustache. My, I seem to have created more questions than I've answered, haven't I?"

"Oh, no, Miss Green. It's color I'm eager for, after all."

"In that case, I hope I've helped. This is my bus coming along now. It's been a pleasure meeting you, Mr. Lao."

I thanked her and stood until the bus swallowed her up. She waved jauntily and took a seat. I turned to head back to my flat, hoping to encounter Dee. I was pleased with my application of his investigative methods and interested in what he would make of Stephen's foreign visitor. A Polish or Hungarian fellow, calling late on the night A. G. Stephen died, was an intriguing event indeed.

CHAPTER FOURTEEN

Soon enough, I shall recount my conversation with Dee, but to keep events in their proper order I'll now narrate the story of Dee's morning, as told to me by Dee himself—after much importuning, for Dee has no particular interest in having his deeds recorded. He is of the opinion that a task, once completed, is of no consequence except in the results and any lessons to be taken. I, as a writer, am of a different belief altogether. Dee indulges my insistence upon being provided with sequences of events leading up to results and lessons, though his indulgence sometimes includes a show of long-suffering tolerance. When someone else has been with him, I count myself fortunate; most people are less reluctant than Dee to talk about themselves. In this case, Dee's story was supplemented with details offered by Jimmy Fingers and Sergeant Hoong.

DEE, HAVING LEFT my flat near Covent Garden, made his way to Limehouse, naturally on foot and unnaturally fast. On his way through the Limehouse streets, he found a boy eager to undertake the finding of Jimmy Fingers for a shilling and the promise of another. At Hoong's shop, he explained his plan to the Sergeant, who sighed and turned his shop sign to "closed."

"Yes, I know, I'm driving you into poverty by constantly interfering with your ability to make a living," Dee said as Hoong turned on the gas ring under the kettle. "Although I think I had a right to expect that, in the six months I was gone, you'd have laid aside savings against the eventuality of my return."

"I was hoping," Hoong said, pouring from the kettle into the pot, "that you'd retired."

A rap on the door soon announced the arrival of Jimmy Fingers, in the company of the boy prepared to accept the second shilling. Dee produced it and the child dashed off.

"Gents!" Jimmy said, doffing his cap as Hoong allowed him entry. "Are we off on another adventure, then? Oh, Mr. 'Oong! That wouldn't be—?"

"Yes, Jimmy, it's the tea you favor. Sit down and have a cup. It's likely we'll need it."

While Jimmy sipped his tea, Sergeant Hoong, whose connections in Limehouse were unparalleled, went about collecting the items they would need. Dee changed his clothing for a workingman's blue cotton tunic and trousers, and they were off.

At the corner, they hailed a taxicab, as time was of the essence; though in the place where they were going it could be said to stand still. The driver, in the way of London taxicab drivers, made no remark upon seeing his cab entered by a Chinese merchant, a laborer, and a Stepney lad—the former carrying a sheet, the latter maneuvering a pole-and-canvas stretcher—nor did he comment upon hearing that their destination was the Westminster Mortuary in Horseferry Road.

Once near, they asked to be let out down the street from that red brick building, at the mouth of an alley. In the shadows of the alley itself, Hoong, sighing once again, lay down upon the stretcher. Jimmy Fingers, with a grin, covered him with the sheet. Jimmy peered out into the street, gave Dee the all-clear sign, and Dee and Jimmy hefted the poles. They carried their cargo out of the alley, down the block, and in through the mortuary doors.

"'Ere!" called Jimmy, to the first attendant he saw inside. "Where d'ye put the fresh ones?"

Looking confused, the attendant stopped his mopping of the floor to point down the tiled hallway to a door marked "autopsy."

"Obliged," Jimmy said, and he and Dee proceeded in that direction. They pushed through the double doors into the autopsy room. Cold air hit them at the same time as the loud hum of the compressors that were making it; the entire room, it seemed, was a giant icebox.

"Oi!" A chubby, white-coated coroner's assistant looked up from the instruments he was laying out. "What do you think you're doing?"

"Got a new one," said Jimmy. "Where do we put 'im?"

The assistant frowned. "I wasn't told." He walked over and lifted the sheet from Sergeant Hoong's face. Hoong had slowed his breathing and displayed no animation whatsoever, appearing (even to Jimmy, it was enthusiastically reported to me) the very picture of death.

"This fellow?" barked the assistant, letting the sheet drop again. "If I wasn't told then the coroner don't want him. Get him out of here."

"What am I expected to do with 'im?" Jimmy protested.

"He's Chinese," the man said with scorn. "Throw him back in the alley with the opium that killed him, I don't care. Just take him out of here." He waved impatiently toward the door.

Dee launched into a tirade of Chinese. The assistant's eyes grew wide. He turned to Jimmy. Over Dee's shouting, he asked, "What's he saying?"

Jimmy shrugged. "Don't know, guv. Probably something about your mam."

"My mother? How dare he!"

"Tell you this, though, 'e ain't gonna stop. Goes on for hours sometimes when 'e gets like this. Best we just leave the fellow 'ere."

"You will not!"

Dee's ranting grew more strident. His face reddened and he bounced on his feet, jostling the stretcher.

"Don't drop that body!" the assistant shouted. "Not in here! I'm off to report this to the coroner. He'll sort you soon enough!" The assistant slammed through the double doors. The slapping of his soles could be heard receding down the hallway.

As soon as he was gone, Dee and Jimmy lowered the stretcher to the tile floor. Tossing the sheet aside, Hoong sprang to his feet.

"Dee," said Hoong, "if your intention was to dislodge my breakfast from within, you came perilously close to success."

"I'll make it up to you," said Dee. "Quick now."

"You won't," Hoong replied, but began, like Dee and Jimmy, to slide open the drawers in the far wall, where the dead, each one numbered, waited their turns to come under the scrutiny of science.

"Mr. Dee, sir," Jimmy said, after opening his third drawer, "I can't say I like this, that I can't. Disturbing these dead folks, it don't feel right at all."

"I doubt they're disturbed, Jimmy," said Dee. "But it's all right if you want to leave. Hoong and I can find—"

"I believe I have," Hoong said. "Is this your man?"

Dee walked over to the drawer Hoong had just pulled out. He looked at the gray face atop the mountain of man A. G. Stephen had been. "Yes," he said quietly. From his pocket, he took out a leather case, which he handed to Hoong. Dee began minutely examining Stephen's cold, rubbery flesh as Hoong snapped the case open, extracted a hypodermic needle, and slid it into the vein in Stephen's arm. He pulled back the plunger, and blood was drawn sluggishly into the tube.

"I think this is all we can get, Dee," said Hoong, removing the needle and capping it.

Dee glanced up. "That will be enough. And here, I've found the place where, if I'm right, the first needle went in."

Hoong bent over the corpse's neck to look at the spot where Dee was pointing. "I agree."

Jimmy was standing by the front wall, as far from the corpse lockers as he could get. He cocked his head to the door. "Whatever you're doing over there, gents, maybe we ought to shake a leg. I think—"

Jimmy's thought went unfinished, but its meaning became clear as the door burst open and the coroner's assistant surged into the room. "The coroner says he'll call the authorities if you don't—" His face went ashen when he saw Hoong. "What—"

Dee cocked his head and smiled. In Oxbridgian tones, he said, "Apparently his condition has improved. Good day." Unhurriedly, Dee slid A. G. Stephen back into the wall and, followed by Hoong and Jimmy Fingers, exited the autopsy room. As Jimmy passed the astonished assistant, he suddenly shouted, "Boo!"

The assistant fainted dead away.

CHAPTER FIFTEEN

I had been waiting so long on the doorstep of Hoong's shop that my nostrils had become inured to the aroma of produce rotting in the gutters, a scent that overlaid that of the latrines of those establishments not yet fitted with indoor plumbing. People came and went, and I studied them as potential material for a story, as any writer might. I was engaged in this project when Dee, Hoong, and Jimmy Fingers rounded the corner. Seeing Dee in workingman's garb took me a bit aback, but Dee was a man of many surprises.

"Gentlemen!" I said. "I'm glad to see you! I—"

"Lao," said Dee as Hoong worked the lock. "Have you had success?"

"I believe I have. I—"

"Let us have a few moments." Dee and Hoong made straight through the shop to the back room.

"But I—"

"Never you mind, Mr. Lao," Jimmy said cheerfully. "We'll 'ave tea." He lit the gas ring under the kettle.

"What are they doing that demands such hurry?" I asked, looking toward the closed door to the back room.

"They've brought a bit o' blood. It needs to be tested now

before it gets old, or some such." Jimmy went to the shelf where Hoong kept the teacups.

"Blood? Where did they get blood?"

"Out of that fellow as was deceased." Jimmy rinsed the teapot under Hoong's tap. He seemed to have become quite at home in the shop.

"They took blood from the body of A. G. Stephen? How did they manage that?"

"At the mortuary. Mr. 'Oong stuck Mr. Stephen with a needle."

"You went to the mortuary?" I felt I was hearing this tale in reverse order.

"I don't mind telling yer, Mr. Lao, I didn't like that place. Mr. Dee said we wasn't disturbing the dead, but I could feel them wishing we'd take our leave. And cold it was! Like the grave itself. But I suppose Mr. Dee, being such a educated man and all, 'e don't believe in ghosts."

Doesn't believe in ghosts, and yet gets his instructions from one, I reflected.

"Jimmy, what are you doing?" I asked, for Jimmy had begun opening tins to sniff their contents.

"Searching for the tea we 'ad this morning," Jimmy said. "Excellent good, it was."

"I doubt it's that one. The label says that's to treat swelling of the lower leg."

"Label?" Jimmy glanced from me to the tins. "You mean these lines and things, it's their names in Chinese? And it says what they do?" He lifted each tin to examine Hoong's calligraphy. "That's a right wonder, that is!"

The door to the back room opened, and Dee and Hoong issued forth. "Ah, Jimmy, you've put the kettle on. Well done," said Dee. He sat on a stool at the low table while Hoong took a tin from the shelf and spooned the contents into the teapot.

"Mr. 'Oong," said Jimmy casually, "if you'd care to show me the label on that one"—he put a small stress on "label"—"I could make meself useful from time to time, fixing a pot."

"You mean, you could drink up my Dragonwell tea at an even greater pace than you do now." Hoong nevertheless turned the tin to present the characters to Jimmy. "Here," he said. "This is how you write them. You can practice and they'll be your first Chinese words." Hoong wrote out the characters on a sheet of paper.

"I will!" said Jimmy. "I'll be the envy o' the lads and no mistake." He pocketed the paper.

"Jimmy," I said, "if my students at the university had only a quarter of your enthusiasm, I'd be a happier man."

"'Ave you thought to offer them Dragonwell tea?" Jimmy asked. "They'll demand to know 'ow it's written, and then Bob's yer uncle."

"Well," Dee said, slapping his thighs, "I'm eager to hear your report, Lao, but first, let me give mine. A. G. Stephen was poisoned."

"Poisoned!"

"There is no question," said Hoong. "When heated in a mixture of certain medicinal herbs, his blood revealed the venom of the Qichun snake, an inhabitant of the forests of north and east Asia. Its symptoms mimic those of cholera."

"Which will no doubt be the official ruling on the cause of Stephen's death." Dee accepted a cup of tea from Sergeant Hoong.

"You must report this to the authorities immediately!" I said.

"Perhaps." Dee sipped from his tea as Hoong poured mine, Jimmy's, and lastly, his own. "First, Lao, tell us your news."

"But—very well, my news. As is probably not surprising, Mr. Thwaite, the butler at A. G. Stephen's household, dislikes

Chinese people. He would give me nothing and shooed me away like a dog."

"Oh, I've met men like that," said Jimmy, shaking his head in sympathy. "Many's the time, as a lad, I was shooed away meself. As though being 'ungry was a crime I'd committed!"

"And mine was being Chinese. Thank you for your sympathy, Jimmy. However, Mr. Stephen's nurse, a charming young woman called Alice Green, was of a different cast entirely. She was thrilled to be helping a writer with his work. Other persons might take a lesson from that eagerness." I looked meaningfully at Dee.

"Oh, yes?" Dee said politely, sipping his tea.

I sighed. "Miss Green maintained that her employer had no final words. That he slipped without stirring from sleep to that state of nonbeing of which we know so very little and yet—"

"You are perhaps growing a bit flowery, Lao," said Dee.

"Your appreciation of the narrative arts is defective," I snapped. "But then, you recited *Romance of the Three Kingdoms* to a horse."

Jimmy grinned.

I went on, "However, Miss Green was able to offer some news, and it was this: the evening of the night he died, Stephen had a visitor."

"Did he now?" Dee said.

"He did. Miss Green described the man as dark and glowering, with a mustache and, most interestingly, an accent. Polish, she said, or possibly Hungarian."

"Polish," Dee said. "Or Hungarian."

"Yes. The young lady is quite observant."

"And what do you make of this?"

"Miss Green is of the opinion the man is some sort of nobility, and he was seeking to do business with the bank."

"Nobility he may be," Dee said. "But I think it unlikely he was pursuing business."

"What do you think was his purpose, then?" I asked, but he didn't answer, just sipped his tea and stared into the air.

For a time after that, all was silence inside the shop. We drank tea while, from the streets of Limehouse, I could hear the shouts of hawkers and the clop of horses' hooves. Over a bit more distance came the honks and tootles of motorcar horns and the tinkle of a streetcar bell.

Finally, with a nod, Dee put his teacup on the table.

"I think," he said, "this is not the time to bring to the coroner's attention the fact that A. G. Stephen was poisoned."

"But Dee—" I said.

He shook his head. "The Metropolitan Police, although an admirable force in many respects, are likely in a case such as this to focus on the dead man's intimates, his friends, and even his household."

"The butler!" exclaimed Jimmy. "It was 'im what did it!"

"As gratifying as Lao would find it if that were true," Dee said, "I don't believe it is. Or, if it is, then I'll put forth that he was acting on someone else's behalf. No, I'm of the opinion that Stephen's death may well be connected to something much larger. Possibly the reason I'm here."

"And what reason may that be, Mr. Dee?" asked Jimmy.

"I don't know, Jimmy. But we might be about to discover it. And any stirring of the pot by the Metropolitan Police at this point would only muddy the stew. I think we must focus on this visitor mentioned by the charming and observant Miss Green. A man who spoke with the accents of Poland or Hungary. Or"—he raised his eyebrows at me—"as likely, Russia."

CHAPTER SIXTEEN

"Bertrand Russell," Dee said, tapping a finger on his empty teacup, "has contacts in many places. Perhaps there's some light he can shed upon the connection between the Russian visitor—"

"Or Polish, or Hungarian," I said.

"Yes, of course. Between this Eastern European visitor, and the death of Stephen. If there's nothing he can tell us about that, perhaps he has an inkling about what Stephen may have wanted to say when he asked me to meet him at the bank."

"You think the two things are related, then?" I asked.

"I'd be very surprised if they were not." He stood. "Hoong, we'll leave you to your shopkeeping, in the hopes that you can find a way to remain solvent."

"I appreciate your consideration for my attempts to earn a day's wage," said Hoong. "However, this day will not be one on which that happens. I've received word that a shipment has come to the docks, and I must go to meet it. If you have no further clandestine work for Jimmy, perhaps I can persuade him to accompany me? If the shipment is complete, it holds six bricks of Dragonwell tea."

"I'm yer boy, Mr. 'Oong," said Jimmy, jumping to his feet. "Unless, o' course, you need me, Mr. Dee."

"No, Jimmy, go right ahead. I suppose then we'll all leave the shop together."

Which we did, and as it developed, that was a lucky thing.

We had just reached the corner of the street that housed Hoong's shop when Dee put out his hand to stop us all. He pointed ahead, and up the street, I saw what seemed a familiar foxlike shape, clothed all in black and hurrying along.

"Dee!" I whispered. "Is that not Isaki? He's meant to be locked up. Why is he out of jail? And where is he going?"

"Your faith in my ability to answer questions such as these does me honor," Dee whispered back. "I suggest we seek the answers from Isaki himself."

We crept forward, remaining the same distance behind Isaki as we had been when we spotted him. My own ability to advance silently was not to be scoffed at, and Dee's, of course, was unparalleled, but Hoong's, given his size, would have been surprising to anyone unfamiliar with the training both he and Dee had received at the hands of Hoong's father in China. Jimmy Fingers was also impressively talented in this regard, which, upon reflection, I realized was to be expected in a young man of his profession. Thus it was that we were able to follow Isaki through a number of increasingly cramped and narrow streets until he emerged onto the wharf.

We stopped in the shadows of decrepit wooden structures leaning toward one another over the cobbled pavement as though telling secrets. Whether or not the buildings had secrets, I didn't know; but Isaki did, for he also stepped into a shadow, this one cast by a fish warehouse whose contents advertised themselves rather loudly to one's olfactory sense. A movement in that same shadow revealed a cloaked figure who, stepping close to Isaki, passed him a folded sheet of paper.

"When they separate," said Dee in low tones, "Hoong and

Jimmy, go after Isaki. Try to retrieve the paper. Lao and I will follow the other."

"How do you know they'll separate?" I asked. "Perhaps this was their rendezvous point and they're planning to go off together."

"In that case, why would the one have passed the paper to the other? Why not wait until they'd reached their destination? No, they clearly—there, they're off."

And, of course, they were.

Hoong, no doubt sparing a sad thought for his shipment waiting on the dock, sped after Isaki, with Jimmy at his heels. Dee and I went in the direction opposite, to follow the figure in the cloak.

The results of each pursuit will be presented here. I'll begin with the one that yielded the least, which was Dee's and mine.

The cloaked figure was as quick as Dee himself as it moved along the narrow lanes. I made my best effort to keep up. We three twisted and turned until the figure reached the top of Coltman Street and rounded the corner. Dee and I arrived there moments later, rounded the same corner, and found the figure had vanished.

To my embarrassment, I was grateful to our quarry for this respite, for my lungs were growing impatient at being deprived of the deep breaths they desired. I placed my hands on my knees and attempted to bring in enough air to satisfy their demands.

Beside me, suffering from no such difficulty, Dee stood erect, scanning the streets in each direction. He found nothing. It appeared our chase was over when, from my low vantage point, I spied movement: the figure, crouched behind a motor-car, was making its way crablike along the pavement.

"Dee!" I croaked, pointing.

My croak was louder than I intended; I did not have

complete control over my vocal powers. The figure whipped its head about and, spotting Dee, rose from the shadow and stood facing us. His features were lost in the depths of the hood.

Dee dodged traffic to race toward him. The figure stood as still as a statue until Dee achieved the opposite pavement. At that point, the cloaked figure sprang onto a motorcar and out into the street, crossing the path of an oncoming bus, barely in time to avoid getting tossed in the air. The bus blasted its horn and screeched to a halt. Dee, chasing the figure back across the street, was forced to run around the rear of the stopped bus to the accompaniment of more horns and screeches from brakes and tires.

Soon enough, unfortunately, he returned, shaking his head.

"Oh," I said. "You've lost him, then?"

"I have."

"I fear my shout alerted him."

"I fear it did." His look was stern. "Lao, you must improve your physical condition. I can't afford to have you not at your best in this matter."

"I—I—as I said, I didn't know to expect you back in London."

"But now you know I'm here. And that I need you. Well. Let's return to the shop and hope that Hoong and Jimmy have had better luck."

I was still digesting the idea that Dee needed me as we made our way back to Limehouse. There, we found that better luck was what Hoong and Jimmy had, in fact, had. This is the story of how that luck was created, as detailed to me later by Hoong, with addenda put in and errata corrected by Jimmy.

ISAKI MADE HIS way along the wharf, making no effort to keep himself hidden. Hoong and Jimmy crept closer, hastily concocting a plan. They stayed in the shadows of sheds and ducked behind cargo pallets until they came near enough that Hoong was able to step into the cobbled street and call Isaki's name. Isaki whipped around. When he saw Hoong, he smiled. As Hoong had predicted, Isaki welcomed an opportunity to engage with Hoong a second time.

Hoong stood, hands at his side, as Isaki advanced.

"So," said Isaki, smiling. "We meet again, old Chinaman, and this time, you are alone. As am I. Let us see who is actually the better man."

Hoong did not correct the mistaken assumption inherent in the first part of Isaki's statement. "It will be my pleasure," Hoong replied.

Barrowmen and teamsters moved aside, less to avoid becoming party to the brawl than to find good positions from which to watch it.

Hoong stepped back into a fighting stance. Isaki, assessing Hoong's position, moved in without haste. As did Jimmy Fingers, unseen by Isaki, for the entire purpose of Hoong's challenge was to distract Isaki while Jimmy freed the ronin of the burden of the folded paper in his trouser pocket.

Isaki stopped, and then sprang forward, executing a flying side kick to Hoong's chest. Hoong went reeling backward. As Isaki landed, Hoong, whose loss of equilibrium had been a feint, slammed a spinning backfist strike. Isaki tried to evade the blow, but Hoong's huge right hand was faster. "Tit moon gwun, crashing iron gate," Hoong called, smashing his fist into the samurai's right side, sending him falling backward to the ground into a pile of discarded fish parts. Isaki, now covered with innards, leapt to his feet, and it was at this point that Jimmy Fingers accomplished his task of thievery, unnoticed by Isaki—but not, as it turned out, completely unnoticed.

"Oi!" yelled a burly longshoreman. "You there! Shorty! You just had yer pocket picked!"

Five men turned about at that cry and fell to examining the contents of their clothing. Four found their possessions untouched.

The fifth was Isaki.

Finding his pocket empty, he whirled around. When he spotted young Jimmy, recognition dawned on his foxlike features. He sped toward the lad, who began to run. As before, Jimmy was fast but Isaki, faster.

"Mr. 'Oong!" called Jimmy, but it was too late: the ronin caught up to Jimmy and snatched the paper back.

Hoong, reaching them, stretched for Isaki. Evading Hoong, the ronin slid on the fish-slippery pier. This time he didn't fall, but while his attention was upon his footwork and diverted from the paper in his hand, Jimmy purloined that paper once more. Isaki flicked out his leg to send Jimmy tumbling. As the lad floundered, Isaki took the paper from him again.

The shrill call of a bobby's whistle cut the air, followed by shouting and the clomp of running feet.

Isaki, paper in hand, swiveled to face Hoong.

"I must be off, old Chinaman," he said. "It will be *my* pleasure to meet again at a later date and finish this."

"I think not, little fox. You will stay." With that, Hoong took two fast strides toward Isaki. Isaki didn't move.

"That," Hoong told me later, over tea, "was unforgivably heedless of me. My father would have had me hauling water late into the night had he seen. I could think of nothing but how I almost had my hands upon Isaki and, therefore, upon the paper. I neglected to consider that such a skilled and highly trained samurai wouldn't let an opponent approach so closely unless that was what he wanted."

"Why, what happened then? It was an ambush?" I asked, my pen at the ready.

"In a way. Isaki ducked under my arms and, in the blink

of an eye, lightly touched several points on my chest with his index and middle fingers."

"That doesn't sound—"

"Oh, but Mr. Lao!" Jimmy burst from across the tea table. "It was the death touch!"

Apparently, this death touch, which I'd heard of but always thought an exaggerated tale of martial prowess, was real enough, for as Hoong described it, he felt himself rapidly becoming paralyzed.

"Paralyzed! What did you do?" I demanded.

"He used the goat-capturing stance!" Jimmy informed me.

Hoong smiled. "Yes, I did."

Managing to assume the goat-capturing stance as he felt the paralysis spreading throughout his body, Hoong inhaled deeply through his nose, rolling back both wrists and squeezing his fists, his forearms, and his entire body. He sank his internal energy downward, using the Iron Wire breathing techniques taught by his father to channel his chi. This allowed him to release, one by one, each point that had been shut down by Isaki's deadly fingers.

Isaki stared at him. "You are more adept than I thought, old Chinaman, but I still have more than enough time to make my escape."

Slapping footsteps and strident whistles heralded the arrival of a truncheon-wielding platoon of bobbies. Isaki, with a grin, leapt to the bar of a lamppost and swung himself onto a roof. The bobbies, seeing Hoong, assumed this was the miscreant about whom they'd been summoned.

"Halt!" one cried. Before Hoong could reply, a ping was heard and another bobby cried, "Ow!" Another ping, another "Ow!" and the bobbies all looked to each other as small stones bounced off their custodian helmets. Hoong looked to see Jimmy crouching in the middle of a group of street urchins, urging them on in their pelting of the bobbies' hats. He waved at Hoong and disappeared behind a lorry. The mob of children scattered also, becoming one with the barrows, boxes, and bags haphazardly populating the wharf.

Hoong took advantage of this confusion to leave the bobbies' company.

"I'm becoming an old man, I fear," Hoong said to Jimmy, whom he found waiting on his shop doorstep when he returned. "I suppose I must begin to get used to failure."

"I ain't seen you fail yet, Mr. 'Oong," Jimmy replied.

Hoong unlocked the door and put the kettle on. "Our charge was to recover the paper. My task was to distract Isaki and, if necessary, render him immobile while you accomplished that. In the event, however, *he* nearly rendered *me* immobile, and I was unable to stop him making off with the paper. I don't know what you call that if not failure."

"A rousing success is what I call it. Though I fear yer will 'ave to write down those tea words in Chinese again." From the pocket of his corduroy jacket, Jimmy withdrew a folded sheet of paper. He handed it to Hoong, who opened it to see, written in English, a name he didn't recognize: *Peng Lian Liang*. Under the name ran three heavy vertical lines sandwiched between two horizontal lines.

"Jimmy!" said Hoong. He clasped the boy's shoulder. "Well done, lad! How did you manage it?"

"I stole it handily enough," said Jimmy, his cheeks glowing with pride. "But then 'e started chasing me to steal it back. I knew I couldn't outrun 'im. That fellow is fast and that's the truth! So I let 'im lift t'other one, with the tea words. Then, I stole it back again from 'im as though 'twere a thing I were determined to 'ave. Then, I let 'im steal it again. Poor fellow will 'ave no idea what 'e's got when 'e unfolds it. Though I 'ave to say, Mr. 'Oong, I 'ave no more idea meself what it is we've got 'ere."

CHAPTER SEVENTEEN

Hoong and Jimmy were celebrating their victory with a pot of tea when Dee and I returned to the shop.

"Mr. Dee! Mr. Lao! Look! Look at this!" Jimmy jumped up, waving a sheet of paper in front of us. On it were Chinese characters, though moving through the air as the paper was, I couldn't make them out. "Dragonwell, it says." Jimmy smiled proudly. "It's the tea. Mr. 'Oong showed me 'ow it's done."

Dee took the paper. "Very good, Jimmy," he said.

To my eye, and I'm sure to Dee's, while Hoong's calligraphy at the top clearly read "Dragonwell," Jimmy's uneven strokes below leaned more to "fruit fly." But following Dee's lead, I also complimented the young man.

"He's a promising student, is Jimmy," Hoong said, "when it comes to things that can fill his belly."

"We must meet a student where he is in order to lead him where he is capable of going," Dee intoned. "As your father often said. But as impressive as Jimmy's brushwork is, I admit to a great curiosity about the other sheet of paper involved in this afternoon's activities."

"Was there another?" Hoong turned to Jimmy. "Do you recall?"

"Well, I can't be sure," Jimmy said. He made a show of going through his pockets, then shook his head.

"Oh!" said Hoong. "Perhaps it's this?" He produced the sheet Jimmy had taken off of Isaki, and held it out to Dee; he and Jimmy both stood and bowed.

"A comedy duo we have here, Lao," Dee said, taking the paper. "Fit for the vaudeville stage. Or possibly the cinema. You gentlemen could talk to Princely Pictures, I'm sure they'd find you something. Would you care to relate the story of how this came into your hands, or would that take too much serious thought?"

"Serious thought?" Hoong answered. "Not at all. It's fairly amusing."

Briefly, he reported on their encounter with Isaki.

"And now you see, Lao, what these two find amusing. Perhaps you should reconsider the comedy act," said Dee. "It may not succeed."

With Dee, I peered at the paper.

"Peng Lian Liang!" I said. "He's the Communist Party secretary in London."

Dee looked up at me. "Do you know him?"

"We've met," I said, and nothing more, for I had no interest in being mocked by Dee for my openness to communist ideas.

"Have you indeed," he said. "And these lines? What do you make of them?"

I considered. "Held one way, it might be the number three in Roman numerals. The other, perhaps a ladder."

"Quite. And have you any guess as to its significance, either way?"

"None," I admitted.

"Nor I. Sergeant Hoong, can you spare a cup of that fruit fly tea?"

"It's Dragonwell tea, Mr. Dee," Jimmy corrected. "Like I wrote there."

Hoong poured tea without a smile. I myself hid mine behind my teacup.

"I think," said Dee, "there will be another change in plans. Lao, I'd like you to go to the Russells' and ask if they can shed any light upon what A. G. Stephen might have wanted to discuss with me, in view of the fact that we now believe him to have been murdered."

The prospect of seeing Dora Russell made me instantly anxious, for I never knew what to expect from that lady. Nevertheless, I agreed. "But what will you be doing, then, if not interviewing the Russells?"

"I? Nothing. Springheel Jack, however, will have a busy afternoon."

THE AFTERNOON AS passed by Springheel Jack will be detailed slightly later in this narrative. First, I will recount my own experiences at the home of Bertrand and Dora Russell.

CHAPTER EIGHTEEN

The Russell home in Bloomsbury was a place that had become familiar to me the last time Dee was in London. Nevertheless, I approached the door with a thrill of nerves, for the great Bertrand Russell was still an idol of mine for the workings of his mind—and his young wife, Dora, a source of unease for the workings of her impulsive personality.

Imagine my relief, then, when the bald butler, Larrimore, welcomed me with a smile and, to my inquiry as to whether Mr. Russell was at home, informed me that both Russells were, at the moment, in the parlor, entertaining Arthur Waley.

"I'm not expected, Larrimore," I said. "Could you inquire—"

He rolled his eyes, as if to say that was a completely gratuitous courtesy, but being a butler, he bustled off. Returning, he said, "Mrs. Russell instructs me to say if you don't come in at once, you'll never be welcome here again."

How like the lady. "Well, then," I said, stepping past Larrimore, "here is my hat."

In the book-lined parlor—hardly distinguishable from the study, or indeed the dining room, from that point of view—I found Bertrand Russell and Arthur Waley occupying upholstered chairs. Dora Russell, in a loose shift dress of pale green, had her feet tucked beneath her on the sofa. As embroidered slippers sat before her on the carpet, I could only imagine those feet were bare.

"Lao!" she said. "What a lovely surprise. Come sit beside me."

Such a position would not have been my first choice—possibly even my last—but as no other chairs leapt forward to present themselves, I put myself on the far end of the sofa from Mrs. Russell. I found myself wishing that piece of furniture had been more commodious, for the far end was not, in fact, very far.

"You've come at an opportune time, Lao," said Russell. "We were just discussing Chinese poetry."

"I've read some of Mr. Waley's translations," I said, accepting a cup of tea from Mrs. Russell. As she delivered the tea, her fingers brushed my hand in a way that I hoped was accidental. Given the lady's past behavior and her general gracefulness, however, that hope was most likely forlorn. I returned stubbornly to the subject of poetry. "I admire them greatly."

"In particular, it was the cat poems of Lu You we were considering," said Russell. "Because of this gentleman." He pointed to the carpet, where a gray kitten tottered, pouncing on invisible enemies. "His name is Xie. He was found at the back door. I was hoping he'd catch mice, but Dora feeds him fish."

"As did Lu You," Waley said, smiling. "And then was forced to ask: who is master, and who is servant?"

"One of the largest and most interesting of philosophical questions," I said. "Pertaining to much besides cat and owner. I wish I had time to debate it with you. However, I've come on an errand."

"Have you?" Dora Russell arched an eyebrow and suddenly smiled. "Lao! Are you and Dee working on a case?"

"We are," I confirmed. "Though we're not yet certain where

it will lead. First, I must tell you—prepare yourselves—that the death of A. G. Stephen was not natural. It was the result of poison."

"Poison?" said Russell. His wife's hand went to her mouth. Waley's eyes widened. Russell asked, "Is that the autopsy result, then?"

"The autopsy hasn't been conducted yet. However, Dee is sure that when it is, the verdict will be cholera. The symptoms are the same."

"Then, how—" said Waley.

"No, don't say," Russell interrupted. "Waley, Dee's methods, in China completely legal, can be regarded here as extrajudicial. We are better not knowing the details."

"You can tell me later, Lao, if you feel you must unburden yourself," Dora Russell said, a smile dancing upon her lips.

"No," I said hastily, and added, "thank you. I feel no such necessity. But I have, as I say, come on an errand, which is simply this: Do you know of any reason such a deed might have been done or anyone who could have done it? Stephen had asked Dee to meet him at the bank this morning. Have you any idea why?"

Russell frowned. "No, I'm sorry, I don't."

Waley shook his head. "I only met the man at Madam Wu's banquet."

I was about to thank them and rise to leave when Dora Russell said, "I do."

All eyes turned to her.

"Alexander spoke to me," she said. "At Madam Wu's, over the cocktails. The third French 75 can quite loosen one's lips." She smiled at me again, then continued, "He's—he'd been—troubled by an anomaly at the bank. Sums, fairly large, have been coming into an account maintained by the followers of Zhang Zuo Lin."

"The notorious warlord?" asked Waley. "Reports are he's a vicious man."

"Yes, he, but that in itself was not the issue. Zhang's people may use any bank they like, said Alexander."

Indeed, I thought, it would not be the way of the Hong Kong and Shanghai Bank to make a moral judgment when it could instead make money.

"His worry," said Dora Russell, "was that roughly equal sums went out after each deposit. They were transferred to an account maintained by the government of Japan."

"No!" I was shocked. "That cannot be. Zhang, trafficking with the Japanese? His single good quality is his patriotism, though it's misshapen in its expression."

"It might not be Zhang himself," Alexander said. He thought Zhang was perhaps being betrayed by his own followers. Alexander had no love for Zhang, preferring the Nationalist government. He felt they'd be easier for the European powers to do business with.

Easier because weaker, was my thought, though I didn't voice it.

"But he was worried," she went on, "that the bank was being used in a way that would ultimately redound to its discredit."

"My dear," said Russell, "why did he tell you this, and neither he nor you told me?"

Mrs. Russell turned to her husband. "You and I have no business with the Hong Kong and Shanghai Bank, but members of your family maintain accounts there. Alexander said he didn't want to worry you. For my part, I thought Alexander a dyspeptic old man—you know I've never liked him, darling—given to fret over things he couldn't control. Not because they were actually worrisome, but because he couldn't control them. I think he was just vexed and wanted someone to tell about it.

We soon went to table, and the conversation that night was so interesting, I forgot all about what he'd said. But if you're looking for people with motives to silence Alexander"—she turned back to me—"you might start there."

CHAPTER NINETEEN

And now, to Dee. Or rather, Springheel Jack.

I would have liked to relay to Dee the intelligence I'd just gathered before he started on his mission, but he and I had left Hoong's simultaneously. Before we did, I'd straightened my tie and brushed my hat while he'd donned the boots, gloves, breeches, and tunic of Springheel Jack. The mask, however, he held under his arm, covered by the billowing cloak.

"And where, may I ask, is Springheel Jack going on this fine afternoon?" I said as we left the shop.

"Springheel Jack," Dee said, "is going nowhere. I'm proceeding to the Roehampton Street Police Station, having ascertained that the good constable McCorkle is hard at work there today. I'll ask him for permission to talk with Vladimir Voronoff. I'll put it to McCorkle that Voronoff has reason to be afraid of Jack, whoever Jack really is, because Jack, whoever Jack really is, dealt Voronoff a drubbing in the park. Therefore, I'll say, I've chosen to present myself as an imitation of the fiend in hopes it will speed our interview."

"A double subterfuge?"

"Springheel Jack could not enter a police station and interview a man in the cells without the annoying interference of numerous bobbies. Dee Ren Jie clothed as Springheel Jack will have an easier time of it."

"You are going to act as an imitation of the man you imitate."

"Precisely."

As I have said, Dee is a man of surprises.

WITH A HOODED, billowing travel cloak encircling his Springheel Jack costume and Jack's hideous mask tucked under his arm, Dee made his way to the Roehampton Street Police Station. There, he swept his hood back and, face plain for all to see, he asked for Constable Timothy McCorkle. McCorkle was sent for, came to the front, cocked his head, and smiled broadly.

"Why, it's Mr. Dee! Good afternoon, sir. What brings you to our station?"

"Good afternoon, Constable. It's a pleasure to see you looking so well."

"It's a wonder, is what it is. I've had a promotion, so now I sit at a desk doing paperwork half the time while the lads go out on patrol. If this is what it's like to be a sergeant, only more of it, I don't know that I want another of these promotions."

"In that case, you are exactly the policeman the Metropolitan Police Force needs and will continue to promote. Constable, is there a place where we can talk?"

McCorkle opened for Dee the door separating public from police. He swept a glance over Dee's odd getup but led him silently to one of the rooms in the station where suspects and witnesses find themselves facing interrogation. The constable gestured Dee to a wooden chair and sat in one himself.

"A pair of men were arrested two nights ago at Richmond Park," Dee began. "A large Russian called Voronoff, who had stolen the mace you so efficiently and discreetly returned to

Madam Wu, and a Japanese man by the name of Isaki, who had sought to buy it. You were the arresting officer."

"I answered the whistle, yes, and was surprised to see your friend Mr. Lao in a clearing with two unconscious men. Between ourselves, I wondered how he had rendered them so, but then I caught sight of that fellow who fancies himself Springheel Jack. It was he who'd laid them low."

"Is Voronoff still in custody?"

"Yes, indeed. Madam Wu has brought charges against him. He'll remain an honored guest at Roehampton Street until the court is pleased to have him at trial."

"I'm glad to hear it, as Isaki is walking free."

McCorkle looked at his hands resting upon the scarred tabletop. "I'm afraid that's true. I protested but could not hold him. A solicitor came for him and, after consultation with his client, announced that Isaki didn't know the mace was stolen when he offered to buy it, and in any case, had never had it in his possession."

"I doubt the first and the second is a lie."

The constable squirmed in discomfort. "The only witness who could reliably swear to that would be that young thief, Fingers, as it was he as Isaki claimed stole it from Voronoff before he, Isaki, received it. And I don't mind telling you, Mr. Dee, a thief's testimony isn't generally accounted reliable, if you can get him to come into court at all."

Which, in the case of Jimmy Fingers, was unlikely. "Ah, well," said Dee. "What's done is done. Tell me, Constable, who sent the solicitor?"

McCorkle rubbed his chin. "Well, that's an odd thing, sir. The gent who came, by name of Hartford, is known to us, for it's he who's generally called when a Chinaman's in trouble."

"Chinese man, young Tim. I'd account it a favor if you'd remember that."

The constable reddened.

Dee asked, "How is it odd that Hartford appeared for Isaki?"

"Well, as I say, he appears for many Chi—Chinese men, as he knows the language. But he's never been seen here for a Japanese before."

"I see." Dee nodded. "Yes, that's interesting. Now I'd like to see Voronoff, if I may. But," he added, sweeping Jack's mask from beneath his cloak, "not as Dee Ren Jie."

McCorkle's features modulated from surprise through confusion to delight as Dee explained his scheme. The two proceeded down an echoing hallway to the locked door behind which prisoners were kept in cells. Before they left the interrogation room, Dee donned Jack's mask, pulling the hood of his cloak forward to shadow his visage.

"If I may say it, sir"—McCorkle, saying it, grinned—"that mask's a right wonder. It's Jack himself, as good as."

"I did my best," Dee answered. "There's a moving picture being shown—a terrible one, but it presents Springheel Jack cavorting. I'm glad to hear from someone who's seen this 'Jack' that I've come fairly close."

"Oh, that you have, sir. Also, Voronoff's only seen Jack late at night. I'm sure your costume will do. I do wonder, though, who this impersonator is."

"An interesting question, Constable."

Reaching the cell they sought, McCorkle slid the peephole door aside. "Look lively, Voronoff. You've a visitor." In a jangle of keys and creaks, the door was pushed open. McCorkle stepped aside and Jack, throwing his hood back, swept in.

Voronoff leapt up off the wall shelf that served as bed and sofa. "You! Come here, I smash you!" However, when Jack raised his batwing arms, threw his fiendish head back, and emitted a hideous cackle, the large Russian shrank away.

(As did McCorkle, though Dee swore me to silence on that point.)

"Now, me Russian, Jack's not wanting to fight ye again." Tossing his travel cloak to a surprised McCorkle, Jack danced about the cell. "It's just some information Jack needs. Two answers to two questions and Oi'll be gone."

"I don't want answer nothing to you."

"Ah, but if yer refuse, this young constable 'ere, 'e'll be so disappointed 'e'll lock me up in 'ere wi' yer. Just us two, me lad, just yerself and Jack." Jack looked at McCorkle, who, having disentangled himself from the cloak's heavy wool, nodded in stern reply. "Now that don't sound enjoyable, do it, young constable?"

"Not to me, sir," said McCorkle seriously.

"Though Jack, 'e'd enjoy it!"

Quick as a flash Jack pounced onto the shelf from which Voronoff had jumped up. He loomed over the Russian, flapping his batwing arms about the startled man. Jack spun and leapt for the bars on the high, tiny window. For a moment, he clung to them, spiderlike, then he flipped a double somersault over Voronoff's head to land beside the constable again. He whipped a circular kick that missed the Russian's nose by a hair's breadth.

"Wot say ye? My budem drat'sya, Gospodin Voronoff?"

Voronoff, in reaction to this display and the invitation to fight delivered in his native language, sagged.

"Now," said Jack, in English once again, "two questions, and meself and the constable will be gone. Set yerself down, me Russian tovarisch." At this command, Jack took a small step forward. Voronoff plopped onto the bench.

"Ah, yer a smart fellow and no mistake! So tell me, why'd yer steal the mace?"

"I don't steal! She give to me. Gospozha Wu. She tell me

Isaki want to buy, but secret. Tell me if I take to park, bring her money, she give me some. Why not? So I try."

Jack looked at McCorkle. "Oh, me constable, 'e don't want to tell the truth."

"This is truth!" the Russian sputtered. McCorkle set his face into grim lines.

Jack rubbed his chin. "Ah, but then, it don't matter wot 'e says, do it? We know the truth about that. Madam Wu 'as already told us."

"She lie!"

Jack leaned close to Voronoff's lumpy visage. "Oi wouldn't say such things about Madam Wu, me Russian bear. She's a proper lady and don't need no kritika from the likes o' yer!"

"*She give it to me!*"

"All right!" Jack clapped his hands and spun about on one foot, returning to lean into Voronoff's face again. "'Ow about this, then. Wot does this mean to yer?" He waved a paper in front of the Russian.

"Nothing."

"Jack thinks yer not thinking 'ard enough."

Voronoff squinted at the paper. "That name, some Chinaman."

"Chinese man," McCorkle corrected him.

Voronoff shrugged.

"And the symbol?" demanded Jack.

"Look like ladder. Or number three, like in British church."

"Jack ain't a church-going man," said Jack. "Wot else comes to yer mind?"

"Nothing else. You think mean something else, ask little rat Isaki."

"Oi don't dispute yer opinion of Isaki-san, me Russian. But 'e's a 'ard man to find since 'e's been sprung from 'ere."

"Sprung?" Voronoff himself sprang, up from the bench.

"Out of jail? Little rat Isaki out of jail while Voronoff rot in this terrible place?" He turned wild-eyed to McCorkle. "You let little rat out?"

Jack inserted himself smoothly between Voronoff and McCorkle, whose eyes were also wide and his truncheon raised. "Now, me Russian, yer don't want a crack on the 'ead from that there stick, do yer? Oi'm told McCorkle can swing wi' the best of 'em. No, yer best to sit and wait. Mayhap someone'll send a solicitor for yer, too." Jack spread the cloak wide again. "Unless yer suddenly remembered something to tell us?"

Voronoff dropped back on the bench. "Da, something to tell you." He looked up and shouted, "Go away!"

CHAPTER TWENTY

Dee and I had arranged to meet again at Sergeant Hoong's shop. While I waited, I sat at the counter, reading a months-old Chinese newspaper. It being the middle of the day, Hoong found himself serving a variety of customers. Some of these berated him for keeping the shop closed so often lately.

"I apologize," Hoong said. "Apparently, I'm needed for endeavors important to the future of China and indeed the entire civilized world. Did you say two meters of the blue cotton?"

The items in the newspaper before me had long since ceased to be timely, of course, but I was enjoying the familiar rhythms of the phrases and the names of the places of home when the bell tinkled and a figure, hooded and cloaked, burst into the shop.

"Ah," said Hoong. "How am I so fortunate that you've come when the shop is empty?"

"What's fortunate is Oi don't mind waiting in the shadows for a quarter 'our so as not to frighten yer customers." With this declaration, the hood was swept back, revealing the dire visage of Springheel Jack. This dramatic action got precisely the reaction it deserved, which is to say, neither Hoong nor I took any notice. Dee sighed, removing the mask. "Such stoic blocks of stone. Very well, I'll return momentarily." At this, he left the front room. In a few minutes, he walked back through the door in his accustomed impeccable tailoring.

"Why, Lao," said Hoong. "Look here, it's Dee Ren Jie. The celebrated judge! Perhaps we can persuade him to join us for a cup of tea."

"I can now say with confidence the comedy act is sure to fail," Dee said. "As to the tea, thank you, but no. I was unsuccessful—or, Jack was—in the attempt to learn the meaning of the marks upon that paper."

"Voronoff couldn't tell you?" I asked.

"He claims not to know. That may be true or it may not, but in any case, I could get no more out of him. He suggested I ask Isaki. That path is temporarily closed to us, but his suggestion gave me an idea. I'll call upon Yoshio Markino in his studio. Perhaps the symbol means something in Japanese culture. Before I leave, tell me, Lao, did you discover anything at the Russells'?"

"I did. Rather than telling you before you leave, however, let me join you and I'll tell you as we go, for as you know, I'm a great admirer of Markino's, and I would welcome the chance to see where he paints."

"You're both leaving?" Hoong asked. "I'll have no use for my 'closed' sign this afternoon?"

"That can't be guaranteed," said Dee. "I'd recommend you do as much business as you can in the next few hours. We might be back."

DEE CONSENTED TO a taxicab, for he deemed Markino's studio in South Kensington to be too long a walk from Limehouse—not in terms of distance to be covered, for I was sure Dee could walk from Limehouse to Peking if he had a reason to do so, but in terms of the time it would take to cover that distance. While we rode, I gave him Dora Russell's account of A.G. Stephen's worries.

"Zhang?" Dee said when I'd finished. His brow furrowed. "Doing business with the Japanese?"

"It seems unlikely, I agree. Completely out of character."

"Or out of the character he chooses to present to the world." Dee's frown continued to deepen as he thought. I had learned not to interrupt him in these reveries. Though they often appeared to result in nothing, it was at these times that his mind started first identifying the outline of, and later filling in, a picture we hadn't yet seen whole.

"Well," he finally said, as the taxicab slowed to a stop, "let's keep this information in mind as we pursue our other avenues. I believe we've arrived."

He paid the driver, and we alighted on Redcliffe Road, a pleasant street of brick homes interspersed with others of limestone. Many had large studio windows on their upper floors, and skylights. Number 39 was of this type.

Dee pressed the bell, and the door was opened to us by the young Mrs. Markino. She wore a tweed skirt and cream silk blouse; her yellow hair was pinned behind her head in a chignon. Dee and I both bowed to the lady. Finding us on her doorstep brought a bright smile to her lips. "*Bonjour*, Judge Dee and Professor Lao! A pleasure to see you again so soon. Yoshio expects you?"

"I'm afraid he doesn't, Mrs. Markino," said Dee. "We promise not to disturb his work very long. We have a question that needs an answer."

"But you must take a coffee! Sit here, I will fetch him." She swept her arm toward the parlor and started for the stairs.

"May we go up, Mrs. Markino?" I asked. "I'd like very much to see where your husband works."

She tilted her head in a charming manner. "Mais oui, of course!" she said and gestured for us to follow.

The staircase discharged us into a single large room on the second floor. A bulge at the rear divulged the location of a water closet; no other walls stood in the way of the light pouring in from front windows that ran from almost-floor to near-ceiling, where they were met by slanted skylights. One window stood open, but despite that, the sharp scent of turpentine filled the air.

"Yoshio, you must stop for a moment," called Mrs. Markino. She walked toward the windows, stepping with assurance along the wrinkled and colorfully splattered tarpaulins laid to protect the wooden floor. A gray cat stood from a patch of sunlight, stretched, and walked with her. "Friends have come."

By the windows, a large canvas rested on a larger easel. Before it stood Yoshio Markino in a paint-streaked smock and trousers. His left hand held a palette dotted with daubs of color; his right, a small brush. He finished a line he was carefully trailing down the canvas and turned.

"Oh! Dee-san, Lao-san! Unexpected pleasure, yes! Happy to see you." We exchanged bows. "But darling"—Markino addressed his wife—"why you have brought guests up here where they can get a mess? Come, come, we all go down. Also, you come, Sasori. Paint already on your head." He set his palette and brush on the charette beside him and reached down to scratch the cat rubbing against his leg.

"No, Yoshio, don't trouble yourself," said Dee. "Lao wanted to see you at your work, and I have a question. If you can answer it, we'll be gone."

"If I can't answer, you will stay? I think then, better not to know answer to whatever question." Markino's mustache crinkled as he smiled.

Dee reached into his pocket for the paper while I looked at the work on the easel. In the brightness of the light pouring in, Markino was painting fog. Specifically, the fog on the Strand in the late afternoon. Women and men, shopfronts, a bus—all emerging, disappearing, there and not there.

"Extraordinary," I muttered. "How you hide what you paint!"

"I don't hide," Markino said. "Fog hides. I paint fog when it hides. So many things look like so far away when really, are right here, just hiding behind fog. Fog, hiding, sometimes more beautiful than things hidden."

Dee unfolded the paper. "Here's a thing hidden, Yoshio. The name at the top we can read—Peng Lian Liang, an acquaintance of Lao's. The symbol, though, we've been unable to crack. We were told a Japanese man named Isaki might be able to read it for us, but he's nowhere to be found. My Japanese is meager, so in case this has a meaning in your language, we've brought it to you."

Yoshio Markino looked at the paper, then threw back his head in laughter. "Meaning? Not in Japanese, but yes, has meaning if you are one of those think most things deliberately hidden!"

Dee and I glanced at one another. "Yoshio, your meaning is right now hidden," Dee said.

Markino shook his head. "Conspiracy, is it the English? Inbo?"

Dee looked at me, then back to Markino. "As I say, my Japanese is poor, but yes, I believe those words mean the same."

"Conspiracy, then. This is railroad track. See, ties and tracks? It is Chinese Eastern Railway."

"This?" I said. "That's what it represents?"

"People say. Between two tracks, three ties, because each section of Chinese Eastern Railway controlled by different country. China, Russia, Japan." He tapped the lines on Dee's paper.

"That's true enough," I said, "and much better off China will be when we ourselves control all the railroads on our own land. But where is your conspiracy?"

Markino chuckled. "In Japan, I see this symbol. People say, 'Oh! Oh! Secret things! China, Russia, Japan, looks like not so good friends, but underneath, have shadow governments! Send assassins, kill each other's enemies, do secret favors, suddenly all overthrow real governments, be big'—word is bloc?—'Big strong bloc. Real governments, look out! Chinese emperor returns! Or maybe, Chinese Communists take over! Russian tsar returns! Or maybe, Russian Communists get even stronger! Japanese emperor never goes away—or maybe, Japanese Communists overthrow emperor! All make alliances! Whole world, look out!'"

"That's the nature of the Railway Conspiracy?" I asked. "A web of intrigue involving revolutionaries, or possibly counter-revolutionaries, from each country? Could such a thing really exist?" My skepticism was clear in my tone.

"I think, no." Markino grinned. "Story like this happens when national identity become more important than sense! Now, come, we all take coffee."

CHAPTER TWENTY-ONE

Dee and I begged off coffee with the Markinos, for Dee had been struck by a worrisome thought. As we left the house, waved on our way by the delightful Mrs. Markino, he said to me, "The cloaked fellow was meeting Isaki to hand him this paper. That clandestine encounter itself implies there is more to this than Yoshio imagines. Yoshio is a good man in a world not always good."

"I'm glad, then, that he has the support of such a charming wife."

Dee gave me a sidelong glance. "Ah, yes, the charming Mrs. Markino. As charming, perhaps, as the charming Nurse Green. Your partiality toward European women is regrettable, Lao. It can only continue to lead to misfortune."

I blew out a breath. "If you are referring yet again to the isolated incident of my misguided friendship with Mary Jones, née Wendell, you might consider eliminating that as a topic of conversation between us."

"I was taking, actually, a broader view."

"I can see only narrowness in your outlook. Many Chinese women are paragons of beauty and allure, of course, but no one—not even you—would maintain Chinese women are alone in this. And Chinese women, I daresay, can be as adept as European ones at the breaking of men's hearts. Perhaps we can drop this topic and return to the subject of our investigation?"

Dee scrutinized my countenance, and then replied, "Very well. I have expressed my feelings."

"Fully," I affirmed.

We walked in silence to Kingston Road. There, Dee hailed a taxicab.

"Two taxis in as many hours!" I said. "Are you sure you're well?"

"Quite well," Dee replied. "I hope we can say the same for Peng Lian Liang."

WE COULD NOT.

Dee's thought had been that Peng's name upon the paper with the railroad track symbol did not bode well. "If I'm right," he said, "Peng might be in danger—or someone else might be in danger from Peng. If I'm wrong, perhaps at least Peng can shed more light on the meaning of this."

But Dee was not wrong.

Peng, who was reading law at the University of London, had a flat in Killick Street, and it was there we hurried. While our taxicab sped—as far as any taxicab, in the midst of London's congestion of buses, motorcars, lorries, handcarts, horses, and precipitous pedestrians, can speed—Dee inquired about Peng: "You've told me he's the Communist Party secretary in London. What kind of man is he?"

"A reasonable one. He's committed to the Communist cause but would prefer a gradual transition of power. To that end, he's studying the evolution of Great Britain from absolute monarchy to parliamentary democracy."

"He sees a parallel?"

"He believes one can be drawn. Though the British, through

it all, have maintained their monarchs, and we have overthrown ours."

Dee said no more until we arrived at our destination. We exited the taxicab at Peng's address and hurried up the path to the front door.

"Don't ring, Lao," said Dee as I reached for the doorbell. "I think we should take care. All may not be well."

The rank of doorbells listed Peng's flat as "ground, left rear." A matter of a meter separated this residence from the structure beside it. Down this narrow chasm, Dee and I proceeded. Making the assumption that of the six windows on that side, the first three were the property of "ground, left front," Dee motioned me low, and we crept under their sills. At each the fourth and fifth, Dee rose just enough to see inside, shake his head, and creep on. I followed him in this popping-up procedure, though I lingered a bit longer, interested in the contents of the flat. Modestly furnished, as befitted a serious Communist, it nevertheless held a good number of shelves groaning with books, magazines, and treatises in both English and Chinese, as befitted a serious scholar. A poem by Wang Wei in beautiful calligraphy hung on one wall; I wondered if the calligraphy was Peng's. Beside it, a framed placard announced the organizing meeting of the London branch of the Chinese Youth Communist Party.

At the last window, Dee rose again. He dropped down, his face grim. With a silencing finger to his lips, he motioned me near. I also rose to look over the sill and was met with a horrible sight. On the kitchen floor, Peng lay in a pool of blood. Above him stood two large men, Europeans, a mustachioed one nodding to a baby-faced one, as though with satisfaction.

"Look at the daggers, Lao," Dee whispered to me, and I did so. Each man held one; the weapons were long and narrow, their blades incised, and their handles inlaid with jewels.

They would have been beautiful had they not dripped with Peng's blood.

"They are Russian Cossacks," said Dee. "Their kindjal blades say as much. We're too late to stop their crime, but I'd like very much to know who sent them. Go to the street and use your whistle to summon the police. Then, hurry to the rear in case these men try to escape. Attempt to stop them." He looked me up and down. "Not both. One will do."

Slightly offended but admitting to myself the truth of the observation behind Dee's addendum, I followed these instructions and crept back again under the sill line to the street. Once there, I blew my bobby's whistle, two mighty blasts, then raced back through the chasm to the cobbled alley behind the building.

The reader, then, will understand why I am forced here to reconstruct, based upon Dee's later (and as always, reluctantly) relating them, the events that transpired inside the kitchen of "ground, left rear."

AFTER I RAN off on my errand, Dee softly and smoothly lifted the window sash. Such was his delicacy of touch that the window made no sound and the men inside were unaware anything was happening until Dee leapt up and crouched on the sill. Both Russians spun to the movement. They lifted their daggers.

Dee dropped to the floor and vaulted across the room to pounce atop the kitchen table. There, he spread himself on his right side and spun like a pinwheel as the Russians stabbed at him. He knocked the knife out of the hand of the baby-faced one with a left roundhouse kick. Flipping back to his left side, he used his right heel to slap away the knife of the other. With that same foot, he executed a rising tiger tail kick, hitting squarely in the Cossack's mustache.

The baby-faced man seized an end of the table and

overturned it. Dee rolled off, landing like a cat on the floor. Beside him lay the red-painted Chinese bench Peng had used for his kitchen seating. Exclaiming, "Ah, Fu Tau Dung, tiger head bench," Dee grasped it with his right hand, used his right foot to kick it up, and smacked the Russian with it under the chin. The man staggered back but remained upright.

Now holding the bench by two of its legs, Dee spun into the baby-faced Cossack in a cartwheel-like fashion, over and down, driving the edge of the bench into the man's temple and following up immediately with a thrusting strike with the right side of the bench to the solar plexus. That man went down, but the mustachioed Cossack had by now recovered. Dagger in hand, he slashed at Dee. Dee deflected the slash. The Russian tried a thrust. Dee shifted into a back stance and hooked the wrist of his assailant with the legs of the bench, sending the dagger flying to the floor to where the baby-faced man was lying.

The mustachioed Cossack returned with a right-handed haymaker. Dee struck the hand hard with the seat of the bench and popped the bench up, changing his hand position to pull out the Russian's foot with the bench leg. The Russian landed flat on his back, but being of a hearty breed, he scrambled up again and punched rapidly at Dee. Dee ensnared his left fist and swept out the man's feet, pinning him to the floor with the bench and slapping both his own hands down firmly on it to control the captive. He threw another tiger tail kick to the Cossack's head. The man stopped moving.

This stasis was timely, for the baby-faced Cossack grabbed the dagger at his feet and leapt up. Dee spun, leaning backward as the knife stabbed down upon him. He crossed his right leg behind himself and laid his palm against the Cossack's forearm. He brought his hands together and locked the Russian's wrist as he twisted his arm. The dagger went flying. Dee swung his left leg over the assailant to restrain him, but the Cossack rolled away.

I AM ABLE now to reinsert myself in the story, for it was at this point that the flat's rear door was thrown open from within. My whistle had raised three bobbies, who had arrived to join me in the alley just in time for us all to share wide-eyed astonishment as a large baby-faced man stared out at us for a moment and then, from the small porch onto which he'd issued, jumped high and forward, wrapping himself into a ball and tumbling over our heads. He landed lightly on his feet behind us and sprinted down the alley.

Dee, brow glistening with sweat, appeared at the door. "Give chase!" he shouted, and the bobbies did, rousing themselves, waving their truncheons, and blowing their whistles as they raced after the man. Dee seemed about to join in the chase, but a clatter from within the flat drew his attention, and mine. Upon racing back inside, we found the table overturned, blocking our path, and the door to the hallway shut. These were minor obstacles, but the delay they caused was enough to enable the mustachioed Cossack to disappear through the front door, for when we reached the street, we found no sign of him.

Dee shook his head. "All you would have had to do was step back, Lao," he said. "His somersault would have landed him right upon you."

In addition to the remarkable unpleasantness of that vision, I found another problem with Dee's remark. "I expected him to run down the steps," I informed Dee. "I had no suspicion he would attempt such a trick."

"He's a Cossack! They're all trained acrobats. That was why I identified him for you. So you'd be prepared!"

"I have spent my life," I said, brushing dust off my jacket sleeves, "in study. Reading, writing. Teaching. I cannot reasonably be expected to be familiar with the athletic prowess and fighting styles of the world's various combat practitioners. Next time you need a human net to insert himself under a circus performer, I will require more explicit instructions."

Dee stared at me; then, surprisingly, he laughed. Slapping my back, he said, "Your point is well made. Henceforth, I'll try to take into account your relative unfamiliarity with aspects of the kind of work in which we're engaged. But Lao, in your turn, you must undertake to familiarize yourself with as many of those aspects as you can. Perhaps," he said, brushing off his own coat, "I shall write a trifling monograph upon the subject."

CHAPTER TWENTY-TWO

Constable McCorkle was not in when Dee and I arrived at the place we had determined was our next port of call: the Roehampton Street station of the Metropolitan Police. Apparently, McCorkle had gotten his wish and was out on patrol. Another bobby escorted us to the cells to call upon Voronoff. A jangling of keys and a creaking of hinges and we found ourselves standing in a cell before the large man.

"You!" he said, seeing me. He jumped up from the cell bench. "I see you in park. Why you here now? Who this you bring? Is advocat, come to tell them this all mistake?"

"What mistake?" I asked. "You stole something valuable, you tried to sell it, you got caught, and now you're behind bars. I see no mistake."

"I don't steal it! Gospozha Wu give me, say take to park, sell to little rat, Isaki. I am not thief!"

"Possibly not," Dee said, to my surprise. "And I'm not a solicitor. But two of your countrymen are killers."

Voronoff's brow wrinkled. "What you saying? Who kill who?"

"Do you remember this paper Springheel Jack showed you, with the symbol of the Chinese Eastern Railway?" Dee withdrew the paper from his pocket. He looked at Voronoff, waiting for confirmation.

"Da, da, so?"

Dee went on, "It also bears the name of a man, Peng Lian Liang." He indicated the Chinese characters. "Peng's just been murdered. By two Russians."

Voronoff scratched his head. "Where you got paper? Who is Peng?"

"Peng was the Chinese Communist Party secretary in London," I said.

Voronoff's lip curled. "Communist! Good he die, then. Who kill this Communist?"

"That's what we've come to ask you," Dee said. "Who, and why, and where can they be found?"

Shrugging, Voronoff sat down again on the bench. He crossed his arms. "So many Russian in London. Most don't like Communist. If I am out of here, can talk to people, ask. From here, sorry, can't help." He looked from Dee to me.

"In that case, I'm sorry too." Dee folded the paper back into his pocket. "We can't help you, either." He banged the door with his fist to summon the constable.

"Wait!" Voronoff jumped up again. "What about advocat?"

"Ask your embassy. Assisting citizens detained in foreign lands is one of the functions of a diplomatic mission," I said.

Voronoff snarled. "Embassy! Not mine, is Communist! This government, not mine! In Russia, real Russia, I am count." He thumped his chest. "Here, nobody. Like serf. But not forever." The door creaked open once more. "You watch, you see! Soon is happening, overthrow overthrowers. Real Russia come back. Real . . ."

We could still hear Voronoff shouting as we followed the constable down the hallway.

"AM I WRONG," I asked Dee as we left the station, "or is that cell area slightly less rank than the one in which you and I met?"

"It may only be that you're getting used to police stations, Lao."

"I sincerely hope not. It's unfortunate this particular sojourn in one was wasted, though, as Voronoff gave us nothing."

Dee glanced over at me. "On the contrary. He gave us two facts, either of which might prove important. Or, indeed, both."

"I don't understand."

"Did you not notice that when I mentioned the Chinese Eastern Railway as the meaning of the symbol, he showed no surprise, but was impatient to get to the reason for our visit? He'd told Springheel Jack that the symbol meant nothing to him. You and I only learned its meaning later."

I thought back to that part of the conversation. "Why, you're right," I said. "It was the response of a man who already knew the information and had forgotten he'd pretended he didn't."

"Quite so."

I was going to comment that Voronoff's response didn't speak as highly of his intelligence as the man might like, but, as I'd had to have his response pointed out to me, I didn't want to give Dee the chance to comment similarly on mine. Instead, I asked, "And what is the other fact?"

Dee's small smile indicated that he understood my strategy, but he merely replied, "Voronoff continues to maintain—rather heatedly—that the mace was given him by Madam Wu. While I don't believe that, I think it's possible he received some instruction he misinterpreted. I'd very much like to know what that was."

Thus, for the third time that day, my astonished self saw Dee hail a taxicab, in this instance to take us to the Bruton Street home of Madam Wu.

As we rode, I mused, "'Nobody. Like serf.' Don't you think, Dee, it was that contempt for the peasants on whose labor the entire wealth of the nation rests that brought Russia to violent revolution? I fear the same prospect for China."

"That fear may be justified," Dee said. "And I think violent revolution giving rise to a Communist government is an alarming prospect."

I glanced at him, growing a bit impatient. "As I've said, that outcome does not alarm me. A larger share of wealth returning to those who labor to produce it would be more just. You, Dee, are famed for your commitment to justice. I cannot fathom why you resist the simplest political path to justice for the peasants and workers of China."

"I resist the untried, as *I've* said. The upheavals caused by the sudden transfer of wealth would weaken the country, leaving us vulnerable to foreign predation."

I sighed. "On that point, you may be correct. Peng was an advocate for peaceful and gradual transition. That view seems in the minority, and the majority is growing restive."

We fell silent, each lost in his own thoughts, until we reached the fine brick house. Dee rang the bell, prepared to explain our mission. To the surprise of us both, however, the door did not immediately open. Feng peered through the sidelight, and then she opened the door to speak immediately.

"Dee Ren Jie! It's good you've come," she said in her oddly accented Mandarin. The hound, Mei Qiang, stood to attention beside her. "I was about to ask Madam Wu if she wanted me to go in search of you."

"What's wrong?" asked Dee, for one could clearly see by the clouds on Feng's countenance that something was.

"Madam Wu received a note this morning. It's upset her. Come in."

"A note?" I whispered to Dee as Feng glanced up and down the street before she shut the door behind us. "I cannot say Madam Wu seemed to me a woman who could be upset by a note."

Following Feng and the hound, we entered the parlor. The lady of the house was leaning forward on the sofa and smoking a cigarette in a carved ivory holder. Once again, she was dressed in men's tailoring: herringbone trousers and waistcoat, white dress shirt with dark blue tie. When she saw us, she dropped the cigarette holder into a crystal bowl and jumped up.

"Dee! And Lao! I'm glad you've come!" She ran to Dee, who took both her hands in his. I had the distinct sense that had I not been present, the contact between them might have been a deal closer.

"What's wrong?" Dee echoed himself.

She shook her head. Returning to the sofa, she retrieved a sheet of paper from the cushion and handed it to him. I looked over Dee's shoulder as he inspected it.

It bore the railroad track symbol and read *Wu Ze Tian* at the top.

CHAPTER TWENTY-THREE

Dee looked from the paper to Madam Wu. "The last person whose name I saw on a paper like this," he said, "is now dead."

"You've seen it before, then?" Madam Wu's eyes met his. "You know what it means?" She shuddered.

Dee glanced at me, then back to the lady. "The symbol, we're told, is the Chinese Eastern Railway. I wasn't sure of the meaning of placing a name at the top and was hoping to ask Peng himself, but he was dead when we arrived. I thought perhaps that was coincidence. Now I'm beginning to fear I see the truth of it."

Madam Wu sat again, as though too weary to remain standing. Dee sat beside her. I took to the chair across the low table.

"I don't know this Peng you speak of," Madam Wu said, "but if his name was on a paper like this, I promise you it's no coincidence he's dead. He was murdered?"

"Most assuredly. By Russians."

The lady's hand went to her mouth.

"Perhaps," said Dee, "you ought to tell us about the meaning of this and the danger you fear."

Madam Wu's elegant fingers withdrew another cigarette

from a silver box on the low table. Dee leaned forward to take a match from a silver striker while she placed the cigarette in the ivory holder. Looking into her eyes, Dee lit her cigarette. She drew in deeply and exhaled the smoke.

"The symbol is indeed the Chinese Eastern Railway," she said. "Who told you this?"

"Yoshio Markino. He also said there's a rumored conspiracy of antigovernment activists in the three countries involved in the railway."

"He laughed at the idea," I put in. "He said it was nonsense."

Madam Wu smiled sadly. "Poor Yoshio. To him, fog is beautiful. He doesn't see the threat it might be hiding."

The door opened, and Feng came in with a tea tray. She poured English tea for me and Chinese tea for Dee and Madam Wu.

"Thank you, Feng," said Madam Wu. "Please stay. Pour some tea for yourself."

Choosing the Chinese tea, the young woman took a seat on the hassock. Mei Qiang settled at her feet.

Madam Wu said, "Yoshio is welcome to his world of lovely illusion. There would be nothing to be gained by spoiling it. But he's wrong." She sipped some tea; as though it had given her strength to go on, she straightened her back and said, "The conspiracy is not nonsense. It's very much alive, operating in many places. It killed A. G. Stephen, it killed this Peng, and now it intends to kill me."

The countenance of young Feng hardened as Madam Wu issued this pronouncement. This would not happen if she could prevent it, I read on her features. Remembering the size of the Russians standing over the bloody body of Peng Lian Liang, I was not sanguine about the ability of the small Chinese retainer to be of any help to her mistress in the event, but it was clear she would try.

"What are they after, this conspiracy?" asked Dee. "Why kill Peng and Stephen?"

"About Peng, I don't know the answer, since I don't know who he was."

"The Chinese Communist Party Secretary in London," I said.

Madam Wu's brow furrowed. "Strange." She thought for a moment and then asked me, "What was his position on violent revolution?"

"He opposed it," I said. "Peng believed in a process of peaceful, gradual reform."

"Ah. That might have been enough, then." She looked from me to Dee. "The conspiracy's objective is the strengthening, in the case of Russia, and then the installation, in the other two countries, of Communist rule. They don't believe it's possible for this to be accomplished gradually." The lady pulled deeply upon her cigarette. "To this end, they send agents to do each other's work of assassination and disruption, thinking—rightly—that it will be harder to identify and trace the culprits. By these means, they also cement trust between and among themselves for the day when all shall arise and China and Japan, with the support of Russia, will declare war upon the imperial enemy—and in China, also the Nationalists and the various warlords—and, defeating them, meet as allies in glorious multinational communism!"

The bitterness with which these words were delivered put a chill into the very air.

"And A. G. Stephen?" I asked. "What is their antipathy to him?"

Madam Wu reached for her teacup, cradling it in her hands. "I'm not sure. I know he was worried about some irregularity at the bank. I think he'd discovered the Chinese Communist Party had opened accounts there."

"The Communist Party also?" I said. "Because we were told—"

But Dee stopped me with a look. He put down his teacup. "And yourself?" he asked Madam Wu. "Why are you now targeted? This is related to the retrieval of the mace, is it not? Stolen from a Chinese by a Russian to be sold to a Japanese. Perhaps it's time to tell us the truth about that."

I looked at Dee in surprise. Was he saying Madam Wu had deliberately deceived us? Deceived *him*? Dee's gaze remained on the lady.

Sighing, she nodded. "My business interests bring me into contact with a great variety of people." She tapped ash into the crystal bowl. "I move freely in many circles. As a woman, I'm perhaps allowed more latitude than I would be otherwise—than I would be, I mean, if I were a man and therefore taken seriously."

Feng, I noticed, tightened the set of her jaw when Madam Wu made this statement.

"I was approached by agents of the conspiracy shortly after I arrived in London," Madam Wu continued. "At the beginning, they were honey-tongued. In China, the Nationalists had failed, they said; it was sad, but it was true. The future was Communist. I must join them, and after the glorious worldwide victory, I would be hailed as a heroine of the revolution! I replied that I was flattered, but as a woman of business, I had no interest in political action."

"But they didn't stop," said Dee.

"Of course not. Blandishment turned to browbeating and from there to veiled threat. Then, the threat became . . . less veiled. Windows were broken at my family home in Peking. My young niece was abducted. She was returned unharmed within the hour, but the point was made."

"What did they want?"

"The mace. For its symbolism." Madam Wu took up her cigarette, but it had gone out. She stabbed it into the crystal bowl. "And . . ."

"And Voronoff."

Madam Wu raised her eyebrows. "Yes. Count Vladimir Voronoff. A leader of the White Russian forces planning the violent overthrow of the Communists and the return of the tsar."

"I'm sorry," I interrupted, "but Voronoff, a leader?"

Again the lady smiled. "Voronoff's intellect is not up to the task, is that your thought?"

"I'm quite sure the man couldn't lead the singing of a hymn with a hymnal in his hands."

Dee shook his head at my imagery but said nothing.

"I agree," said Madam Wu, "but it doesn't matter. Others do the actual planning. Voronoff's value, like that of the mace, is symbolic. His family were among the largest landowners in Imperial Russia. His death at the hands of the conspiracy would send a message to the world."

"And what was your involvement to be?" Dee asked.

"Voronoff is too vain to be wary, but he has protectors. The conspiracy operates in the shadows. They had no wish to engage in a battle, their men against his, on the streets of London. Voronoff must be isolated, and then the conspiracy would send someone to dispatch him."

Dee nodded. "Your role was to get him to trust you, and so leave his guards behind."

"Abominable," I said. "To make such a demand upon you!"

"I felt I had no choice," Madam Wu replied. "But then, I learned you were in London, Dee." She turned to him, contrition in her eyes. "I created a desperate plan."

"You gave him the mace," Dee said. "He's always maintained you did."

"I told him I was being threatened by the conspiracy, who were demanding the mace. I asked Voronoff to take it to Richmond Park and give it to Isaki."

"Isaki was to be the assassin?"

"Yes." She took both Dee's hands in her own. "But I knew if I told you it had been stolen, if I asked you for help, you might both retrieve the mace and stop the assassination. The agents of the conspiracy wouldn't be able to fault me—everyone knows Dee Ren Jie has eyes and ears everywhere, and I'd tell them that your . . . regard . . . for me had not only caused you to stop this plan but made me no longer a useful instrument for them. I'd be free."

"If that was your plan, why not just tell Dee the truth?" The question came out perhaps more harshly than I meant it to, but the lady had gone to quite some lengths to hide her real intentions and, in doing so, had put us all in danger.

Dee smiled. "Lao is speaking on behalf of the bruises he sustained in the retrieval."

"Oh, Lao, I'm so sorry." Madam Wu leaned forward and put a gentle hand on my arm. "For such a distinguished scholar to be hurt on my account!"

My cheeks burned. "Really, no, it was nothing," I muttered.

Madam Wu picked up her teacup, though the tea must by now have gone cold. After a moment, she said, "I was ashamed. I should have had the strength to oppose them, not try to defeat them by guile. However, I didn't. The strength I tried to borrow was Dee's."

"Whatever strength I have is always yours," Dee said. The lady looked gratefully into his eyes. I myself turned away to study the abstract canvases on the walls.

After a moment, Dee gestured to the paper on the table. "But now you've received this. It must mean your deception has been discovered."

Madam Wu nodded. "I don't know how. But as you see, they have a different idea of what it means to have no use for me."

CHAPTER TWENTY-FOUR

Feng was dispatched to fetch Hoong. Although reluctant to leave her mistress, she agreed once it was made clear that Dee intended to remain in the house at the side of Madam Wu.

"Also," Madam Wu said to Feng, "Chung is here. Chung Kao Kun, my chef," she said to Dee and myself. "You met him at the banquet. He's not a trained fighter, but he's large and quite handy with a cleaver." She offered a brave smile.

I left also, with instructions to search out Ang Chun. While none of us suspected the fiery young man I'd encountered at the meeting of the Chinese Youth Communist Party of being personally involved in the murder of Peng Lian Liang, or even of being a member of the Railway Conspiracy, it was still possible his connections among the international communist movement could help us confirm Madam Wu's theory of the motive behind Peng's death.

Which might have happened, had I been able to find him. Ang was not at the university, nor at the rooms nearby that he shared with two fellow revolutionaries. I spent a fruitless hour searching the undergraduate drinking establishments in the university's vicinity and another wandering in and out of the Chinese dining places in Pennyfields and Limehouse, pausing in one for a plate of pork dumplings to offset the pangs of hunger beginning to plague me.

Finally, having exhausted all my resources and also myself, I made my way to a corner on which stood a telephone kiosk. I slipped two pennies into the slot and lifted the ear trumpet. The switchboard operator snapped, "Number, please!" Perhaps she was as hungry and vexed as I.

"Mayfair 1818," I replied.

I heard some pips, some rings, and then, in English, "Mayfair 1818. Wu Ze Tian speaking."

"Madam Wu," I replied in Chinese. "This is Lao She. I trust all is well?"

"Yes, thank you," said she, also in our native tongue. "Have you been successful in your search?"

"I have not. Ang Chun might as well be a ghost as a man, for all I've been able to see of him."

"That's unfortunate. Let me bring Dee to the telephone for a reconsideration of the next steps, then."

I waited. The next voice I heard was Dee's. "So, Lao. Ang Chun has vanished?"

"As neatly as any magician's assistant. Unless you can offer fresh water to fish in, I'll reel in my line."

"I really would be careful of that tendency to express yourself in imagery, Lao. But no, I think nothing more can be done on that front tonight. Madam Wu tells me an Autumn Moon Festival is to be held tomorrow, sponsored by the Chinese Consulate. Many of London's Chinese residents are expected to be in attendance. Perhaps Ang Chun intends to be among them. Although, as he is a devoted Communist, perhaps he doesn't."

"The event," I informed Dee, "is being held in an attempt to bring all London's Chinese together. The university's Youth Communist Party have received an invitation. I myself was hoping to attend." I had forgotten about the event in all the recent excitement and was reinvigorated by the thought of the festivities to come. "I hope you have no brief for me that would interfere with that."

"Quite the contrary. If, with your sympathies, you're planning to be there, it's possible Ang Chun is also. Or at least we may find someone who can improve our understanding of the fatal attack on Peng Lian Liang. No, Lao, I'll not interfere with your revels."

"Excellent! Then, if no more angling is to be done tonight, I'll come back to Madam Wu's to join the protection brigade."

"Thank you, but I think there's no need. Hoong is here, in the garden, and Jimmy in the downstairs, keeping watch at the entrances to the kitchen and pantry."

"Is that not setting the fox to guard the chickens?"

"Lao, if you're going to insist upon imagery, you will have to learn to be precise. Jimmy's not charged with guarding the food in the larder. If he should feel in need of sustenance and make himself a pot of tea, where's the harm?"

It was not the depletion of Madam Wu's tea supply that had been my worry, but, chafing at Dee's continued criticism—it was I, after all, who was the writer—I said nothing.

"Also," Dee continued, "Feng and Mei Qiang are watching the street. The chef, Chung Kao Kun, lives in, with his quarters at the top of the house. And I am here myself. I think our task would be better served if you were to retire to your own flat and put up your fishing gear, allowing yourself to be lulled into a good night's rest on the calm seas of sleep."

"That," I said as I heard the pips declaring the post office would expect another penny if I desired to continue this call, "is worse than any imagery I ever myself attempted. Good night, then. I'll see you in the morning."

I replaced the earpiece with a certain finality, hailed a taxicab, and was soon at my flat, where I searched the cupboards until they yielded a bit of bread and a tin of sardines. Making do with these as supper, I tumbled into my bed and was wafted off on a breeze of slumber.

CHAPTER TWENTY-FIVE

Having slept soundly and eaten a full English breakfast at the tea shop two doors down from my flat, I reported to the Bruton Street home of Madam Wu at midmorning. The sky still sparkled blue, and the clear air moved with a fresh sea breeze, rare occurrences in London once the sun had spent even an hour's time above the horizon.

"Good morning!" I said with emphasis to Feng, who answered my knock. "And to you, Mei Qiang." I offered the hound my hand to sniff.

"Good morning, Teacher Lao," Feng said, considerably more subdued than I. Her eyes darted up and down the street before she closed the door behind me.

"All is well?"

"Yes, sir. Madam Wu is in the parlor, and Judge Dee is in the kitchen."

"Is he indeed? Doing what, if I may inquire?"

"Madam had planned to attend the Autumn Moon Festival this afternoon and was to bring the mooncakes. Because of the threat delivered yesterday, however, she's decided to remain here. Nevertheless, as she doesn't like to break her word, she's having the mooncakes prepared. Mooncakes, it seems, are a kitchen specialty of Judge Dee." Saying this, she offered a sly smile. "Although, as I understand it, making them is a tedious business. Chef Chung prepared the lotus paste filling two days ago and set it to age in the pantry, but this morning, as they began the rest of the process, he was quite willing to step aside."

"I'm not much of a hand in the kitchen," I said, "but perhaps I can be of assistance. First, I'll just pay my respects to your mistress, if I may."

"Of course." Feng showed me to the parlor. There, I found Madam Wu pacing in a double-breasted jacket and trousers with a shirt of western cut but fashioned from Chinese embroidered silk. Its gold phoenixes formed such an elegant pattern that I almost missed the pendant about her neck: hanging there on its gold chain was Dee's bat-carved bi.

"Lao," the lady said, rising. She bowed, and I returned the courtesy. "Thank you for coming."

"It's my pleasure. Though it appears I'm not needed, which I'm glad to see. Feng reported everything has been calm."

Madam Wu's hand went to her pale throat, where she fingered the bi. "Yes, it has. Though the people who issued this warning can be expected to strike without a further one."

"Why do they send the threat at all? Why warn the intended victim?"

"Perhaps to offer a final chance to change their ways? Or just for the sake of frightening them. That's the effect it's had on me." She gave a wan smile.

"I can't imagine anything frightening you for very long, Madam Wu," I said. "Nor can I think these villains would have the temerity to actually attack a woman of such eminence as yourself. People who would deliberately frighten are cowards."

"And yet, they do seem to have dispatched A. G. Stephen, if Dee is correct."

"Ah," I said, deflating a bit. "Yes, you're right about that.

Still . . ." My bolstering argument having lost its struts, I was not sure how to replace them.

"Still," said Madam Wu, smiling, "I'm well taken care of here. May I offer you tea?"

"No, thank you. With your permission, I'll go to the kitchen and see if I can be of assistance in the mooncake preparations."

Thus, having taken my leave of Madam Wu and been shown to the door to the area below stairs, I emerged into the chaos that was the Bruton Street kitchen.

There, I found Jimmy Fingers, his nimble cutpurse hands encased in great kitchen mitts, sliding a pan of golden-brown mooncakes out of the oven. Chung Kao Kun, happily serving as sous-chef in his own kitchen, had the delicate task of molding almond and lotus paste around the salted egg yolk for filling. Hoong, wearing one of Chung's chef's jackets over his merchant's attire, opened the door to the pantry so Jimmy's pan could lay to cooling with a number of others already crowding the marble counters. Dee, also in a jacket of Chung's—and looking a bit swamped in it—was carefully and precisely wielding the piston that shaped balls of paste-filled dough into inch-thick round cakes and applied a carp pattern on top. The whole room was filled with the sweet odor of baking, browning, and cooling pastry so reminiscent of home I felt I must have a mooncake immediately. I started for the pantry but was stopped by Jimmy.

"I wouldn't, if I was you, Mr. Lao," he said. "Mr. Chung says it's bad luck for us all if anyone was to eat 'em before the party. There might be a cleaver coming yer way if you try."

"Oh, but surely—" I started to remonstrate, but my complaint was cut off.

"No, Lao," Dee said, not looking up from his work. "You know the proverb, 'Eating Din's Mooncakes Before Ji's Banquet.'"

I frowned. "I'm very sorry to say that I don't."

"It's a story Mr. Chung told us," said Jimmy, "about this bloke 'oo 'elped 'imself to a few o' these beauties 'e was supposed to be delivering." Jimmy lifted another tray of cakes, these with bats on them, into the oven. "When 'e got where 'e was going and they saw 'e was short a number o' cakes, they lopped off 'is 'ead, along with the 'eads of everyone 'oo'd come with 'im. Mr. 'Oong explained it means it ain't worth a big risk for a small reward." He looked to Hoong, who nodded. "So since then, it's been bad luck in China to eat the mooncakes before the party," Jimmy finished triumphantly. "I'm surprised to find this is a new one to yer, Mr. Lao."

I looked from Hoong to Dee. "But that's not—"

Dee spoke to me in Chinese. "Of course it's not. Chung quickly appreciated that Jimmy's appetite is a floodgate that once open is hard to close. He invented the story, and Hoong and I supported it. As it is, we'll barely have enough to feed the crowd. Also, I understand the hound, Mei Qiang, is a fiend for mooncakes. Feng does not easily rouse to anger, but if she learned mooncakes were being devoured early and her dog was not included, I fear we'd encounter her wrath. Now be so good as to put on an apron and knead that dough."

Jimmy was observing us quizzically; out of courtesy, we rarely spoke Chinese in his presence. "Dee was telling me the whole story," I told him. "Now I understand."

Thus, the commotion continued, Dee acting as kitchen general, organizing his troops and taking various roles in the battle himself until, at the end of the morning, Dee, with Hoong, Chung, Jimmy, and myself, stood gazing victoriously about at the depleted flour canisters; crusted saucepans of syrup; empty baskets that had held dozens of eggs; and the neat rows of honey-colored pastries with patterns of carp, bats, or the double happiness symbol embossed on their faces.

Feng and the hound came down the stairs, as they had a

few times through the morning, to check the progress of the mooncakes and to assure us that all was well upstairs. Mei Qiang, smelling the mooncakes, sat and raised her paw, yipping as her tail swept the floor, but Jimmy said even the dog must not have one until the party, as we would otherwise all suffer from bad luck.

"Now," Dee said, "it is time you all got ready to leave for the festival. I'll pack the mooncakes into their tins."

"I'll help with the packing," I said, "so that you can get ready also, Dee."

"Oh, I won't be going," Dee said. "I'll remain here with Madam Wu. That way, Feng will be able to attend."

"Oh, but Mr. Dee," said Jimmy. "After all this work?"

I thought of Dee's bi around Madam Wu's pale throat, and I smiled. "Someone must make that sacrifice, Jimmy," I said.

CHAPTER TWENTY-SIX

As the entire kitchen brigade had been uniformed in Chung's chef's jackets to protect our clothing, we required but the briefest time to collect ourselves. The below-stairs powder room was made good use of, and soon, polished versions of Hoong, Jimmy, and Chung, each toting two large round tins of mooncakes, paraded through the pantry and up the kitchen steps to the pavement. Hoong's blue merchant's tunic and trousers appeared fresh and pristine. Jimmy had slicked his hair back under his flat cap. His attire consisted of a shirt and the standard three pieces of a man's suit—jacket, trousers, and waistcoat—though entirely unmatched as to color and cloth. Chung had chosen to make the delivery in a clean set of chef's whites, prompting me to wonder whether Madam Wu had invested in one of the new laundry machines that had recently become available.

Following after were myself, Feng, and the hound. Feng and I carried mooncakes also, but ours rested in cloth-covered baskets, Madam Wu's supply of tins having been exhausted. I felt that if my two-button tweed suit had become slightly rumpled in my efforts to contribute to the preparations, no one but myself was the wiser. Feng, who had largely avoided the clouds of flour and drips of egg by the sensible precaution of staying above stairs, wore her black tunic and trousers, and over those, her usual padded green waistcoat.

Madam Wu kept no chauffeur, but apparently, Chung was accustomed to serving in that role. Piling his mooncake tins onto those already held by Jimmy Fingers, who fairly staggered under the tower of them, Chung made the trip around to the lane to fetch the motor. He tooted into Bruton Street a few minutes later in a seafoam-green Bentley. We loaded the tins in the boot, though not the baskets—these, Feng and I held on our laps as we sat, not trusting the cloth covers alone to keep the pastries safe within. Hoong took the front seat beside Chung, while Jimmy and I sat in the rear and Feng faced us from the central folding seat. Mei Qiang lay across the feet of the three of us.

Our destination was the Sailors' Palace, a grand name for what was, in fact, a grand building with, however, a humble mission: the improvement of the lot of sailors fallen on hard times through bad luck, age, or injury. I had passed by the multiwindowed brick-and-stone edifice many times on strolls through the Limehouse dockside after a repast at one of the Chinese eating establishments that dotted the area. As many of the attendees at the Autumn Moon Festival were, in addition to sailors and laborers, expected to be students or diplomats, a premises had been sought for the event in a more salubrious locale than the East India Docks. But it was a sad truth of England in those times that Chinese persons, even diplomats with ready cash in hand, could not count upon finding an assembly room in which to gather in number. Thus, the Sailors' Palace, maintained by the British and Foreign Sailors' Society, was settled upon, for the management, being accustomed to foreign sailors, apparently had no fear of the Yellow Peril the gathering represented.

As we motored east across London, Chef Chung spoke. "I've been asked to convey this instruction from Madam Wu.

I'm to return immediately after leaving you all at the festival. She bids you enjoy yourselves, and while you, Sergeant Hoong and Teacher Lao and your young friend, may of course do as you please, Madam Wu requests that Feng"—he smiled—"and especially Mei Qiang refrain from eating any mooncakes. We were able to make barely enough for the gathering and she has ordered a new stock of ingredients. I'll make some for ourselves later in the day."

Feng smiled also and scratched the ears of the hound. "Poor Mei Qiang," she said.

Jimmy, having been quite taken with the mooncake story related by Chung, asked if I would tell some more Chinese tales as we went. I obliged, though mine were not ersatz: I offered "Wielding the Axe Before Ban's Door" and "Kua Fu Chasing the Sun." I chose stories with morals that might prove helpful to Jimmy, if he understood them. Feng's frowning concentration as I spoke was a bit unnerving. She seemed not to know those tales, though they were part of the upbringing of every Chinese child.

"Feng," I said, as we pulled to the curb in front of the Sailors' Palace and Chung silenced the motor, "where is your home in China?"

"My ancestral village is near Wutong Mountain, I'm told."

"Told? Your family lives elsewhere?"

"I no longer have a family, Teacher Lao."

Feng offered this disquieting statement in her usual direct manner. I was on the point of questioning her as to the meaning of it when Hoong opened the motorcar door. Mei Qiang jumped out onto the pavement. Feng and her basket followed, and then Jimmy. Last came myself, carrying my own basket. The boot lid was raised and the tins removed. Chef Chung, with a smile, bid us all enjoy the festival and drove off again.

The tins, carried by three men out of the kitchen, had now to be carried into the Sailors' Palace. I handed my basket to

Feng, so as to participate in the carrying. Hoong, Jimmy, and I each lifted two tins. Feng, a basket over each arm, watched this operation, and in this, Mei Qiang saw an opportunity.

In a flash, the hound snatched the cloth cover from one of Feng's baskets.

"Bu yao! Ting zhu!" Feng shouted, but the hound did not obey, for the lure of mooncakes proved too great.

Or *nearly* too great. With her jaws open wide above the basket, as if to gather every mooncake in at once, Mei Qiang stopped. She drew back, bristling. Slowly, she stuck her muzzle near the pastries again—this time, jaw closed—and sniffed. She retreated, approached again, sniffed once more. Dancing a series of agitated steps on the pavement, she growled, then began to bark.

"Something's wrong," said Feng, in English. "Mei Qiang's warning us. I was afraid she'd eat every mooncake before I could stop her, but look—she won't touch them." Feng crouched to scratch the ears of the troubled hound. Mei Qiang stopped barking but began to whine.

Sergeant Hoong dropped his tins into the arms of Jimmy Fingers, who found himself staggering under the weight of the mooncakes for a second time. Reaching into Feng's basket, Hoong withdrew a mooncake, broke it in half, and sniffed it. The golden egg yolk shone from the dark filling like the full moon in the night sky. Hoong pinched off a piece of that yolk, smelled it, wiped his fingers on the linen cloth, then pinched a piece of the filling. This he also smelled. He frowned and touched the filling to the very tip of his tongue. He snatched the cloth from Feng's basket, wiped his mouth and hands, and spat.

"The dog is correct," Hoong said. "There is cyanide in the mooncakes."

CHAPTER TWENTY-SEVEN

"Mr. 'Oong? Mr. Lao?" came the plaintive voice of Jimmy Fingers as he tottered under the weight of mooncake tins. "What's 'appening?" Hoong relieved him of three tins, and the lad's face was visible again. "I thought I 'eard you say 'cyanide.' What was it really you said?"

"I said exactly that, Jimmy. These mooncakes are poisoned. There's cyanide in the filling."

"Poison?" Jimmy dropped the remaining tin, which clattered to the pavement with a great noise. Mei Qiang jumped back and began again to bark. Feng gave her a gesture to silence her, though the dog continued to whine. "These cakes we was working on all morning?" said Jimmy. "They was meant to kill people?"

"Fiendishly clever," I said, "putting such a thing in almond paste, which would naturally hide the scent. But how was it possible? The house has been guarded like a fortress."

Hoong shook his head. "Only since the threat came yesterday. Chef Chung made the paste two days ago to give it time to age. Anyone could have gotten to it."

A black Mercedes touring car stopped, and three Chinese diplomats emerged. They bowed to us, smiling, and entered the building. I shuddered to think we could have been their unwitting executioners.

"All right!" said Hoong, and again, as in the kitchen, we had an officer in command of the troops. "The first task is to dispose of these noxious items."

"I must go back to Bruton Street and make sure all is well," said Feng.

"Dee is there," Hoong reminded her. "And Chef Chung will arrive shortly. You may, of course, do as seems right to you, but this intended assault was upon the festival attendees, not upon your mistress. I believe our duty lies here, to ensure no other danger surfaces." To Feng's still-worried look, he added, "There will be dustbins in the alley, and I see a telephone kiosk between here and there. I'll telephone Madam Wu. We can ascertain that nothing there is wrong, and she and Dee must be told of this attempted assassination. After that, we can proceed to inter the mooncakes."

Feng, with a nod, took up both baskets. Hoong and I gathered some of the tins from the pavement, but Jimmy blanched at touching them. "Go on, Jimmy," Hoong said. "The mooncakes are locked inside. In any case, they can't hurt you unless you eat them. Come, you've been handling them all day."

"That's as may be," said Jimmy, "but now I know what they are."

"Your knowledge makes them no more dangerous," Hoong said, but still Jimmy hesitated until Hoong lifted two tins and thrust them at the lad's chest. Instinctively, Jimmy clutched them. He sighed, holding them out in front as far as his arms would stretch, and followed. Hoong led us in a march to the back alley in the hopes of finding a bin into which we could place the lethal pastries so none would be poisoned but rats.

As he had promised Feng, Hoong stopped our march at the telephone kiosk. He dropped his tins onto Jimmy's stack once again. While Hoong slipped two pennies into the kiosk slot, I asked him, "Do you think the poisoned mooncakes are connected to the murder of Peng? To the Railway Conspiracy?"

"I think it highly unlikely," Hoong responded, "that they are not."

Jimmy, Feng, the hound, and I waited for Hoong's conversation with Madam Wu to come to an end. Upon replacing the earpiece, Sergeant Hoong stepped out of the kiosk and addressed his troops. "Nothing amiss at the house demands our attention, and Chef Chung will be arriving there soon. Therefore, after the mooncake disposal is complete, I suggest we continue on to the Autumn Moon Festival, which we will attend not as guests but as guardians. Except for you, Feng. Your mistress asks for you to return." He looked to Jimmy and myself. "Each of you must do as seems right."

"I'll come with you, of course," I said to Hoong.

"I will too," said Jimmy. "But I won't eat nowt."

"That will be novel," said Hoong.

Continuing on to the alley, we found a grouping of bins and, on Hoong's orders, took the precaution of not merely depositing the tins in them but emptying the tins and mixing the mooncakes with the bins' contents to make them lose any attraction even to the most down-and-out passing tramp. It was a sad sight: the brown egg-glazed dough, the purple filling, the golden yolks all being smashed into an ugly refuse-covered paste. It was an even sadder resulting scent. Hoong preserved one mooncake in a cloth in his tunic pocket for Dee to examine.

When our task was complete, we left the alley to make our way back to the Sailors' Palace. It was our intention to flag down a taxicab for Feng and Mei Qiang and for the others of us to continue into the building to take up our posts as sentinels.

• • •

NOW, IT MIGHT seem that from here, this story could continue uncomplicated in the telling. In the natural flow of narrative, those of us in Limehouse would enter the Sailors' Palace. Whatever happened there could be told, leading eventually to our return to Bruton Street, where we would expect to find Chung had arrived, followed by Feng and Mei Qiang, and that based on Hoong's telephone call, precautions had already been doubled. At that point, the account of events could resume there.

However, things did not proceed along those lines.

On the contrary, the events that followed the discovery of this attempt upon the lives of all attending the Autumn Moon Festival were characterized by such complexity that I am here forced to split this chronicle into two—and to do it thrice before we all converge again.

CHAPTER TWENTY-EIGHT

At the moment of Hoong's telephone call, Dee and Madam Wu were in the parlor. When the instrument rang in the entry hall, the lady jumped up, though from what activity, Dee would never say.

"Mayfair 1818. Wu Ze Tian speaking," she answered, and then, in Chinese, "Sergeant Hoong? Is everything—No, nothing has happened here. Why should—" A pause. "Oh, surely not! How can that possibly—but—yes, all right, I'll tell Chef Chung when he arrives. Will you come back here? Yes, I see. I suppose you're right. But please, send Feng back. Thank you, and please be very careful."

Dee, by then, was on his feet. "What's happened?" he asked, coming into the entry hall. Madam Wu spun to him, pressing her finger on the switch hook. She had not replaced the earpiece, but she did so now. Her face as pale as the moon itself, Madam Wu whispered, "The mooncakes were poisoned."

Dee's body tensed. "Poisoned? How? Is anyone—"

"No one ate them. Apparently, there was cyanide in the filling. Mei Qiang smelled it first, and Hoong confirmed it. Moments before they were going to go into the building, thank goodness. Chung is on his way back here. He left them before the poison was discovered, so he doesn't yet know. Feng is also coming back. The others will stay to make sure no harm comes to the festival attendees."

The next few minutes in Bruton Street, while those of us in Limehouse were pounding mooncakes into mush, were spent with Dee, Madam Wu at his side, examining every door and window to make sure all were secure. Soon, the sound of a key turning in a lock was heard from the rear. Chung, having returned the motorcar to its accustomed garage in the mews, entered the house by the back door.

"It was not long thereafter," Dee told me later, "that I realized what a besotted fool I'd been. I've never agreed with your assessment of women as incomprehensibly complex, Lao, but if, extrapolating from myself, you were to proclaim men incomprehensibly simple-minded, I don't think I could find fault with your conclusion."

What could have made Judge Dee Ren Jie pronounce such a verdict upon himself? It was, in sum, the following.

Dee, having instructed Madam Wu to remain in the parlor, hurried down the hallway to assure himself that it was, in fact, Chung who had entered the house. Finding that it was, he conducted the chef to the parlor, to receive the bad news about his pastries from Madam Wu.

The lady, standing, spoke calmly. "Sergeant Hoong has called," she said to Chung. "They've discovered poison in the mooncakes."

Chung startled. "Discovered—"

"Before any were eaten. The mooncakes have been disposed of."

Puzzled, Dee turned to face Madam Wu, for these words, which he might have expected to be delivered in tones of relief, instead rang with exasperation.

"Before," echoed Chung. "Then—"

"Yes," Madam Wu said. "Wait here." She nodded to Dee

and left the parlor for the hallway, where she lifted the handset on the telephone.

"What are you doing? Ze Tian?" Dee said. He started toward her.

"Madam Wu said to wait here." Chung stepped in front of Dee. He poked two beefy fingers into Dee's shoulder. In a swift move, Dee clasped Chung's wrist, twisting it slightly to dissipate the energy of the touch. Chung spun and brushed Dee's left hand away with his right. For a long moment, they regarded each other.

Dee, not wishing, as he said later, to escalate the situation but equally not wanting to be kept from an understanding of what, exactly, the situation was, gently but firmly pressed Chung's shoulder with his right palm to move the man aside. "Excuse me," he said.

Rather than stepping aside, though, Chung blocked inward with a left mirror hand and spun around to execute a chopping knife hand strike to the base of Dee's neck.

Evading, Dee shifted back onto his left leg, taking a high tiger stance. He used black tiger raises the head, capturing Chung's wrist and elbow and applying a low stomping kick to the chef's right knee. "I wanted," he said later, "to control him without hurting him, as I was still not quite sure what to make of this turn of events."

From the hallway came the murmuring voice of Madam Wu. "The first plan has failed. Move to the second."

Dee's eyes met Chung's. Chung twisted his body backward and shifted into a unicorn stance with a left knife hand slicing Dee's locking hands from his wrist. He launched a right punch at Dee's head.

Dee's mind raced back to Hoong's father's martial arts training hall in Yantai. In a pattern he'd learned on the Muk Yan Jong, the wooden-man fighting apparatus, he cut down

Chung's punch and struck at his solar plexus with a chopping fist, following up with a reverse tiger palm to the ribs and cutting inward with both right and left hands to a cross position. He struck out at the chef's right leg, breaking his position. Chung fell to his knees.

As Dee straightened, Madam Wu returned to the parlor. "Dee," she began.

Chung leapt to his feet, grabbed Madam Wu from behind, and produced a knife, which he pressed to her neck. The lady gasped.

Dee stopped all movement. He lifted his hands. Chung, with his paring knife to the throat of Madam Wu, moved slowly across the room. "Sit," he told Dee.

WITH APOLOGIES, IT is here I must pause and return to the events ongoing in Limehouse so as to keep all things in proper order.

CHAPTER TWENTY-NINE

After the successful, though tragic, disposal of the mooncakes, we four—Hoong, Jimmy, Feng, and I, plus the hound—retraced our steps. We reached the corner and hurried along Commercial Road toward the Sailors' Palace. I had just spied a taxicab that might take Feng back to her mistress and was signalling to it when a tremendous boom echoed off the wharf.

Next came a shuddering of the air. With a sense that I'd been hit in the back by a sandbag, I tumbled forward and found myself on the pavement. Debris rained down. Glass tinkled and people shrieked. A great cloud of dust rolled out from the Sailors' Palace.

After a few moments, my head cleared. I shook it, pushed myself to a sitting position, and found Jimmy Fingers lying unmoving beside me and covered in fragments of brick.

"Jimmy!" I shook the lad. Around us, people were running from the building as dust and smoke continued to bloom. "Jimmy!" I cried.

Jimmy groaned. I felt a great surge of relief.

"Jimmy! Are you all right?" I helped him to sit. He wiped at his face, and I realized the brick and stone powder frosting his features must also be adorning mine.

He coughed and opened one eye to me. "Well, Mr. Lao, I

can't say I enjoy being knocked arse over tip, but it ain't the first time." He peered around at the smoke and chaos. "What's 'appened?"

I looked to the Sailors' Palace, where a corner of the structure was missing. Clanging bells announced the approach of the fire brigade. "I know no more than you, Jimmy," I said, "but there appears to have been an explosion."

"Not just an explosion," corrected Hoong, emerging out of the smoke above us. He offered a hand to help me up. Feng, beside him, offered one to Jimmy. Mei Qiang danced and yipped. All of us, covered in dust as we were, could have been mistaken for gritty ghosts. "I believe," said Hoong, "it was a bomb."

A BOMB IT had been. Of this, we were assured by the stalwarts of the fire brigade who, in their concentration on their work, tried at first to shoo us away. Obediently, we began to back to a distance, but as we did, Mei Qiang whined and pawed at her mistress's leg. The hound pounced on a pile of rubble and attempted to dig at it as though burying a bone.

Or searching for one. Feng and Hoong fell to digging at the same pile until they exposed a hand. The fingers moved. Jimmy and I joined in, frantically lifting lumps of brick and stone and throwing them aside while bells clanged and the shouts of firemen filled the air. After more digging, the face of a young woman was revealed. She blinked and looked around. In another few minutes, her torso and legs were freed of their stone carapace. Jimmy lifted her and conveyed her to one of the ambulances arriving along Commercial Road.

After that, there was no more thought of leaving. Following the hound, we dug four more unfortunates from the rubble. I say "unfortunates," but all five lived, whereas six people in total were killed that Autumn Moon Festival afternoon.

The fire following the explosion was quickly extinguished by the men of the responding brigades. Once that was done, they joined in the digging. They brought in dogs also, trained for that at which Mei Qiang was merely a gifted amateur. Satisfied then that the professionals had the situation in hand, we took our first pause since the explosion. A young woman with a Red Cross armband brought tin cups of water to us, and we all drank eagerly. I looked at my watch, thinking hours had passed, but I was astonished to discover it had not been twenty-five minutes from the time Hoong had made his telephone call to Wu Ze Tian. My fatigue and the ache in my muscles told a much different story.

Yet another story was told when Jimmy pointed across the road to a warehouse building on Beccles Street. Busy in our rescue work, we had not once looked up, but we now saw through the dissipating smoke a banner hanging over the building's wall. In blood-red paint, in English and Chinese, it read, "Revolution!"

CHAPTER THIRTY

Here, leaving we four (plus the indispensable Mei Qiang) wetting our parched throats in Limehouse, I must resume my tale in Mayfair.

DEE, HAVING BEEN ordered by Chung to sit and encouraged to do so by the fright in Madam Wu's eyes as Chung's paring knife pressed to her throat, lowered himself to the sofa.

"May I ask," he said in calm tones, "what's going on?"

"No," snapped Chung. "You'll remain there, and silent, until my friends arrive."

"I give you my word I shall, if you'll release Madam Wu."

Chung glanced down at his prisoner. Dee noted an odd thing: the captive with the knife to her throat met her captor's eyes, and something seemed to pass between them. Only after that did Chung lower the knife and let her go. Gruffly, he demanded that she sit in the chair across from Dee. She did so, Chung remaining near enough to plunge the knife into her should he deem it necessary.

Dee, true to his promise, stayed silent at first, but he directed a steady and inquisitive gaze to Madam Wu. "I didn't suppose," he told me later, "that her eyes alone could answer my questions—except in one regard. If they could meet mine only briefly, and then she was forced to look away, I would have the most important answer."

And indeed, that was what happened.

After Madam Wu's gaze broke from his, Dee nodded to himself. He glanced about the parlor and reviewed in his mind the placement of rooms, windows, and doors in the house. Satisfied that he was prepared, he spoke.

"You've played me for a fool," he said.

"Silence!" barked Chung. He waved his knife menacingly toward Madam Wu.

Dee shook his head. "Madam Wu has nothing to fear from you. In fact, she's directing your actions, is she not?"

Chung, after a moment's hesitation, said, "No!"

But Madam Wu said, "Yes. It's all right, Chung."

Chung frowned. He didn't lower the knife but, in two strides, crossed the room, implying that if the knife were to be employed, now it would be Dee who was its target.

Madam Wu shook her head and softly spoke. "I didn't play you for a fool, Ren Jie. What went on between us was not a game."

"Not to me," he replied. "You seem to have thought of it quite differently."

"No."

"I should have realized," Dee went on, "when you admitted you hadn't told the truth about the mace. The second story about that wasn't any more true than the first, was it? Since it seems clear that when Chung's 'friends' arrive he intends to kill me, I'd like to be on my way, but before I leave, I think I deserve an explanation."

"You'll go nowhere!" growled Chung, with a glance at Madam Wu.

The lady didn't respond to him but spoke to Dee. "I will give you your explanation," she said. "And I hope that once you've heard it, you'll no longer want to leave."

CHAPTER THIRTY-ONE

Once more, now, I must return to Limehouse, briefly and for the final time.

COVERED WITH SWEAT-DAMPENED dust, we drank more water from tin cups. Feng cupped her hand to give a share to Mei Qiang. Wiping her brow, Feng said, "I must telephone Madam Wu. She must learn what's happened here. Originally, she'd intended to be here, after all."

Around the block once more we went, avoiding the fire-hoses and the canvas stretchers on which the men of the fire brigade were carrying out the injured—and the dead. At the telephone kiosk, Feng fed pennies into the slot, lifted the earpiece, and spoke, leaning close to the mouth opening. She listened, frowned, spoke again, then stepped back. Stepping in again, she spoke once more, but I could tell clearly there was no longer anyone on the line.

She replaced the earpiece, stayed unmoving for another few moments in the kiosk, then pushed open the door.

"Feng?" I said. "What's happened?"

"Betrayal. We must get back."

Feng began to run in the opposite direction from the Commercial Road. I grasped her strategy: a taxicab would only be found away from the site of the emergency. I ran with her and found Hoong and Jimmy doing the same. Mei Qiang loped along. "Feng?" I cried, but the young woman didn't answer. It wasn't until we four were seated in a taxicab, Hoong in the front, Jimmy, Feng, myself, and the dog in the rear, and the driver, as Feng instructed, was racing toward Mayfair, that she told us what had happened.

CHAPTER THIRTY-TWO

And here, for the final time, I return my narrative to Bruton Street. Soon will come the moment when we all converge.

MADAM WU STOOD and paced the room, as though collecting her thoughts. Dee followed her with his gaze while maintaining, at all times, an awareness of Chung's location and movements.

Stopping her pacing, Madam Wu turned to face Dee. "China is at a crossroads," she declared.

"In five thousand years of history, we have traversed many crossroads," Dee replied.

The lady shook her head. "Never before have the world's other powers been in a position to overcome us, to occupy our land, to sweep us away."

"To the contrary. The Mongols overcame us and occupied our land. Far from sweeping us away, they produced the Yuan Empire, one of China's most glorious. China prevailed; it was Mongol culture that was swept away. The Manchus overcame us and, in short order, became like the Mongols, completely Sinicized. Our culture is ancient and strong, capable of absorbing any who attempt to conquer us."

Madam Wu looked at him with sorrow in her eyes. "No, Ren Jie, you're wrong. At this very moment, while ill-considered democratic reforms weaken the Nationalist Party's ability to rule, the Russian Communist government, the Japanese emperor, and every European power are standing over the map of Asia with knife and fork, ready to carve up China amongst themselves with no regard for the Chinese. Even America is drooling for a piece. We won't Sinicize these enemies. China will disappear."

In steady tones, Dee said, "I assume it's this fear of China's disappearance that's driving your actions, including the attempted poisoning of the Autumn Moon Festival attendees?"

"They are, to a man—and woman—Nationalists or Communists."

"Or merchants or laborers with no special leanings. And three of my friends. And Feng, who has been devoted to you."

Again, Madam Wu smiled sadly. "Feng is on her way back. She's been told to avoid the mooncakes, though not why. As for the others . . ." She shook her head. "People die in war."

War. Madam Wu's parlor vanished, replaced by the mud and icy rain of a French battlefield. The cries and whimpers of dying men filled the air along with smoke, shouted orders, and bursts of gunfire. Blood soaked the earth. A ragged voice begged for help; Dee looked frantically about but couldn't find the source. He felt himself begin to tremble, overcome with a longing for the sweet oblivion of opium.

"Dee Ren Jie!" roared a voice. Dee looked up to see not a battlefield and not Madam Wu in her parlor, but Commissioner Lin, standing high in the empty air, pointing an accusatory finger. "Stop these imaginings! That war is long over. A new one is coming. Look to the future. Do what you've come here to do."

With that, Commissioner Lin vanished, and Dee found himself in the Bruton Street parlor once again. Madam Wu stood regarding him as though waiting for him to speak.

With a tremendous effort, Dee gathered in the memory that had assaulted him and folded it into the furthest recesses of his mind.

"War," he said to Madam Wu, in a voice not as strong as he liked but growing stronger, "is something you know nothing about. Your failed attempt to kill the festivalgoers—of what was it in service? What are you working toward?"

Madam Wu began pacing again. After a few turns, she stopped once more. "The times demand a strong leader. China needs Zhang Zuo Lin."

"Zhang Zuo Lin," Dee said, "is an opportunistic, cruel strongman. A tyrant and a would-be dictator. Emphatically not a leader."

"Zhang can unite China! And he will. Understand: his position in Manchuria has given him the opportunity to make friends, behind closed doors, among the Russians and the Japanese."

"This is connected to the Railway Conspiracy, is it not? Which is not, as you said it was, being directed by an international network of Communists. The opposite, if I'm not wrong."

Triumphantly, she smiled. "Connected to it? No. It *is* the Railway Conspiracy. And you're not wrong. Zhang is behind it. It's true, as I said, that killing one another's enemies makes discovery less likely and forges bonds of trust. White Russians kill Japanese Communists, Zhang's forces dispatch Russian Communists, and White Russians and Japanese together squelch China's nascent Communist movement. As our alliance strengthens, the communist strains in China and Japan will be destroyed before they can engulf those countries. That of Russia will be weakened."

"'Our' alliance. You speak not as an interested observer but as a participant. What is your role in this?"

"Zhang is a powerful and capable military leader, but he is

not a political strategist," said Madam Wu. "As a woman of business, I've had to learn cunning. Subtlety. Patience. Zhang's abilities and mine are perfectly fitted."

Dee looked at her with a new and bitter understanding. "Zhang is behind the Railway Conspiracy, but the idea wasn't his."

Madam Wu's smile broadened and she tipped her head as though acknowledging a compliment, although Dee had intended the opposite of praise.

"And your ultimate goal?" Dee asked.

"In Russia, the Communist revolution will be reversed and the tsar reinstated. Japan will retain its emperor, and China will crown another, ushering in a modern dynasty, a strong government that can take its place beside Russia and Japan to keep the Europeans and Americans at bay." Clenching a fist, she raised it high and declared, "The East will be ours!"

Dee stared. "You're mad."

Again the lady smiled. "No. No, I'm dedicated to our cause. I'm certain we'll win. And I'd like you to join me."

Dee considered these words. Madam Wu's dedication and certainty, he had no doubt, were ill-placed. What she was hoping for would not come to pass and would be nothing other than a disaster if it did. Russia and Japan could do as they liked and as they would, but to have such a man as Zhang Zuo Lin ruling China—worse, attempting to crown himself emperor and begin a family dynasty—would spark such internal violence and conflict that the country could well dissolve back into the mosaic of fiefdoms that existed in the Warring States era.

"The strength China needs," he finally said, "is the strength that grows out of justice and opportunity."

Madam Wu's smile faded. "Your friend Lao is a Communist. I didn't take you for one, but perhaps I've been wrong?"

"Many people, including Lao, can see no route to supporting the peasants and workers in their desire for fair dealing other than the communist one. I can; after all, I remain an agent of the Nationalist government."

"The Nationalists are weak and about to be defeated."

"By Zhang?"

"By Zhang or the Communists. One way would be to China's glory, the other to further humiliation. You must choose, Dee."

"A false choice. Neither way you present is inevitable or would be good for China."

Madam Wu frowned. She looked down at the carpet and pressed the tips of her fingers together. When she looked up again, she spoke. "Ren Jie. You know I admire you. I care for you. I want you at my side. Your skills—and your fame, I won't deny it—would be tremendous assets in this fight. If you join us, I can promise you a role—a major role—in the government to be established. Minister of Justice, perhaps. You'll be in a position to mitigate some of Zhang's . . . less temperate inclinations." She held his eyes. "On the other hand . . ."

Dee stood slowly, ignoring the glowering Chung, who waved the knife a bit but seemed to have no plan for how or when to use it.

"On the other hand," Dee said to Madam Wu, "what?"

"If you don't join us," the lady replied, "I know better than to hope you'll stand aside and let the game play out."

"That you call the future of China a game puts an end to any doubts I had, which were few."

"Is that it, then?"

"Do you need to hear it said? I will not join you."

Madam Wu, her eyes fixed on Dee's, put her hand to her throat and touched the bi. "I'm sorry," she said. She spun and raced across the room to the cabinet on which the dragon-taming mace stood in its carved cradle. As she seized it and ran out the door, a force of large Chinese men poured in.

CHAPTER THIRTY-THREE

Dee was a talented and disciplined martial artist. That he now found himself outnumbered was neither unexpected—Chung had said his "friends" were on the way—nor unprecedented. Dee had fought unequal battles before this, prepared to do so by the rigorous training provided in the kung fu studio of Hoong's father.

Though it turned out the battle in Madam Wu's parlor was not so very unequal after all.

As Madam Wu vanished down the hallway to the rear of the house, Dee leapt to the back of the sofa to consider the men now surrounding him. He probed for weaknesses, for evidence of poor training: unbalanced stances, strained shoulders, loosely held hands. These things would tell him where to attack first. All the men had stopped, looking like nothing so much as a pack of overgrown jackals, waiting for a command from the pack leader to set upon their prey. Chung raised his knife to give that command.

FROM THIS POINT forward, this narrative is once more the product of my own experience and not dependent upon accounts prized out of Dee.

• • •

AS WE RACED toward Mayfair in the taxicab, Feng told us this: that her telephone call had been answered not by Madam Wu but by Chung; that he'd inquired in concerned tones whether she was all right before she'd told him about the explosion; and that when she did, he asked whether the building still stood, as a bomb under a corner could bring an entire structure down.

"I never said bomb," Feng told us grimly. "I never said corner. I never even said the Sailors' Palace. I said only that there'd been an explosion."

"Perhaps Chef Chung learned about this another way, before your call?" I said.

"He acted surprised when I told him. Shocked, even. And yet he asked questions that indicated knowledge."

"Your inference, then," said Hoong, "is that he already had this knowledge."

She looked at him. "Does it seem unreasonable to you, Sergeant Hoong?"

"No, Feng, it does not."

"Knowledge," I said, "might, in turn, indicate involvement."

"And involvement with the bomb," said Hoong, "might, in its turn, indicate involvement with the poisoning of the mooncakes."

"Chef Chung made the filling," said Feng. "And kept everyone from eating any mooncakes before the festival."

"By that Chinese story 'e told!" Jimmy said.

"Which he invented," said Hoong.

"Invented?" Jimmy frowned. "Are you saying it ain't a true legend, Mr. 'Oong?"

"I thought, at the time, he'd found a clever way to circumvent your appetite, Jimmy. So I supported the story."

"As did I," I said. "And Dee."

"But it weren't real? It were for fooling me? Oh, gents, yer've disappointed me."

"Don't look so downcast, Jimmy," Hoong said. "We did save your life."

Jimmy, lips pursed, tilted his head. "That's fair," he said.

"And Chef Chung told me not to eat any mooncakes at the party, or to feed them to Mei Qiang, because there were so few. He claimed these were Madam Wu's instructions," Feng said. If she could have growled like her hound, I believe she would have. "I now think it's more likely he was concerned about having to explain my death to my patron."

"Patron?" I was confused by her choice of words. However, she would say no more.

Soon after, we arrived at the Bruton Street home of Madam Wu. Feng leapt from the taxicab, threw open the house door, and with Mei Qiang beside her, dashed inside. The others followed. I started after, but the cabman shouted out that he required payment. I thrust a pound note at him and raced into the house after my companions.

Our fear had been that we'd find Madam Wu and Judge Dee in danger from Chef Chung. As Feng threw wide the door and we issued into the parlor, we encountered an unexpectedly different situation. Madam Wu was nowhere to be seen, and Dee stood on the back of the sofa surrounded by a crowd of large Chinese men.

At the sound of the door being flung open, all eyes turned to us.

The eyes of all but Dee looked briefly baffled, possibly as much by the makeup of our phalanx—three Chinese, one large, one small, one smaller yet and female; a British lad; and a dog; all of us sweat-streaked and covered with stone dust—as by the question of whether we were friend or foe. That last was answered, and the first shunted aside, by Chung's command. "At them!"

Immediately, all the men stepped into fighting stances.

Hoong, eyes blazing, threw his arms skyward. His sleeves fell to his shoulders. I saw what I hadn't known him to be bearing—iron rings, five on each arm. He crossed his hands overhead, crashing the rings together with a loud clang. Stretching out his arms, he raised his index fingers in the classical Shaolin bridge hand position. He roared, "Yat ji jing jong!"

Heroes united? Did this also mean me? I needed, then, to meet this trust, outnumbered though we were. Untrained in classical fighting techniques, I was not, however, untried on the streets of Peking. I took a fighting position of my own.

In response to Hoong's roar, our opponents were briefly silent until one yelled, "Scum!"

I saw Dee smile, almost as though he knew what was to come.

Hoong leapt in, crashing through the crowd, his size matching theirs but his power greater. He cut a swath through the men, who seemed helpless to stop him. I relaxed my stance and watched as—arms outstretched, brandishing the iron rings—he swung to and fro and spun like a whirlwind, smashing everyone and everything in sight. He knocked down one, two, three of the attackers as easily as a tidal wave pounds the shore.

I cried, "Sergeant Hoong, please take care! The room holds delicate pieces of artwork."

Hoong bellowed a laugh. "My little brother is an art lover, but nothing stands in the way of my righteous fists." He battered through the crowd with seven star slashing blows. I stood agape, watching a Hoong I might have suspected but had never seen before.

Despite Hoong's declaration, not a bowl or a scroll was damaged in his rampage across the room. I had hopes of all the treasures staying intact until I spotted Jimmy Fingers on the room's opposite side. Wise lad, staying out of the way of danger; but as I thought this, he jumped up onto the chaise longue, lifted one of Madam Wu's large artworks from the wall, and smashed it down over the heads of three of the attackers, dazing them and encasing them in it. "Got 'em!" he exulted.

"Oh, no, Jimmy!" I said. "That was a Le Corbusier!"

Dee smiled. "Calm yourself, Lao. It was a print. An original print, signed and valuable, but not unique. Jimmy!" he called. "A good choice."

In all the chaos, I was late spotting a flash of movement. "Dee!" I cried. "Behind you!" One of the pack was stealthily but speedily creeping up on Dee, dagger raised.

Feng saw him too, but Feng did more than shout a warning. She pulled a dagger of her own from her brocaded waistcoat and sent it spinning through the air. It embedded itself in the would-be assassin's wrist, forcing him to drop his knife.

Dee turned without hurry. "Very good, Feng. Your training included the fei do ban, the flying dagger, then."

Feng acknowledged the compliment with a small nod.

With a cry, the assailant yanked the dagger from its resting place. Blood gushed onto the carpet. No doubt considering himself now useless and vulnerable, he tried to dash out the door. Unfortunately for him, he had to pass me to reach it. I thrust my leg out. He tumbled over it, fell to the floor, and did not rise.

One was at my feet, three knocked down by Hoong, three imprisoned by Jimmy in art. But all was not over. There were attackers still standing.

Another man rushed at Dee. Now the general joined his troops in battle: Dee spun his body into the attacker with a golden flying leopard leap. He landed in a crouched position and applied a tiger fist strike to the assailant's groin. The fellow buckled over into a heap.

A second came racing over. Dee took a crane stance and executed a thrashing backfist strike followed by a cutting tiger claw palm strike to the attacker's rib cage. Shifting backward, he picked up the man and slammed him to the ground.

With a loud growl, Chef Chung charged into the combat.

Dee met him with a tiger tail reverse kick, sending Chung reeling back. Chung, red with rage, scrambled up and came in with a left hook, followed up with a straight right hand. Dee destroyed both with his iron forearm.

"Chung," Dee admonished, as though he were the teacher and Chung the student. "You're letting anger drive all skill from your fighting technique." This comment, of course, had the effect of further incensing the chef. He aimed a kick at Dee's right thigh to destabilize him. Dee shifted back into his tiger stance and parried, launching a right arrow kick and punch simultaneously. Chung deflected the technique. His counter was ham-handed—but someone in the crowd had had enough.

A figure leapt across the room: Mei Qiang, who, in a flash, attached her teeth to Chung's ankle. "Good puppy!" Dee said, smiling.

Within an instant, another flash followed: a dagger, thrown by Feng. It buried itself in Chung's hand, and the chef found himself nailed to the floor by dog and dagger. As soon as the knife landed, the young woman somersaulted over the sofa to drop onto Chung's chest with a thud. She knelt astride him, shaking him by the neck and demanding, "Where is Madam Wu? What have you done with her?"

CHAPTER THIRTY-FOUR

The hound, Mei Qiang, had released her hold on the chef's ankle but stood growling over him, looking ready to rip out Chung's throat should Feng release her hold on it.

Sergeant Hoong put a restraining hand on Feng's arm. "He can tell us nothing if he can't speak."

Dee dealt a final blow to one of the attackers who'd started to rise. He leapt up and looked around. "Feng!" he said. "Stop."

"He must tell me what he's done with Madam Wu!"

"No." Dee came and knelt beside her. "Feng, I'm sorry."

"What happened?" she cried before he could go on. "Where is she?"

"Come," said Dee. Hoong restrained the half-dazed chef while Dee led Feng to the sofa. "Sit," he suggested.

"No! Tell me!" The young woman leaned toward him, her body taut.

"Madam Wu is well. Unhurt. I'm afraid, however," he said as Feng's features began to relax, "that that's the extent of the good news." He glanced at me. "It's to my shame that I didn't understand this sooner. Madam Wu, far from becoming a victim of Chef Chung, has been behind his actions. It was at her command that he poisoned the mooncake filling. When he returned here and she told him that plan had failed, she made a telephone call to initiate a second plan. I don't yet know what that might be—"

"The bomb," said Hoong, rising, having bound Chef Chung hand and foot. "Madam Wu was responsible for the bomb."

"That can't be," said Feng.

"A bomb?" Dee asked.

I realized he would have no way of knowing what had happened at the Sailors' Palace—or why we four looked as disreputable as we did. I explained in short order about the explosion. "Across the street," I said, "a banner had been unfurled that read 'Revolution!' It appears to all that the Communists—led by that fiery young student, Ang Chun—are responsible."

Dee's face grew hard. "Fiendishly brilliant," he said. "The Communists are not responsible, Lao, but they will be blamed. The murder of Nationalists brought about by Communists sets the two groups upon each other. There will be more killing, making much more distant the possibility of a negotiated reconciliation. While those two are battling each other, Zhang Zuo Lin will attempt to seize power, for which he's been busy setting the stage. Or rather"—Dee looked at us all—"Madam Wu has been."

The account Dee proceeded to give of Madam Wu's actions and intentions was difficult to reconcile with the generous and self-possessed woman I knew. I said as much, and Dee responded, "She's a true believer, Lao. Zhang hopes to use the upheaval in China to give himself power. Madam Wu hopes to use Zhang to give China power—power to withstand the predations of foreign governments."

"At a time when, having recently overthrown the imperial line, China has two promising paths to follow," I said, "to be supporting a man who'd return us to dynastic rule with himself as emperor—it's unconscionable!"

"I agree," Dee said. "But Madam Wu doesn't see the situation in that light. She believes a strong hand is required—and she believes she can control that hand. That is, I think, a tragic underestimation of Zhang's brutality and his ruthlessness." At a sound from behind him, we all turned. "Feng?" said Dee. "Feng, are you all right?"

The young woman had fallen back onto the sofa cushions. Putting her head in her hands, she started to tremble, then to wail.

Women, as I had discussed with Dee, befuddled me. Add in tears and I never had any idea at all of my proper role. Dee glanced at Hoong, who started tentatively toward the young woman, but to the surprise of us all, Jimmy Fingers straightaway crossed the room to sit close beside Feng. He wrapped an arm around her shaking shoulders and whispered words of comfort.

While Jimmy held Feng, Mei Qiang put her paws on the lap of her mistress and licked her face, whining. Feng hugged the dog tightly. Jimmy continued his soft words. Hoong, after a moment, stepped over the struggling Chung and continued to the powder room, from which he brought a damp hand towel to offer to Feng. Slowly, her sobs subsided. She scrubbed at her face and then folded the cloth carefully in her lap.

"There," said Jimmy. "Better now?"

Feng didn't respond but continued to stare at the cloth.

Jimmy looked up to three sets of eyes on him. "I 'as four sisters," he said. "Nobbut this to do, really, when ladies is crying."

"I'll remember that, Jimmy," I said.

Dee crouched before Feng. "You've had some bad shocks," he said. "And you're exhausted. The poison, the explosion, the digging, the fighting—"

"No," she whispered. She looked up and said in a stronger

voice, "No. Those things are true, yes. But . . ." She fell silent again.

"Come," said Jimmy. He nudged her with his elbow. "Yer'll feel better for telling us. We're yer pals, and I'll take on as many as says we ain't!" He made fists and a fierce face.

Jimmy's bravado drew a small smile from the young woman. After watching her in the recent melee, it was clear to me—and no doubt to Jimmy—that her fighting ability far surpassed his.

She looked at the cloth in her lap again. Then, straightening her shoulders, she began. "I am from Mexico," she said. "From Torreón."

"Torreón," I breathed.

Dee said softly, "I see."

Hoong frowned.

Jimmy looked from one of us to another. "Mr. Dee? I don't see, meself. And," he added, to Feng, "if yer a Mexican, I'm a Lascar!"

Feng shook her head. "I'm not Mexican. I'm Chinese. My grandfather's father left China for Mexico. Later, he sent for his wife. My family has—had—been in Torreón since then. Four generations. I lived there until my tenth year." She stopped and looked away, meeting no one's eyes.

"And then?" said Jimmy. "Wot 'appened then?"

Feng's eyes suddenly filled with tears again. She pressed the cloth to her face and sobbed quietly.

"What happened," Dee said, "was a massacre. Chinese were caught between two sides in the Mexican Civil War. When the rebels entered Torreón, three hundred Chinese people—not soldiers, not partisans of either side, but farmworkers, laundrymen, shopkeepers, bankers—were killed in the space of two days. Butchered, brutally, inhumanly."

"My parents," said Feng. She lowered the cloth and spoke with force. "My grandmother. My two brothers. I was saved by the Mexican tailor who lived next door. He hid me in his home and told the mob there were no others in the family but those they'd already killed."

"Why, that's terrible!" Jimmy frowned and hugged her more tightly.

"Your speech," I said. "I wondered where in China would give you those accents in your speech."

"Nowhere in China," she said. "In Torreón, we spoke Chinese at home, but I spoke Spanish with my friends and among the people of the town. That is also, Teacher Lao"—she took a gulping breath—"why I don't know, and am eager to learn, the stories and proverbs of China. To make our family's lives in Mexico easier, my grandfather converted to the Roman Catholic faith. Those are the stories I learned."

"You're a Christian, then?" Though my own conversion had been made in the Church of England, our Savior teaches us to love one another broadly.

Feng looked at me with a shadow of her old stoniness. "I left my faith in the ruins of Torreón."

"Feng," Dee asked gently, "how did you come to be in the employ of Madam Wu?"

One of the attackers on the floor of the wrecked parlor began to stir. Hoong strode to the window, tore down the sash holding back the drape, and bound the man's hands.

"I fled Torreón with scores of others," Feng said. "We made our way to Mazatlan hoping to find passage to China. I'd been given money by the tailor, all he could afford to spare. It wasn't enough to buy passage, but I was hoping to work and earn what I needed."

"To earn—but you were ten years old and alone!" I said.

"I had no choice. Mexico had become unsafe. I was a strong child, used to working in the fields. I'd never seen China. But all I could think was to go there."

Hoong, having tied the hands of another thug as a precaution, returned to our circle.

Feng straightened her shoulders and continued, "A ship had recently docked in Mazatlan from San Francisco. It was spending two days in port while it took on cargo, and the passengers had disembarked. Hoping to find work carrying purchases as they shopped or perhaps tailoring garments, I went to one of the hotels where they were staying. Among the passengers was a small group of wealthy Chinese merchants. Madam Wu was one."

Here, Feng stopped. She scratched the ears of Mei Qiang, who nuzzled her hand. Jimmy also scratched the ears of the hound, which brought forth from Feng a slight smile.

"Madam Wu inquired as to my situation, how I came to be seeking work so young and alone. As soon as she understood, she offered to take me with her. She said I could be useful in her household and that if I were willing, she'd have me taught—not only schoolwork but the martial arts."

Dee smiled. "Your knife skills. Plus what we saw here today." He gestured around the room.

The young woman nodded. "Madam Wu said she was embarked upon a path that would bring power to China, real power, and that I was welcome to join her in the journey. She told me she was building a China whose citizens would never again have to worry about humiliation, about persecution. Chinese wouldn't have to go abroad to earn their living, and any who did choose to travel would be greeted with respect and even deference." Feng's eyes filled once again with tears. "I joined and followed her. I believed in her. But now you say she's killed randomly, without care, murdering innocents, putting the blame on others—if this is true, my patron is no better than the killers of Torreón." She lifted the cloth and began sobbing into it once more.

"Feng," said Dee, "I'm so very sorry."

"I am also," I said. I sat awkwardly on her other side and embraced her as Jimmy had. The surprise in her tear-filled eyes when she turned to me was almost enough to cause me to retract my arm, but her small smile convinced me to let it remain.

Wiping her eyes with the cloth, the young woman nodded.

"Power," Dee said, "is a dangerous desire. Those who possess it often come to feel they've done something to deserve it, and that therefore, their choice of how to employ it is beyond questioning. I believe Madam Wu wants the best for China. But her vision has been warped by the power she wields. I won't promise you power. But as Jimmy says, we're yer pals."

Feng looked up in wonder at hearing Dee so perfectly imitate Jimmy Fingers.

Dee smiled, and then, his face serious once more, said, "We have a task to accomplish. People have died, and unless we can stop what is happening, many more may die. You, Gao Feng, can be valuable in this undertaking. Are you willing to join us?"

Feng met Dee's eyes wordlessly.

Dee said, "And Mei Qiang, of course."

The hound, upon hearing her name, lifted a paw to Dee and wagged her tail.

Feng nodded. "Yes. Yes, if you think I can be of use, I'll join you."

"Thank you," said Dee. "I can't offer you power, but we'll try together to find justice."

CHAPTER THIRTY-FIVE

Dee stood. He briefly put a hand on Feng's shoulder; then he turned to the chef, Chung Kao Kun, who was struggling on the floor in his bonds. "Where is Madam Wu?"

"She's escaped you," Chung sneered.

"So that she can murder again in the name of her love of China?"

Chung's sneer turned to a smirk.

Dee set his mouth into a hard line. "It disgusts me to talk to this man, someone so willing to murder strangers—and those who thought they were his friends. He'll tell us nothing. Hoong, Lao, Jimmy, search his pockets and the pockets of the others. We may find something of interest."

We fell to the task. I began with the man still unconscious—he was, after all, closest to me. In his pockets, I found nothing but a leather wallet with a few pounds and some papers in Chinese issued for the purposes of identification.

The man who'd stirred earlier was searched by Jimmy, who, as his profession might lead one to expect, made quick work of the job. As the thug made feeble protestations, I saw Jimmy glance to Dee, who stood, back to us, at the cabinet where the dragon-taming mace had rested. Jimmy then quickly relieved the man's wallet of its pound notes.

"That's fine, Jimmy," said Dee from across the room, not turning, "but leave his identification papers. The police will want to know who it is they've got."

Jimmy reddened and, shrugging, grinned at me. Turning his attention to the pockets of another man, he said, "We'll be calling the officers, then? It won't bother no one if I take my leave before they come, I 'ope."

"We'll all be gone by then," Dee said. Turning back to us, he shook his head. "Though I can't say I'm sure where it is we'll be going."

"This may suggest a course of action." Hoong held out a piece of folded paper he had taken from the pocket of the chef. Dee opened it. With raised eyebrows, he showed it to the rest of our group. It held the railroad symbol and, above that, words in Chinese.

"Wot's it say?" Jimmy asked.

I told him, "Anthony Cartwright."

"Who might that be, when 'e's at 'ome?" Jimmy asked.

"Even at home, he's Anthony Cartwright," Dee said.

I said to Dee, "And that home? How are we—"

"At the start of the war," Dee said, "Cartwright began his explosives experiments in a laboratory in Hazlitt Road."

"Yes, I remember. He mentioned that at the banquet."

"This work was sponsored by the British government and produced great success for the military." I detected in Dee's voice a note of ambivalence about this great success; no doubt he was remembering the percussion of blasts on the battlefield. "I understand he keeps a flat above the laboratory for the times when he returns to London." Dee looked at the paper in his hand. "This indicates that he's a target of the Conspiracy. If he's fortunate, this instruction might not yet have reached the intended assassins. But we can't depend on fortune."

Dee, using his Oxbridge tones, then called the Metropolitan Police Force from the telephone in Madam Wu's hallway. He suggested they come to Bruton Street to collect some gift-wrapped thugs who had attempted a robbery. He apologized that he himself had been called away from home but promised to leave the door open for them.

"Quick now," he said to us all. He threw the front door wide for the police and led us down the hall and out the rear door into the alley. "The fastest way to Hammersmith is likely to be a taxicab." He started for the end of the alley but was interrupted by Feng.

"The fastest way will be by motorcar, yes. But why not take Madam Wu's motor?" Feng pointed to a closed stable door with a lock on it. "Chung will have driven it in there when he returned."

Dee looked from the stable door back to her. "Have you the key?"

"No. But surely all of us working together can break it."

"Oh, miss, no need for that." Jimmy grinned and took two thin strips of metal from his waistcoat pocket. "'Alf a second," he said. Dee nodded, and Jimmy set about his trade.

I didn't take out my pocket watch, but I believe I can fairly say Jimmy exaggerated; the snapping open of the padlock came a full three seconds after he first touched it.

"I shall—" Dee began, but Feng had already lifted a key on a silver fob from a hook on the wall. She stepped on the running board and, with one hand on the chassis, swung her legs over the Bentley's doorless side. Having achieved the bench, she slid behind the steering wheel.

"Feng," said Dee. "You can drive a motorcar?"

"Madam Wu requested that Chef Chung show me how. Chef Chung was a patient and expert teacher. Until today, I thought him a good man." Feng's voice remained even as she turned the key, but she pushed in the ignition button with possibly some unnecessary force.

We once more filled the motorcar. This time, Hoong joined me in the rear seat, though he occupied rather more of it than I. Jimmy faced us from the fold-down. Dee, as Feng settled behind the wheel, stepped without hesitation through the door into the front passenger seat. Mei Qiang, also without hesitation, leapt up after him and curled at his feet. I assumed, given Dee's height and the size of the well, the hound was lying *on* his feet, though I couldn't see it; but if so, Dee gave no indication that her position troubled him.

"Dee," I called from the rear, "I had no idea before now that you were an animal lover. Yet you recite poetry to a horse and permit the advances of a hound."

"I've said, Lao, that I make use of whatever is available to me. At times, I grow rather fond of it."

The first time I'd heard these sentiments from Dee he'd been referring to myself. Now he was using the same words when discussing Mei Qiang. I chose to interpret the smile in his speech with generosity of spirit.

Feng changed the car's gears and smoothly, without the slightest shake or jiggle, we slid from the stable into the alley, where she executed a partial turn and entered onto Bruton Place. Thence to Berkeley Square, and we were racing toward Hammersmith.

As a writer, I have, throughout my career, suffered the occasional accusation of hyperbole. In my novels, I've attempted to portray the situation of my fellows with truth but also humor, and because of that aim, I plead guilty to the judicious use of elaboration and embellishment. Thus, I feel it important to clarify that when, in this chronicle, I use the term "racing" to describe our journey to Hazlitt Road, I am keeping to the bare, unaided truth.

Gao Feng drove the Bentley the way she fought. No wasted action, rapidly decisive. Upright in her seat, her hands smoothly moving through the required sequences, her feet adroit on the pedals, she seemed to have a preternatural sense of the locations of every motorcar, horse cart, barrow, and pedestrian for many streets around. I saw Dee watching her with great interest as the motorcar slipped through openings I hadn't noticed and sped along avenues that had not seemed clear when we turned their corners. Between Mayfair and Hammersmith sat a number of intersections equipped with the newest in red-and-green traffic lights, but though we slowed once or twice, we were never forced to stop at one.

In other words, our trip to Hazlitt Road took only half as long as I'd expected.

And even at that, we were barely in time.

CHAPTER THIRTY-SIX

"This is the place," Dee said, pointing at a two-story brick building clearly built, in its time, to be a warehouse. Feng turned the wheel and slid the car to a smooth stop. We all leapt out, ready for action.

Surprising me, Dee pressed the bell.

I said, "But Dee! If Conspiracy agents are within, you've now alerted them to our presence."

Dee shook his head. "They would already know we're here. That motorcar is handsome and fast but hardly silent. Our lack of stealth will convince them *we* don't know *they're* here."

Dee rang again. He turned and nodded to Feng. She returned to the motor and started it up, driving it some distance down the street while an anxious Mei Qiang whined quietly under Dee's restraining hand. Feng parked the car and hurried back to us.

"I see!" I said. "Now they'll think we've gone again!"

"They will, unless they hear you," Dee said. "Please speak no more."

When no response came to Dee's ring, he signaled Jimmy. The lad once again produced his metal strips and silently gained us entry. He opened the door inch by inch to prevent the hinges squeaking, a practice no doubt perfected in his previous career.

Within, we found a high-ceilinged hallway with glass-paneled walls on either side. Glancing about, I saw through the pebbled glass vague outlines of laboratory equipment and such structures as were required to hold it in place. At first, nothing else; then, a moving shadow could be seen through the glass on the left side, and following it, another.

I thought Dee would lead us there, but he chose a door on the right side instead. We entered that laboratory noiselessly and closed the door behind us. Full of questions, I nevertheless heeded his admonition to remain silent.

Bringing us deeper into the room until we were some distance from the door, he whispered, "It's undoubtedly an ambush. We'll meet it. Then, we'll find Cartwright."

"How do you know they haven't found him already?" I asked. "And . . ." Though we all knew what the result would be if indeed the Conspiracy had found their target, I could not bring myself to speak the words.

"Because," Dee said, "they're still here. You three," he said to the others, "and Mei Qiang, stay low behind this table. Lao, come with me."

I followed Dee to a wide stone-topped table in a far corner where our activities were unlikely to be observable from the laboratory across the hallway. Lining up four glass flasks, Dee directed me to find and bring him tins of saltpeter, charcoal, and sulfur.

"How do you know they'll—" I stopped. Cartwright's expertise was in explosives. I understood what Dee was planning and why he knew I'd be able to find what he asked for.

From the canisters I brought, Dee measured the ingredients together. "Now," he said, "we're prepared."

Chinese Taoist monks invented gunpowder while trying to discover the elixir of eternal life. The irony was as unavoidable as the formula was simple, and Dee and I made short order of combining the three ingredients to create the proper mixture.

We each carried two powder-filled flasks to the bench nearest the door, behind which our friends crouched.

Dee spoke while lighting four Bunsen burners. "We'll heat these flasks briefly to activate them. When we enter the other laboratory, we're likely first to encounter thrown weapons, possibly shuriken. They may be poisoned; I believe I detected an odor of tetrodotoxin when we entered the building."

Feng turned a curious look to Hoong, who whispered, "Blowfish poison. I smelled it too."

Dee went on, "Each of you, take an instrument tray from that stack and use it as a shield. When I pull open the door, stay low and lift your shields with a yell. The darkness will be our ally. Jimmy, stay here. On my command, hurl the flasks across the hallway where I direct you. Is everyone ready?"

Everyone was. With our shuriken-shields raised, we crept across the dark hallway. We arrayed ourselves. Feng whispered to Mei Qiang. Dee put a silent hand on the door pull.

A motionless, soundless moment.

"HI-YAAA!" Dee yanked the door open.

In a cacophony of "HI-YAAA!" we rushed into the room, ourselves low, our shields high. Mei Qiang barked wildly as metal clanged on metal. A blizzard of shuriken flew through the air, hitting our trays, either piercing them through or bouncing off them and clattering to the floor.

A moment of ominous quiet.

Dee shouted, "Jimmy! There!"

I lowered my shield and turned to see Jimmy, in the room across the hall, seize the heated flasks and, with a juggler's skill, send them spinning one after the other across the corridor to the place where Dee pointed. At the same moment, from that same spot, several shadows leapt up onto the laboratory tables with katanas drawn: black-clad ronin about to spring. Dee had perceived them, though no one else had.

Loud booms percussed the flash-filled air. Three of the darkly clad assassins spun backward onto the floor, their swords clattering away.

The fourth was Isaki.

That masterless samurai leapt into the air and spun around to gain momentum to lop off the head not hiding behind its shield.

Mine.

I felt a blow and crashed to the floor, though when I reached up, I found my head still joined to my neck. Feng, wearing leather gloves and wrist braces I had not seen her don, had kicked me over and ensnared Isaki's sword with a rising X-block. She wrestled the sword down, and it skittered across the room. Giving Isaki a kick to the torso, she sent him tumbling.

"Excellent, Feng," Hoong said. "But remember: that one is mine."

Feng looked sharply at him. "If possible."

Hoong glared but said nothing.

"Danger!" I called, as I saw the three Japanese assassins reassemble.

Hoong stepped forward and laughed. "Xiao laoshu! Little rats!"

The three ronin all rushed Hoong at once. One threw a roundhouse kick. Hoong met it with a backfist to the shinbone. I heard a crack, and the man fell at the same time the second ninja thrust a dagger at Hoong. Hoong came in from the outside, ensnaring the hand and crushing it, forcing the man to drop the dagger as Hoong's right hand smashed diagonally down on his jaw. He staggered and collapsed. The third assassin attempted to jump on Hoong from behind. Hoong's massive left hand smacked his face with a power slap that, I was quite sure, rattled his brain. Hoong followed it with a blow to the side of the head. The man keeled over.

I shouted my approval and swung my attention to movement on the other side of the laboratory.

Six persons clothed in the black tunics and trousers and wearing the black bowler hats of the boo how doy—those Chinese triad members called in English "hatchet men"—were creeping forward. My heart thumped, but before I could call out, I saw Mei Qiang, Feng, and Dee stepping out to confront them.

Mei Qiang stood quivering and growling, waiting for the order to strike. Dee extended two fingers in the classical Chinese gesture and rebuked the triad men: "As people of the Han, you should be ashamed of yourselves."

The six snarled and attacked.

Dee went left, Feng right, and Mei Qiang down the middle, each taking two assailants.

On the left, the men rushed in, both with their lather's hatchets raised to chop down on Dee. Dee shifted back into a bow stance, deflecting both blows simultaneously. He grasped the attacking arms at the wrists, twisting them inward as he turned his body. One man, he threw over the other. Both came crashing to the floor, their weapons flying in different directions. The first man to land shook a table of apparatus; the second slid into the same table, causing beakers to break and liquids to mix, foam, and sputter. One of the men shouted in alarm as drops spattered and burned through his sleeve. "Aiyee!" He stood and ran, peeling off his tunic. The other didn't seem to have been hit by the drops, which was as well, as he was unconscious.

The two center assassins ran at Mei Qiang. The hound snarled and leapt, latching her mighty jaws onto the hatchet arm of one of them. Spinning around, trying to shake her off, he dropped his weapon. The second man chopped at Mei Qiang, but the hound's head flashed back and forth as it would if she had a rat between her teeth. Missing her, the man's axe landed in his partner's imprisoned arm. Mei Qiang let go her grip and jumped back, growling as one man screamed and the other, yanking the axe free, slipped on spilled blood and crashed to the floor.

The hound turned her attention to her mistress. Feng was squared off with the two other attackers, one closer and one farther behind. The first charged in with a vicious chop downward that Feng evaded by dropping low. She hooked his leg with her ankle, and with a scissorlike action, twisted that limb in a way I was sure had broken his knee. He fell, releasing a long, low moan that reinforced my certainty. As the second man attacked, Feng rolled to her left. She waited until he closed the distance and hit him squarely with a ground fighting kick. As he reeled back, she sprang up and threw an inside crescent kick to his head, which sent him crashing to the floor. She pulled a dagger from her waistcoat, ready to stab him, but he had ceased all movement.

Peace reigned for a moment, weapons and unconscious fighters were scattered about, and I thought perhaps the battle was over.

But Isaki was not done.

Isaki's katana had been lost in the dark, and Isaki himself had been lost in grogginess from Feng's kick, but Isaki's enmity toward Hoong had gone nowhere. I watched him rise to his feet and spy Hoong across the room. They stared at each other.

With a movement so fast I barely saw it, Isaki launched two shuriken at Hoong's head. Hoong twisted away nearly as fast, and the spinning blades whizzed by him and crashed through the glass corridor wall.

Isaki, incensed, let out a loud yell and rushed Hoong, swinging with his left hand.

Hoong deflected the blow outward, saying, "Ghat muk. Wood block."

Isaki followed up swiftly with a right.

"Pek choi. Chopping strike." Hoong thumped on Isaki's forearm. He followed with a hammer strike to the samurai's head, but Isaki blocked it with his left palm.

"What are you saying, Chinaman? Stop singing this little song." Isaki launched a roundhouse kick to Hoong's thigh. Had it connected, it would have crumpled Hoong, but Hoong dropped his right hand, brushing the kick aside. He followed up with a left hooking foot sweep, capturing Isaki at the ankle. As Isaki tottered, Hoong spun about, slamming his elbow into the ronin's torso and stealing all his breath. Hoong followed up with a double tiger claw strike to Isaki's jaw.

At that moment, we heard bobbies' shrill whistles and there came heavy footsteps charging down the hallway. Isaki seized the moment to leap onto a laboratory table, and from there to another. He pointed a finger at Hoong. "When next we meet, Chinaman, it will be your end." He jumped to a third table and out a now glassless window.

CHAPTER THIRTY-SEVEN

The timely arrival of the Metropolitan Police was explained later by the man who led them in: Anthony Cartwright. The constables, appalled and somewhat confounded by the wreckage of equipment, apparatuses, and men, were of a mind to pile us all into their arrest van. Cartwright stopped them. "These people are here to provide security for my laboratory." He indicated our party.

One of the constables frowned. "The girl? And the dog?"

"I hire effective personnel, Constable. If they happen to be female or canine, that makes no difference to me. Now please see to the removal of these intruders. And do be careful. How they managed hand-to-hand combat in here without detonating the entire building, I don't know. Come!" he said to us, as though we were in fact in his employ. "We've got pressing business, as you know!"

He led us at a gallop out the door, leaving the men of the Metropolitan Police gaping.

When we reached the street and slowed, Dee said to Cartwright, "What pressing business is it that we've got?"

"I have no idea. Whatever business brought you to my laboratory. By the mess you've made, I assume it was pressing."

"How did you come to arrive simultaneously with the constables?"

"I brought them. I was headed here to look in on a research experiment—one now in shards on the floor—and saw the flashes of small explosions. I was about to summon the fire brigade when I saw figures moving in the smoke. At that point, the police seemed the better bet."

"And why did you claim us as your employees?"

"I could see there were two sides to whatever went on, and I chose yours. Was I wrong?"

The question seemed simple curiosity, with Cartwright's next action dependent on its answer.

"No," Dee said, "your assessment is correct. Those men were there to kill you."

"In that case, thank you all for dispatching them. Are you able to tell me why they came after me, and why you came after them?"

"We will," said Dee, "but first, perhaps we ought to leave here, in case they had men in reserve."

"Also"—Cartwright grinned—"we wouldn't want the constables, when they begin bringing their prisoners out, to see us standing here. They'd be disappointed at the way we're handling our pressing business."

We rounded the corner where the Bentley sat waiting. "I think it would be best to retreat to a quiet place and consider our situation," said Dee. "Gentlemen, can you find space in the rear of the motor for another passenger?"

"If Sergeant Hoong can see his way to occupying only half of the bench," I said, "I'll happily share the other side with Mr. Cartwright."

"A challenge I accept," said Hoong.

Cartwright, as he climbed in, looked at Feng behind the wheel. "You also drive?" he said with admiration. "Truly a woman of wonders."

Feng, without answer, started the engine. When all seats—and the floor at Dee's feet—were occupied, the young woman turned the wheel. The motorcar, as though it took no notice of its ever-increasing passenger load, slid into the traffic. Feng inquired what our destination was to be.

Dee answered, "I think we would do best to make our way to the home of Bertrand and Dora Russell. The day's activities—many of them violent, all of them confusing—require consideration, as does our own position in relation to them. If all agree?"

None disagreed, but as Feng began to pilot us with smooth speed east across London, Cartwright spoke. "If no one explains to me what you and those other men were doing in my laboratory, I'll begin to suspect myself of being a participant in my own kidnapping."

Dee said, "Lao, will you enlighten Mr. Cartwright as to the circumstances that led to the current situation? If so, I shan't have to turn around to address him."

Feng bristled. "If you feel you must watch the road—"

"No," said Dee. "I feel I must watch you drive. I make it a point to study the methods of those with excellent technique, no matter the skill they are practicing."

"Oh." I saw a flush creep up her neck. "I apologize."

I couldn't see her face to read its expression, but Dee was grinning.

I proceeded to my assigned task, explaining the paper with the railroad symbol to Cartwright and expanding my discourse to encompass all that had happened that day. He listened with focused intensity. Despite what Dee had said, he did turn to explain in greater detail the events at the home of Madam Wu.

"The Railway Conspiracy!" Cartwright said when all explanations were finished. "What a how-de-do! When we discussed that at Madam Wu's banquet, none of us knew what it meant, or whether it was even real."

"It seems to be quite real," I said.

"And I'm a target? Any guess as to why?"

"Because of your time in Manchuria, I imagine," said Dee. "The experience provided by your war work for the British military would make you an asset for any side you chose. The respect for the non-Han Chinese your travels demonstrate would suggest to the Conspiracy that side would not be theirs."

"So they decided to eliminate me, without even the courtesy of asking me first? That seals it, then." He thumped fist into palm. "Whatever you're planning, Dee, I'll be part of. People of such incivility can't be allowed to rule the world!"

WHEN WE REACHED the Russell home, Feng stopped the motorcar. All remained within with the exception of Dee, who hurried across the pavement and pressed the bell. The bald butler, Larrimore, greeted him and drew him inside. Soon, Larrimore came out again to speak to us through the window of the car.

"If you'll just go around to the mews," he advised Feng, showing no surprise at the sight of a small, young Chinese woman acting the chauffeur, "you'll find the garage available. Lester has been sent to move the master's automobile. I'll meet you at the rear entrance of the house."

Feng did as she had been instructed, driving the car into the former stable. Jimmy pulled the doors closed, and we crossed to the house.

Dee's thought had been that such a striking car discharging such a motley collection of passengers would draw attention on the street. The same, of course, was true of the mews, but fewer people would see us, and those who did would likely be servants, accustomed to keeping their thoughts to themselves.

"Right now, staying low, that would be the ticket," Bertrand Russell said, once we were all seated in the Russells' parlor and holding brandy snifters. The Russells had shown little surprise at the size of our congregation and no consternation whatsoever at the idea of our dusty, bedraggled clothing perching on their parlor furniture. Quite the opposite; close on the heels of the brandy snifters came plates of sandwiches prepared in the below-stairs kitchen. A bowl of water was procured for Mei Qiang, who slurped thirstily.

"Yes, with assassins from the Railroad Conspiracy loose in London, staying low sounds very sensible," I concurred.

"It's more than that," said Dora Russell. "Dee, you're a wanted man."

CHAPTER THIRTY-EIGHT

Everyone was shocked to hear that the Metropolitan Police Force was on the lookout for Dee, except Dee himself.

"I suspected something like this when Madam Wu escaped," he said. "She will have gone to the police with a story about my being the one who made the mooncakes. She'll then say that, once I learned my first attempt at mass murder had failed, I instructed my confederates"—he looked around at us—"to trigger a bomb I'd previously planted. Then she'll say I and those same confederates attacked her in her home. Chung will bear that out, and as there's no one to bring a charge against him or any of the others we left behind at Bruton Street, they'll be let go."

"Surely they will not!" I said.

"That's 'ow it is with coppers," Jimmy said, shaking his head. "They chase down those as are innocent and let go those that need jailing." Jimmy himself had been chased down a fair few times in his young life—though rarely innocent, I was sure. The irony in his statement seemed lost on him, however.

"That appears to be what's happened," Dora Russell concurred. "You're considered a person of interest, Dee. They're hoping you'll help them with their inquiries." The irony Jimmy had been unable to find abounded in the tone of Dora Russell's words. “The news reports tell us that a certain large man of your acquaintance, a Chinese merchant, is also being sought, and a young woman with a dog has been mentioned.”

Dee sipped his brandy. “In that case,” he said, “I propose to throw myself on the mercy, not of any court, nor yet of the Christian Lord”—he lifted his glass to Russell, a well-known atheist—“but of you, my friends. Additionally, I propose similarly to throw Hoong, Feng, Cartwright, and Mei Qiang.” The hound, now resting at Feng’s feet, picked up her head and swept the floor with her tail. “If you can see your way to enduring such a situation for a day or so, not longer—keeping in mind none of us has brought so much as a toothbrush, so there will be no dressing for dinner—my gratitude will be almost more than I can bear.”

“Splendid!” said Bertrand Russell, slapping his knee. “We’ll close the blinds and play at spies. As to toothbrushes, I can send Larrimore out. Yes, this will do quite nicely. Though after your day or so, what is it that you mean to do then?”

“Then,” said Dee, “we shall see.”

“Dee,” I said, “I notice that Jimmy and I were not mentioned as being thrown anywhere. I know you too well to think this was an oversight. What is your intention?”

“Ah, Lao, you’re a perceptive fellow. I think, as neither you nor young Jimmy seem to be of any interest to the Metropolitan Police, nor indeed to the Conspiracy—”

“—though if I were you I would take that as an insult, Lao,” said Cartwright.

“—it would be best if you went about your normal lives,” Dee continued. “This would avoid your looking suspicious and enable those of us here to have eyes and ears in the world outside. I’ll send word when circumstances have changed and it’s time for action.” He added, with a certainty I found myself glad to hear, “It won’t be long.”

• • •

THUS IT WAS that Jimmy Fingers and I left the house of Bertrand Russell by the rear mews. He went first, I some minutes later; he turned south, I north. Where Jimmy went, I didn't know, but I took the bus to my flat, eager to bathe, change my clothes, and consider all that had happened that day. It seemed nearly inconceivable that a day that began with a morning of cheerful mooncake-making should end in death, destruction, and flight from both assassins and the police.

I was so deep in thought, trying to sort out all these events, that I failed to notice two constables at the entrance to the block of flats that contained my own until it was too late to avoid them. "Gentlemen," I said, tipping my hat as I attempted to move past.

"Well, don't 'e look a mess?" the stout one said.

"I dunno," the thinner one responded. "Maybe Chinamen dress all dirt-covered natural-like."

"If you'll pardon me," I said stiffly, making to insert my key in the outer lock.

"Don't think so, guv." The stout one barred my way. "Yer this Lah Ow Shee, I'm betting. See, now, the Metropolitan Police is looking for yer good friend Dee Ring Jee." Despite the bobby's mangling of both of our names, I was not put to any pains to understand whom he meant. "So our guvnor, 'e says, Buck and Coyle—I'd be Buck, and 'e's Coyle"—this was accompanied by a pointing thumb—"the guvnor says, go see that fellow Lah Ow Shee, as 'e most likely knows where to find this Dee chap."

"That I don't," I said with dignity. I prefer not to lie, but as I'd already referred to Buck and Coyle as "gentlemen," I felt myself sufficiently compromised that another falsehood would barely register upon my immortal soul.

"And wot if we don't believe yer?"

"I can do nothing about that. I've come from the ill-fated Autumn Moon Festival, where I anticipated a joyous celebration but instead found myself digging people out from the rubble of a bomb. Dee was nowhere to be seen." This, in fact, was true, although misleading.

"We 'ear from the guvnor as it was this Dee as planted the bomb."

"In that case, your 'guvnor,' whoever he be, has a very wrong idea about Judge Dee."

"Ooh, the fellow's a judge, is 'e?" Buck grinned at Coyle, his smile bringing to mind the blades of a sawmill. "We'll 'ave to doff our caps right enough when we grab 'old of 'im, then."

"Whatever you do is of no concern to me," I said. "Now, please step aside."

"Ah, but Chinaman, yer doings is of great concern to us."

So much for the Metropolitan Police having no interest in me. I wondered if Jimmy had been similarly confronted at his rooming house in Silver Street.

Evidently considering their threat adequately made, Buck said, "'Ave a good evening," and the two bobbies separated, allowing me to enter the building.

Rattled anew by this unpleasant encounter, I collected my mail and made my way up to my flat, thinking how grand it was going to be to bathe and lay my weary body down to sleep. The Russells' sandwiches would have to do for supper, as I was far too tired to go out again in search of it. I might, however, pour myself one more small brandy before I shut my eyes on this day.

As it turned out, this splendid finale had to be postponed, for I opened the door to my rooms to find a large man sitting in my upholstered chair.

Even in the twilight darkness, it was impossible not to know that form. "Voronoff!" I said, astonished. "How did you get out of jail, and how did you get in here?"

"Hah! Little rat Isaki not only person can find advocat. Good to see you, Chinaman. No, really not so good. Just came so you tell me where to find your tovarisch Dee. Also, that silly Cartwright. You tell me where he is, also."

"I have no idea. Please leave." I also had no idea what I would do if this large Russian thug failed to obey my instruction, but it seemed wise to hide any trepidation I felt.

"No, you tell. Those two sukiny deti, they both dead men. Just not dead yet. You tell where to find, maybe you don't be dead man, too."

"I can't help you."

Without haste, Voronoff pulled a piece of paper from his pocket. Holding it on two corners, he showed it to me. "You know what is this?"

I nodded. "The symbol of the Railway Conspiracy."

"Very good, Chinaman. Any name on it, name of dead man. You don't tell me by tomorrow where Dee and Cartwright hide, your name go here." He tapped the paper and folded it carefully to replace in his pocket. He stood to leave.

"How do I contact you? If I should find them?" I thought this would be a useful piece of information.

"Oh, you don't worry. I contact you. Think hard about what I say." He nodded his bear-like head and went out my door.

I sank onto the chair Voronoff had vacated. I was overwhelmed to the point of numbness by the events of the day, and yet, I found to my dismay that one more disagreeable surprise awaited me.

Voronoff had finished my brandy.

CHAPTER THIRTY-NINE

I did, finally, get my bath and my long, heavy sleep. I awoke to sunlight pouring through my window along with the whooshes, clip-clops, horn blasts, and hawkers' shouts that made up a London morning. My limbs ached, though not as badly as I thought I deserved. I dressed, wondering about my friends at the Russell home in Bloomsbury. They were, I knew, in as safe hands as any in London; and yet, the connection between Dee and Bertrand Russell was not unknown. A clever inspector might go round for a look.

I could, however, do nothing on that front for now. I did have a task before me: a flyer I'd taken from my mailbox the previous evening informed me that the Chinese Youth Communist Party was to meet today to discuss the tragedy at the Autumn Moon Festival. I hoped to find Ang Chun at that meeting, both to assure myself of his safety and to warn him of the danger to himself and to the other members of the Youth Communist Party.

That meeting was scheduled for the noon hour, which left me time for a meal. Feeling sorely in need of one, I locked my flat door, trotted down the stairs, and found, on the pavement outside, a pair of bobbies. Buck and Coyle must have been relieved of duty by these fresher but no more refined constables. I responded to their sneers with a tip of my hat and stepped speedily along.

Neither bobby spoke, but they kept pace with me. I ignored them and made my way by bus—in which vehicle the bobbies joined me—to Limehouse, where I entered Wu's Garden and ordered a double plate of pork dumplings. I thought perhaps my bobby disciples would also take a table, thereby at least earning Wu a few shillings more, but they entered only long enough to ascertain that I sat alone. Looking at each other, they wrinkled their noses at the aromas swirling about the restaurant and retreated.

Calling a waiter over, I instructed him to go into the street and find a likely looking lad for an errand. He returned with a red-haired boy of perhaps nine years. As he was led to my table, the child stared about in wonder at the hanging paper lanterns and the scrolls on the walls. The waiter indicated to the child that he was to approach me.

"'Ere," the boy protested, "I don't speak no Chin-ee."

"No matter," I said. "We will converse in English. What's your name, child?"

"Well, I never," marveled the boy. Rapidly, though belatedly, he removed his cap. "I'm Ben."

"I'm pleased to make your acquaintance, Ben. I am Professor Lao from the university. Do you know your way about London, Ben?"

Ben puffed up his chest. "With me eyes shut!"

"You may keep your eyes open for this errand," I said. I gave the boy a note I had written in Chinese, detailing for Dee my constable companions and my plan to attend the meeting. I also handed over a shilling. "Take this to 31 Sydney Street," I said, "and another shilling awaits you once you've delivered it."

The lad stuffed both note and shilling deep into a pocket of his corduroy trousers. "Am I to wait for an answer, sir?"

I considered. "No. Once you've collected your second shilling, your duty will be done."

Beaming, the lad replaced his cap upon his red head and ran off. I turned my attention to my newly arrived dumplings.

AFTER MY MEAL and a considerable amount of tea, I left Wu's Garden, handing an extra shilling to the waiter who'd brought me young Ben. As I issued onto the street, I saw the lounging constables straighten up and nudge one another.

"Good day," I said, though I refrained from calling them "gentlemen." "I, as I presume you know, am Lao She, lecturer in the Department of Oriental Studies at the University of London." I bowed. "Apparently, I can expect to enjoy your company throughout the day. Might I therefore have your names?"

The older constable, a rotund man with a wide mustache, scowled at me. "What d'ye need our names for?"

"They could come in very handy," I said. "Supposing one of you falls behind. Shall I say, 'You there, bobby, bobby-the-other is missing?' Or if a lorry were to bear down upon you, would you not respond faster to a cry of alarm if I included in it your names?"

He continued scowling, but the younger, taller constable scratched his head and said, "Why, that sounds reasonable enough. Don't it, Ritts? I'm Tucker, he's Ritts," he told me.

Ritts now enlarged the scope of his scowl to include Tucker. I wondered if that presaged a dressing down for the younger man once I was out of earshot.

"Well, then, Constable Tucker and Constable Ritts, it's time we were off."

"Where are we making for, then?" Tucker asked as they fell into step behind me.

"The university," I said. "Please put on some speed. I have a meeting to attend."

Had I been alone, or pressed for time, I'd have taken a bus from Limehouse to the university. As it was, heeding Dee's admonition to improve my physical conditioning, and wondering in a scientific way about the conditioning of the Metropolitan Police Force, I elected to walk, and fairly rapidly, at that.

"Here," I said finally, approaching the classics building where, as before, the meeting was to be held. "Will you accompany me inside? I'm afraid the meeting is for members only, but the hallway has benches in case you care to sit." Without waiting for an answer, I entered through the double doors.

I could hear by the slap of leather soles that Ritts and Tucker had, in fact, followed me into the building. Perhaps they were enticed by the promise of a place to rest their bobby bones. I wouldn't have minded a brief respite myself, but first I had a message to deliver.

I entered the meeting room. Again, the banner of the Chinese Youth Communist Party had been hung at the front. Tea and biscuits were available, and small groups of men and women were standing about speaking in low voices to one another. All conversation was in Mandarin. It took a moment, as on the earlier occasion, for my ears to adjust to what had once been an everyday experience. I glanced about and, to my great relief, saw Ang Chun.

"Ang," I called. "Ang Chun! A word?"

The young man separated himself from the group he'd been with and walked to meet me. "Teacher Lao. I'm glad to see you here to join in our deliberations. This is a sad day."

"Sadder, perhaps, than you know. You are referring, I presume, to the bomb at the Autumn Moon Festival?"

"Indeed."

"Are you aware of what's befallen Peng Lian Liang?"

Ang Chun nodded. "Peng is dead. Killed, as I understand it, during a robbery at his flat."

"Killed, yes. But those were not the circumstances." I sketched for Ang Chun in outline the events of Peng's death.

Ang frowned in disbelief. "Russians? Cossacks? Teacher Lao, I'm sorry, but that sounds absurd. Why would Russian Cossacks desire the death of Peng Lian Liang?"

"Are you familiar with the Railway Conspiracy?"

"Oh, that's nonsense."

"No, you're wrong. It's quite real." I gave him such details about the conspiracy as we now understood. "Peng was their victim," I said. "They also made an attempt yesterday on the life of Arthur Cartwright."

"The chemist?"

"The same. The attempt was unsuccessful, and Mr. Cartwright is now in hiding. Ang Chun, it is the Railway Conspiracy that is responsible for the bomb at the Autumn Moon Festival and the banner hung across the street from it."

He fixed his dark stare on the quadrangle beyond the windows. Returning it to me, he said, "If this is true, what is their aim?"

"The conspiracy intends to establish an autocratic leadership in each of the countries involved. With the bomb, they hoped to kill a good many of the Chinese Nationalists in London. With the banner, they hoped to lay the blame for those deaths on the Chinese Youth Communist Party. Zhang Zuo Lin cannot succeed in China unless both the Nationalists and the Communists are weak and fail to unite. The Nationalists are better established, and the senior diplomats here in London are all of that party. Educated youth, as in this group"—I gestured around me—"are, on the other hand, the future of the Communist Party. What better way forward for Zhang than to kill them and blame you?"

He considered what I'd said. "I've heard the Metropolitan Police are searching for a man named Dee Ren Jie in connection with the bombing. Is he a member of the Conspiracy?"

"No, he is its enemy. It was they who made him appear culpable, for the same reason they hung the banner at the bombing site. They hope, in this way, to make their enemies eliminate one another."

Ang Chun trained his piercing eyes on me for some more moments. Then, he turned and strode to the front of the room.

CHAPTER FORTY

"Comrades! Your attention!"

All eyes turned to Ang Chun, who clapped his hands as he stood under the banner of the Chinese Youth Communist Party, and talk quieted to an expectant hush.

"Comrades, we've all heard about the murders—indeed, the assassinations—of our countrymen at yesterday's Autumn Moon Festival. There is other news you must hear. Most of you know that one of our own, Youth Party Secretary Peng Lian Liang, died two days ago. I've been told his death was an assassination also."

A stunned moment, and then a shout: "No!"

"Yes, and here's the worst of it. There appears to be evidence these deaths were orchestrated by a multinational group intent on reversing the revolution in Russia, strengthening the Japanese emperor, and declaring Zhang Zuo Lin emperor of China."

"Zhang!"

"No!"

"Impossible!"

Ang Chun held up his hands and quiet reigned again. "Additionally," he told the crowd, "as a technique to discredit and ruin us, these crimes are deliberately being laid at our feet."

This time, the shocked exclamations and shouted questions

threatened to break out into chaos. Ang Chun held his hands up again. "This is Teacher Lao She, from the Department of Oriental Studies. He will give you the details on the situation as it stands."

I hadn't expected to be asked to address the crowd, and I was impressed at Ang Chun's immediate willingness to share the spotlight. I stepped to the podium in the front of the room. "Please take your seats," I said. When all were seated and the room more quiet, I told the assembled Young Communists what I had told Ang.

"I think," I finished, "the wise course would be for your group to remain as unobtrusive as possible over the coming days. Hold no public events, issue no statements. If any of you is questioned by the police, answer honestly. As you are innocent of the murderous events at the Sailors' Palace, and equally of Peng's death, the investigation will soon veer off down other paths."

"No!" shouted Ang Chun. Sharing the spotlight apparently put him under no obligation to agree with me. "Innocence guarantees nothing. The authorities, looking for someone to blame, will settle easily on us. We're Communists, and we're Chinese. We'll be accounted responsible for shedding innocent blood. I say we must hunt down the members of this conspiracy ourselves and shed some guilty blood!"

A young woman jumped to her feet. "Ang Chun! Remember the cause! We must keep our focus on building the international party!"

"No, I agree with Ang!" yelled a round young man. "We must find the persons responsible to avoid being blamed ourselves. We cannot build the party from jail!"

The argument continued along these lines. To my alarm, Ang's faction appeared to be carrying the day, until at last, the envoy who'd come from Paris, Zhou En Lai, stood.

"Comrades," he said, and all quieted to hear him. "Feelings are running high. That's to be expected in grave circumstances such as these. Still, I believe Teacher Lao is correct." He was a year my senior, but he bowed to me. "We must bide our time and wait to see what develops. Hunting down the members of the Conspiracy has a fine ring to it, but we haven't the skills for this task. If somehow their names become known to us, the situation could change. But for now, I'd encourage everyone to go home, study, and wait."

Chaos threatened once more as people in the crowd turned to one another and discussed Zhou's words. After a brief time, the young woman who'd asked Ang Chun to remember the cause stood and called for a vote. I was much relieved when the results went strongly along the lines suggested by Zhou En Lai. Zhou's status as European envoy, I reflected, as well as his half-decade advantage on most of them, could well have influenced this young crowd. They might be revolutionaries, but they were still well-brought-up Chinese.

Ang Chun, for his part, was less than pleased, but the will of the majority was clear. As the meeting broke into small whispering groups, he approached me. "Teacher Lao," he said. "You must keep me informed of any developments."

"Yes," I said. "I shall." Given the young man's fiery temperament, the wisdom of this was questionable, but he and the others, I thought, deserved to know. "Also, I'd advise you to take care. We have no evidence you yourself are a target of the Conspiracy, but you're one of the leaders of this group. I suspect they'll likely take notice of you."

In the hallway, I found Ritts and Tucker on the wooden bench where I'd left them. Tucker was smoking a cigarette and Ritts, arms folded, stared at the ceiling. They nudged each other when they saw me.

"Oi!" snarled Ritts. "It's about time. What d'ye Chinamen talk about in there, all packed together? Though was I packed in with some o' them China-women, I'd not much mind." He elbowed Tucker and leered in the direction of two female students emerging from the room. Tucker said nothing, but he smiled.

"We talk about the manners of London policemen," I said, "and how to improve them." Upon which I spun on my heel and made for the door.

I heard the footsteps of my attendants following me down the hall. My thought was to go round the shops, purchasing such bits and pieces as I required. Thus might I replenish my stores of various items, show these policemen that Chinese people lead normal, quiet lives, and possibly convince the Metropolitan Police Force that following me was a bootless and boring endeavor.

That plan did not immediately change but was made less attractive when, leaving the building, I and my constable companions encountered the original bobby pair, Buck and Coyle, whom Tucker and Ritts had replaced in the night.

"Oi!" the several bobbies hailed one another.

"Wot're you two rascals doing here?" Ritts inquired. "Our shift ain't done yet."

"The guvnor thought the more, the merrier, keeping track o' this Chinaman," said Buck, the stouter of the two. "See, the guvnor, 'e went to the pictures last night, and it seems 'e saw this new feature, *Man of a Hundred Faces*."

"Ah! I've seen it meself," Ritts said. "Quite good, it is."

"The guvnor was reminded that these Orientals, they 'as dark magics they can use. 'E was worried that you two might fall victim, see."

"Us? Me and Tucker? Bosh. We ain't afraid of no magic tricks!"

Tucker took a glance at me and seemed a bit less sure. Nevertheless, he didn't contradict his partner.

I blew a frustrated breath between pursed lips. "Yes," I said, "bosh, and humbug besides. It's an absurd and, indeed, offensive idea. Dark magics! That picture was as much a fairy tale as"—an impulse came upon me to blurt out, *as Spring-heel Jack*, but as that man had recently been seen in London, I thought better of it—"Father Christmas."

"Yer bound to say that, ain't yer?" Buck said. "But we know better. Don't yer try it, I'm warning yer. Come on, then, lads, let's all join in on the do!"

"What would happen," I asked them, "if I just stood here all day?"

They exchanged frowning glances. "Well," said Tucker, after a few thoughtful moments, "I suppose we'd all stand here with you."

As Tucker was the only one of the group who seemed even marginally thoughtful, I assumed his supposition correct. I sighed. "Much as I'd like to hear your guvnor's response when your report on the day's activities is 'We stood round,' I have things I must do. Come on, then! Look lively!"

I led the charge down the sidewalk. My escorts were not the most graceful of men, though it's also possible the deliberate speeding up and slowing down of my own pace in a herky-jerky manner could have contributed to the collisions and pileups happening in my wake. I refused to turn around, and therefore only knew about these events from the confused exclamations of "Pardon!" and "Clear off!" the former addressed, I assumed, to members of the general public and the latter to one another.

I decided to turn and reprimand the constables for failing to keep formation. As I started to do so, I felt someone bump into me. This was no good example to set for my bobbies. I quickly turned back and apologized at the same moment as the bumper, who tipped his cloth cap, winked, and moved on. The wink I might have taken for insolence but for the fact that this was not the first wink I'd ever gotten from Jimmy Fingers.

CHAPTER FORTY-ONE

I walked resolutely on, not looking back at either Jimmy Fingers or the constable squadron, until we came to a bustling street of shops. Here, as the bobbies did their best to keep up with me, I was able to examine my pockets to learn into which Jimmy had slid his note, for note I was sure there was. I found, in my waistcoat, a folded paper bearing words in Chinese.

It told me that Dee had intelligence to share and would appreciate my presence in an hour at the Bale Road Stables in Stepney where Feldman and Sons boarded their horse. *I'll be in disguise*, the note read. *Bring as many bobbies as you like.*

In truth, my preference would have been to bring none, but as that was an option not available, I changed course and set out for the bus that would carry me and my convoy of constables to the East End. I briefly thought about using a taxicab as a means of possible escape, but it seemed to me likely the bobbies would commandeer another and demand the driver follow mine without, in the end, paying him for his trouble. I didn't want to be the cause of a workingman losing a portion of the day's livelihood. Accordingly, we all boarded a Stepney bus. As can be expected anywhere in the world, I paid my fare and the men of the Metropolitan Police Force did not pay theirs.

"What're yer up to?" Buck inquired suspiciously as we took seats.

"I'm proceeding about my necessary errands," I answered with dignity. "You lot, on the other hand, are wasting ratepayers' money by unnecessarily following me."

"Only yer better not use any of those dark Oriental magics on 'ere."

To that, he received no answer. We continued the ride in silence.

Alighting in Stepney, I inquired as to the location of the stable in question. The young fellow who gave me directions to Bale Street looked upon my escort with some doubt, even hostility, but I whispered to him, "You have nothing to fear from these gentlemen. They're not constables, but actors, rehearsing for their roles in a soon-to-be-produced moving picture similar to the American pictures about the Keystone Kops."

The lad lit up. In a voice as hushed as mine, he said, "Oh, I've seen some of those! I'm keen on the pictures. Full of belly laughs, the Keystone Kops." He raised his voice. "Good luck to you, gentlemen," he said, doffing his cap. "You're almost believable!"

The Keystone Konstables, having no idea what he might mean by this, scowled, with the exception of Tucker, who—though no more knowledgeable than his brethren—politely touched the bill of his helmet in return.

I led our parade to the stables, where I inquired for the horse of Mr. Feldman. "She's over there with some new groom," I was told by a stall-mucker. By the note of doubt in the boy's voice, I was led to believe this new groom was something of an oddity at Bale Street. With confidence, I marched into the stable and on to the stall that had been pointed out to me. With considerably less enthusiasm, the bobbies pulled faces and followed. The mucker had not yet found his way to the dirt floor between the stalls, and clouds of flies arose along with a strong aroma from the piles of horse-leavings plopped here and there.

Feldman's young mare stood quiet in her stall, being brushed by a disheveled old man with thick, unruly eyebrows and unkempt white hair pushed down around his face by a cloth cap. His back was bent, but his movements were sure and gentle. The horse seemed appreciative.

"Ah," the groom said, casting a glance at me, "ye'd be the gent interested in buying this fine bit o' horseflesh, then?"

"Oh," I said, looking about for Dee. "I'm afraid you've—"

"Come, Lao, play along," the groom whispered in Chinese.

The inclination to turn to the bobbies to see if they'd heard this old man speak Chinese was strong, but I defeated it. "Dee?" I whispered, though if this were not Dee, I couldn't imagine who it might be.

The groom raised his caterpillar-like eyebrows. I recognized that amused glance, though the eyes themselves were almost hidden. The fur, or whatever it was, that Dee had attached to his visage cloaked the shape of his eyelids—the only thing that could have given him away.

"Yes, indeed," I said, in English. "I've been discussing with Feldman the possibility of such a purchase."

Dee responded, "Aye, she's a fine one. She'll haul many a cart before she's done. I guess ye'll be wanting a look round at her?"

"Ah. Yes, of course."

"Come this way, then."

Dee opened the gate to the horse's stall to admit me.

"She's quite docile," I whispered. "Have you been reciting to her again?"

"From *Journey to the West*. She enjoyed learning about the White Dragon Horse." He led me around to the stall's rear.

"Would you care to join us, constables?" I called. "In case Dee Ren Jie is hiding in the water trough?"

Ritts jeered. "The trough's at this end, Chinaman. We can see it fine. The end where you are contains a bit o' something else. Mind yer shoes." All laughed, and they remained outside the stall.

Dee gestured with his hands as though he were pointing out this and that feature of the young mare, all the while whispering to me in Chinese. "We've worked out a plan. Feng reported having seen Madam Wu going off at odd times at night, often in the car with Chung. As the car is quite eye-catching, I sent young Jimmy to inquire among his acquaintances if anyone had noticed a seafoam-green Bentley reappearing in the same location on different nights. We now have reports of the car having been seen on multiple occasions outside the entrance to the London Necropolis Railway."

"The Necropolis Railway?"

Although we spoke in Chinese, my surprise at this odd news had caused my voice to rise. The constables swivelled their heads as one at my exclamation. I quickly made a gesture at the horse's rump and shook my head.

"A fair recovery, Lao, but you must learn to control yourself better."

"But Dee," I whispered. "What on earth would they want with the Necropolis Railway?"

In my time in London, I hadn't found myself passing the Necropolis Railway terminal often, yet it had made quite the impression on me. The Railway had begun seventy years before as a means of transporting caskets and mourners to the vast new Brookwood Cemetery in Surrey—and, of course, bringing the mourners back. In the early years, it was quite a success, and eventually, a large new station was required to replace the original. The new building, built, as was the first, behind

Waterloo, purported to be a modern, attractive structure, meant to contrast favorably with the somber gloom of most buildings related to the funeral trade. I was not alone, I was sure, in thinking somber gloom not inappropriate; still, this second Necropolis Railway building featured large windows, bright sconces and hanging lamps, and white-tiled walls.

However, after the war, the popularity of this train service waned, as automobiles and motorized hearses became available for Londoners' funeral needs.

"For the last few years," Dee told me, "the cemetery trains have run only once a day in either direction. The gate is pulled down at night and the building empty. The waiting room is large, and, significantly, it's neutral territory. The Conspiracy members, though they're doing one another's dirty work, are each unlikely to trust the others enough to meet at a location one of them controls."

"But—"

"Also," he continued, "if shrouded lanterns in the closed and locked Necropolis Railway waiting room nevertheless emitted enough dim light to be seen from the street, who would come to investigate?"

I had to admit the compelling nature of his logic. His final remark put paid to my doubts: "And after all," he said, "they are the Railway Conspiracy."

"Very well," I said. "What is your plan?"

"Considering the events of recent days, we expect the members of the Conspiracy will feel an urgent need to meet again tonight. We propose to be there when they do."

Dee lifted the horse's hoof and looked up at me as though we were discussing the ease with which she allowed herself to be shod.

"Yes," I said in conversational tones and in English. "Her leg is quite shapely."

As expected, the bobbies greeted this with snickers and elbow nudges.

"They're eminently predictable," I whispered in Chinese to Dee. "It's quite tiresome."

"I'm sorry our acquaintance has brought you these boring companions," he said. "Will you be able to rid yourself of them in time to join us at midnight at the Necropolis Railway?"

Many another place—indeed, almost any other place—was more enticing for a midnight rendezvous than a room where, in daylight, mourners waited for the call to board a train carrying their loved ones out of London for a final time. However, if this was truly to be the end of the Railway Conspiracy, then the words I uttered could not have been more sincere: "I wouldn't miss it."

Dee smiled. "I counted on that."

I considered. "To your point of ridding myself of this private army"—I tilted my head toward the bobbies—"might I borrow Hoong for an hour or two? If you deem it safe for him to leave your sanctuary at the Russells', I have an idea that might well work." I explained my thinking to Dee.

"Why, Lao," he said. "That's quite devious. I had no idea academics could be so wily."

"Is that compliment or complaint?"

"Oh, it's high praise. Hoong is equally wily and will no doubt find ways to evade notice as long as he's not seen with me. I'll send him round with the necessary items as soon as possible. Do you think you can keep the interest of your uniformed friends for an hour or so before you go back to your flat?"

"I'm afraid I can. Are you familiar with the Book of Ruth, from the Old Testament? 'Whither thou goest, I will go'? These gentlemen seem to have quite taken it to heart."

"We shall have to shake their faith, then."

"Indeed." I smiled in answer to the smile he was offering

me. "Before we set out to do that, though, I must tell you this: I've had a visitor." I detailed for him the social call paid by Voronoff and the deadline fast approaching. "I'm afraid the Metropolitan Police are not the only group seeking to apprehend you, Dee. The Conspiracy are taking an interest."

"I expected they would. Madam Wu will not have been happy to hear I escaped the attentions of Chung's friends. Lao, you must take care. They will be watching you."

"It's one of the reasons I haven't yet worked to shed my honor guard. They're not impressive, but their numbers might cause an assassin to bide his time."

"I agree. And after tonight, we can hope that the Conspiracy—at least its London branch—will cease to be a threat. To any of us."

I left the stall, assuring the groom that the young mare was indeed a fine horse and promising to have a word with Feldman. I reversed course and walked past my bobbies. "I'll be continuing my errands," I informed them, "upon the completion of which I'll be going back to my flat. You may follow me if you like, but I'm sorry to say I'll not be inviting you up for tea."

me. "Let's set out to do that, though I must tell you one—I've had a visitor." I detailed for him the social call paid by Vorobeitr and the deadline fast approaching. "I'm afraid the Metropolitan Police are not the only group seeking to apprehend you, Dex. The Conspiracy are taking an interest."

"I expected they would, Madam. You will not have been happy to hear I escaped the attentions of Curtis's friends. I ask you must take care. They will be watching you."

"It's one of the reasons I haven't yet worked to shed my honor guard. They're not impressive, but their numbers might cause an assassin to bide his time."

"I agree. And after tonight, we can hope that the Conspiracy—at least its London branch—will cease to be a threat to any of us."

I left the cell, assuring the groom that the young mare was indeed a fine horse and promising to have a word with Zellman. I reversed course and walked past my bobbies. "I'll be continuing my errands," I informed them, "upon the completion of which I'll be going back to my flat. You may follow me if you like, but if anyone asks I'll not be inviting you up for tea."

CHAPTER FORTY-TWO

An hour and a quarter later, uneventful except for the occasional repeated warning about not using my "dark Oriental magics," I left my bobby brigade at the door of the building that housed my flat. Ritts endeavored to shoulder his way in, but I'd anticipated such an attempt and quick-stepped inside, shutting the door in his thick face. Proceeding upstairs, I let myself into my living quarters.

The upholstered chair that I'd found accommodating Dee upon my return from Richmond Park, and later discovered to have been subjugated by Voronoff, was again occupied, but this time not by either of those men.

"Sergeant Hoong," I said. "It's a pleasure to see you. May I offer you some tea?" I set water on to boil.

"Indeed," Hoong said. He indicated a large bundle wrapped in brown paper on my kitchen table. "Between Jimmy's consuming my Dragonwell tea at a great rate and your requiring these items from my shop, I begin to wonder if the entire goal of this mission is to bankrupt me."

"If that were it," I said, "I'd have asked for your best silks."

"It's a feint," he replied. "You're thinking I'll drop my guard. I won't, you know."

Smiling, I retrieved teacups and a pot.

"Having observed you and your constables come up the street," Hoong said, "I must congratulate you on attracting quite the least appealing of that brotherhood."

I sighed. "I have no control over who is sent after me. The control I'm hoping for is the ability to make them scatter."

Now Hoong smiled. "Like rats from a cat."

I poured the tea. We raised our teacups and drank to the scattering of constables.

IN DUE TIME, our tea finished, I changed my clothes, replacing the jacket, waistcoat, and trousers of a respectable academic with the Chinese merchant's blue cotton tunic and looser trousers Hoong had brought me. Finally, I donned the brightly embroidered Chinese slippers he'd included in the package. "An excellent touch," I said when I saw them. "My compliments."

"Your instructions, as I received them, were vague. I was forced to interpret them to the best of my meager abilities."

"You have risen to the occasion." I bowed.

I left Hoong in the flat and went out to greet the bobby battalion. As I'd expected, my attire occasioned a good deal of laughter and mockery.

"Ooh, 'e looks a proper Chinaman now."

"Only 'e don't 'ave the long plait down the back. Where's yer Chin-ee plait?"

"Nah, lots of 'em is cutting 'em off these days. Gets in the way when they eat their rats."

Jeering of this sort continued as I made my way along the pavement to the next street. At the corner, I turned. "Constables," I said sharply, "I've endured your presence, and your disagreeable behavior, since yesterday. My patience is wearing thin. I fear my good nature may at any moment desert me. You would do well to desist."

"Desist!" Buck slapped his belly. "'E wants us to desist! Wot d'ye think, lads? Shall we *desist*?"

A loud chorus of negatives, some of them quite rude, answered him. I spun about again and continued. As I walked, I began to hum my favorite folk melody, "High Mountain and Flowing Water." Gradually, as their mockery continued, I raised my voice and started to sing.

"'Ere, wot's this?" Ritts cried. "Stop that wailing, yer 'urting me ears!"

Another few steps brought us to the alley beside the King's Turnip, a pub whose sign bore a painting of one of the Tudor monarchs with a very large nose. I halted my forward progress and turned to shout at the men harassing me.

"You must stop!" I squeezed my hands into fists. "I cannot listen to any more of this!"

"Oh, 'e cannot listen," said Coyle, oozing with sham sympathy. "Poor Chinaman. 'Ave we upset yer?"

"You're not doing yourselves any good," I growled.

"Is that a fact, then?"

I lifted my arm straight out and pointed a finger at them. "It is."

"Oh, no, lads. We've got 'im angry."

I clenched my jaw and my arms and shoulders, which always makes my face its reddest. "Yes," I hissed. "You've made me angry. Quite angry."

I began shaking. The bobbies took each a step back. I started to spasm like a puppet with a madman pulling his strings. With a howl, I ran jerkily down the alley, until I dove behind a rubbish bin.

"'Ere!" shouted Ritts. "Where d'ye think yer going?" A rush of footsteps indicated that the entire foursome had entered the alley to follow.

The footsteps stopped suddenly as my companion behind the

bin, Sergeant Hoong, rose up with a howl of his own. His clothing was the match of mine, down to the embroidered slippers, with the difference that, in his case, everything was shredded and rent, the trousers and sleeves too short, the closures popped open, toes jutting from the slippers. He waved his arms and twitched his legs in these rags like the lunatic puppet I had just been.

"Gor! 'E's growing!"

"Burst out 'is clothes, 'e 'as!"

"It's 'is magics! 'E's using 'is Oriental magics!"

"Bigger, lads, 'e's growing even bigger!"

Hoong had stretched to his full height and, laughing like a maniac, loomed over them. The most satisfying shout of all came next, however. All four voices in concert yelled, "Run, lads, run!" and, if the slap of leather on cobbles could be trusted, they did.

I peered above the rubbish bin to see Hoong halfway along the alley, still howling. He made his way to the pavement and peered in both directions. Then, laughing, he returned to my refuge.

"They've scattered," Hoong said.

I stood, brushing dirt from the knees of my trousers. "Like rats from a cat?"

"Mice, rather. Small and squeaking. I congratulate you, Lao, on an excellent scheme. Not only was it effective, it offered scope for my dramatic endeavors."

"You're still thinking, then, of a career on the stage? The comedy duo with Jimmy Fingers that Dee mentioned?"

"Or possibly a strongman act, now that Ben Hur has retired. I've learned, Lao, that the world is rife with opportunities one had neglected to consider until they present themselves."

When I thought of the serene and predictable academic life I'd been leading before Dee arrived in London six short months earlier, I had to concur. Surprising myself, I found the prospect of this uncertain future not disagreeable.

CHAPTER FORTY-THREE

The terminal station of the London Necropolis Railway was every bit as foreboding as the name implied. Even the label "terminal"—at other railroad stations, merely descriptive—was portentous here. Hoong and I were hiding in the shadows on the opposite pavement, waiting for the signal that our companions had arrived. I felt well-fueled for the occasion, having gone with Hoong to Wu's Garden for beef noodles and cockles with leeks. I also, I confess, felt better for being in the company of Sergeant Hoong. He had always acquitted himself well in a physical confrontation, but what I'd seen in Madam Wu's parlor when he revealed the iron rings was on a different plane to what had come before.

"Hoong," I whispered, "are you wearing the iron rings?"

"This seemed an appropriate occasion," he replied.

"I had no idea—"

"No. Few people do."

The signal came, a light blinking three times from near the gate at the entrance to the railway. Beyond, one would find access to the first-class mourners' waiting room, and farther along, the waiting room for mourners whose tickets entitled them to carriages of the second and third classes. From those rooms, doors opened to the platform where the trains pulled in with caskets already loaded into hearse van carriages. These carriages were separated, as were the passengers, by class (though whether accommodations in the hearse vans differed as greatly from class to class as those of the passengers, I had never heard.)

All this could be accessed, of course, only if the gate were open. From the shadows where I stood, I could see that it was closed, and see its large bronze lock.

If the members of the conspiracy were inside, they had either relocked the gate behind themselves or found another way in. As Hoong and I crossed Westminster Bridge Road, I saw a shadow slip away from the others that loomed nearby. Apparently, however the Conspiracy had entered, we were to go in through the gate, courtesy of Jimmy Fingers.

While Jimmy was working his dark Stepney magics upon the lock, Hoong and I nodded greetings to the company. In addition to Jimmy and to Dee, who, with a finger to his lips signaled us—rather needlessly, I thought—to silence, we were met by Feng, Mei Qiang, and Anthony Cartwright. At the feet of the party sat three duffel bags, such as soldiers used for carrying their kit.

All nodded to all and waited for the triumphal swinging of the gate. Jimmy turned with a grin and gave the two-thumbs-up sign of the British Tommy—which, of course, he had never been—before he bent to the shadows and withdrew an oilcan, with which he treated the hinges. Quite the foresighted lad, I thought. It would be a shame for a squeak of hinges to derail, as it were, our plan.

It occurred to me, as I thought thus, that I didn't know what plan we were following.

"Dee," I whispered, "what is to be our course of action?"

He motioned for Hoong to join us. "These bags," Dee said, speaking in a voice as soft as mine and indicating the duffels at his feet, "contain a number of interesting mechanisms devised by Cartwright. Some, we will place in the corridor before we enter the waiting room, where we believe the meeting will be held."

"Will be? It's not underway, then?"

"According to Feng, the nights Madam Wu went out, midnight came and went before she called for the car. We expect the Conspiracy members to arrive within the hour. We'll be in place, and when they're all here, we'll emerge. The remaining mechanisms will be for our use then."

"What are they?"

"The ones in the corridors are largely smoke, plus some that will delay any attempted escapes. The ones for our use, should we need them, are mechanical advances on throwing stars and the like." He smiled indulgently at Feng. "Feng refuses to have anything to do with them. Her waistcoat contains weapons she has been trained to use. She disdains the use of untried equipment in actual fighting situations."

Feng, who had been listening to Dee's explanation, met my eyes and nodded seriously.

Dee turned to Hoong. "I see you've brought your tiger tail three-sectional staff. Your father was a master of that weapon."

"Indeed."

"And Lao"—he raised his eyebrows—"you're carrying double sabers?"

I stood straighter, feeling the comforting weight of Hoong's swords strapped to my back. "Sergeant Hoong suggested it. Though I fear the use of two at once is beyond me, Hoong felt one would suffice to attack, and the other to intimidate."

Dee glanced at Hoong, then nodded in a thoughtful way, though I had the uncomfortable sense he might have been suppressing a smile.

"Lao," Dee said, "do you still have your police whistle?"

"Of course."

"Excellent. You'll have need of it soon."

With that, Jimmy opened the gate, which made not the slightest squeak. We entered through the archway and into the shadowed, cobbled passage.

CHAPTER FORTY-FOUR

I freely admit to a shiver of trepidation as our company made its silent way through the arched entry. The confrontation to come seemed to worry my companions not at all: Hoong appeared confident, Jimmy excited, Feng determined, Mei Qiang alert, and as for Cartwright, I gathered his interest was more in the effectiveness of his mechanisms than any other factor. Dee, of course, as was his way, carried an air of calm assurance. For myself, though, the unanswered questions were many, which made calmness and assurance hard to come by. How many Conspirators could we expect? What weapons would be at their disposal? What was our next step if they didn't come at all, or if they escaped our attempt to capture them? And what was my own role to be, and could I depend on myself to fulfill its responsibilities satisfactorily?

Dee has had, at certain times in the past, an unnerving way of seeming to read my mind. What talent gave him that ability, I didn't know, but he employed it now.

"You will be, as usual, invaluable, Lao," he said. "When the fighting begins, take on whatever opponent seems likely to you. Your chief charge, however, will be to blow your police whistle through the platform door when I give the signal."

"Through the platform door? Dee, we're behind Waterloo

Station. What bobbies will be near enough to hear, much less come running?"

"The bobbies I asked Russell to request. They're on their way and will be in position. One," he added, "will be young Tim McCorkle. He finds languishing at a desk disagreeable." He smiled and left me open-mouthed as he pushed through the door.

Had we continued on straight, we would have achieved the train platform without passing through the waiting rooms. We did not, though. Rather, following Dee, we all veered to our left.

The corridor we entered had a glass roof, a lucky thing for the topiary trees growing in pots on the tiled floor. Cartwright stopped to arrange devices behind two of these potted trees, in places where they would not be seen by anyone entering but could, and we hoped would, be easily tripped over by a person rushing for an exit. Then, he came to join the rest of us at the door to the first-class waiting room.

We gathered about Dee as he issued instructions. "Each group of you, take a duffel bag of Mr. Cartwright's incendiary devices and smoke bombs. Release them into the room on my signal, to distract and confound our enemies. Surprise and confusion will be our key advantages." Looking at each of us in turn, he said, "Remember, my friends: we will attempt to incapacitate them. By no means are any of us here to kill. This conspiracy goes deep. We must capture as many of these conspirators as we can and deliver them to the authorities. Conduct yourself as you see fit, but try your best not to take a life."

Hoong, Jimmy, Feng, Cartwright, and I all murmured our assent. I fancied I heard Mei Qiang softly growl hers, but that was probably an effect of my nerves.

Dee pulled the door and we entered the waiting room.

The large area was well, if somberly, appointed, with brown upholstered armchairs and low tables settled upon thick carpets of the sort all consigned, in Europe, to the label "Oriental," though the origins of these particular ones I believed to be Turkmenistan. Electric lamps, unlit, hung overhead, and electric sconces lined the walls, similarly at rest. Wainscotting, wallpaper, and watercolor paintings of meadows and seashores connected the floor to the high arched ceiling. All was dim and shadowed; the only light came from the windows in the wall through which we had entered from the corridor, and in the corridor itself, what light there was had made its laborious way from the streetlamps on the Westminster Bridge Road.

As Dee had instructed, our group split into thirds, concealing ourselves behind chairs along three of the walls. Dee, with Hoong, selected a row of seats along the north wall, and Cartwright, accompanied by Feng and Mei Qiang, a set near the south wall. Jimmy and I crouched behind the line of chairs on the west, opposite to our entry point, to await Dee's signal.

Jimmy's excitement was palpable. I feared he might leap out too soon, eager for the battle, and though I myself felt a thrill of nerves as I heard the squeak of hinges—clearly the Conspirators had not had the foresight to bring an oilcan—I laid a hand on his arm at that point. The lad turned with a grin but made no other move.

Dark shapes issued into the room, not from the entrance we'd used but rather from the north, through the door that gave onto the train platform. With the shapes came a bit more light but not enough to make out faces. My heart jolted when I spotted a foxlike form stealing across the carpet, accompanied by other similarly graceful shapes, and I'm afraid my jaw briefly dropped when a bear-man lumbered in, other large men with him. The last group to arrive was clothed in the tunics, trousers, and bowlers of the boo how doy. I suppressed a shiver as I imagined the lather's hatchets hidden up their loose sleeves. They were led by a cloaked figure, possibly—in fact, I admitted to myself, quite probably—the man Dee and I had followed and lost along the wharf.

When the last of the shadows accompanying the cloaked figure had entered and the door shut behind them, the figure stood at the center of the room and spoke quietly, but forcefully, to the silent assembly.

"Friends!"

I doubted the sentiment behind that word, but I did not doubt my hearing.

This cloaked figure was no man.

It was Madam Wu.

"We've done well in our endeavors in London," she continued. She spoke in English, no doubt the only common language among the representatives of the three countries involved in the Railway Conspiracy. "I congratulate you all: those who eliminated the threat of A. G. Stephen, those responsible for the actions at the Sailors' Palace, and those who attended to Peng Lian Liang. To those whose mission to eliminate Anthony Cartwright met with interference, I can tell you I have complete faith in the success of your next attempt." I imagined Cartwright silencing a snicker across the room. "All of you, and those who are continuing our fight on all fronts, you have the thanks, I know, of your respective *legitimate* governments and the appreciation of us all." She looked around the room. "We have been hampered, here in London, by the interference of a man by the name of Dee Ren Jie and his minions." I found it necessary to bite my tongue to keep from voicing a strong protest against this label. "However, I believe we now have him in check. The Metropolitan Police Force are searching for him as a suspect in the actions we have taken—a fine irony. He will either be captured or forced to flee the country. In either case, our operations in England and later across the Continent will be able to continue free from his intervention."

A chorus of approving whispers in three languages began to arise. It was cut short by a shout in English: "Madam Wu, you are wrong."

The cloaked figure whipped around toward the voice. It was, of course, Dee's; and when he spoke again, it was from another side of the room. "As a lover of English poetry, you will be familiar with Thomas Howell." A moment later, from yet a different place, "It was he who said, centuries ago, 'Count not thy chickens that unhatched be.'"

And with that, chaos erupted, for those chickens were our signal. Jimmy and I reached into our duffel and tossed incendiary devices high into the air to join those soaring from other quarters. With clouds of smoke and flash-bangs of light and noise, everything turned topsy-turvy. Men shouted, drew their weapons, scrambled for cover as they attempted to decipher who was nearby: friend or foe or swirl of gases.

Out of the commotion and clouds before me, the fox face of Isaki suddenly appeared.

I leapt up, swept a saber from the pair I carried, and thrust at him. The force of my lunge carried me forward, and I stumbled as my sword drove into empty air. While I peered about for the vanished Isaki, I felt the second weapon slide from the scabbard upon my back. I spun only to find the smoke cloud before me as void of solid matter as the first. A clang of steel upon steel and the jarring of my arm from wrist to shoulder, however, announced the knocking from my grip of the saber I'd been clutching. As I looked about wildly, Isaki stepped out of the smoke with a saber in each hand. His teeth glowed with a smile.

"These weapons may not be of Japanese make, but they are quite fine," he sneered. "A poor swordsman such as yourself dishonors them. Even your worthless blood would sully them; thus, I disarmed you instead of cutting off your hand."

I was in a dilemma, for I objected to this insult, but had I convincingly affirmed the value of my blood, Isaki might abandon his objection to staining the sabers with it. I was not called upon to respond, however, as the voice of Hoong boomed through the smoke:

"Lao She may not be a fighter, but he's a warrior whose heart far surpasses yours, Isaki." Hoong whipped the three-sectional tiger tail staff off his back. "The time has come to finish what we began."

"I am most happy to oblige, Chinaman," Isaki answered.

The two began to stalk each other. Standing between them as I was, I felt my position a possible hindrance to Hoong's success. I tried to back off into the smoke and shadows. However, I stumbled over the carpet and sent a cigarette table flying. Isaki laughed at me.

Hoong took advantage of the distraction I'd created—unwittingly, but usefully—to swing the free left section of his staff at Isaki's head. Isaki, just in time, caught the movement and ducked. Hoong followed with a sweep to the ronin's legs, but Isaki sprang catlike into the air, slashing out with both sabers at Hoong's head. Hoong spun around, cutting downward with the staff's free section. He stepped back into a ready position. Isaki landed, also poised for the attack, and leapt forward with a slashing cut of his right saber at Hoong's neck. Blindingly fast, he spun around to also use the left. Hoong deflected both attacks using the staff's free right section. Isaki chopped at Hoong's head, but it was a feint: he shot out low with a left stab to Hoong's leg. Hoong blocked each blow with the middle section of his staff, high, then low.

The two glared at each other. Hoong said, "You're a sneaky little rat." The taunt had the desired effect: Isaki, enraged, slashed wildly at Hoong's leg again. The two men spun away from each other, resuming their ready stances. I was fully engaged in watching this battle, but the sudden nearby blast of one of Cartwright's devices let loose such a cloud that I lost sight of the combatants.

Out of this cloud dashed Mei Qiang. The smoke was thinnest down near the floor; I could see the scurrying hound as she zigzagged in and out of the conspirators' positions, nipping and gnawing at the ankles of Russians, Japanese, and Chinese. She slipped through the mist like a ghost, frightening her victims as much as paining them. It was as though she fully grasped the subtleties of Dee's strategy of "surprise and confusion."

I could not see Madam Wu, but ice filled my veins when I heard her snap, "This dog is a nuisance. We must be rid of it."

I leapt up to chase after Mei Qiang, to keep her from Madam Wu's clutches, but immediately lost her in the melee. As I stumbled forward in search of her, a shouting Cossack hurtled out of the smoke, kindjal dagger drawn. I jumped back, but I was not his target. His goal was Dee, who had also emerged from the clouds and taken a fighting stance, ready to meet his attacker.

I leapt aside. The Cossack, dagger in a reverse grip, slashed at Dee's head. Dee shifted left and parried with his right arm. The Russian swept his dagger from the other side for a second slash. Sliding his hand inside the Cossack's arm, Dee trapped the wrist. He wound it inward while turning his own body, then spun in underneath and executed a sharp lateral elbow strike. He twisted again, contorting the man's arm. The Cossack, fighting the movement instead of turning with it, shouted in pain. Dee threw a chopping kick to the inside of the Cossack's left knee, breaking his footing, and followed up with a heavy downward iron palm slapping strike to the jaw.

The man dropped to the floor.

But as one fight ended, another threatened to begin. "Dee!" I shouted as from the smoke a second Cossack rushed in.

"Thank you, Lao!" Dee leapt backward as the attacker slashed from right to left. A quick third stab came in low, the acrobatic Cossack supporting himself on his left hand while the dagger in his right thrust at Dee's midsection. Shifting his weight back, Dee executed a double hand cross block, trapping the wrist. Then, he swung his right foot in a semicircle, sweeping out the Cossack's supporting hand and simultaneously relieving him of his dagger. The Cossack, attempting to regain his balance, stumbled into a side table. Dee leapt forward and plunged the dagger into the back of the Cossack's hand, pinning him to the wood.

"Poshel ty!" the Cossack howled. "Moya ruka!"

Dee shook his head. "Knives make dangerous toys." He stepped back from the immobilized Russian. "As I said, Lao: you are invaluable."

"Is it time for the whistle?" I asked.

At that moment, the voice of Voronoff boomed. "Guard the exits!"

Madam Wu shouted, "Yes, guard them! Let no one leave this place alive!"

How different, I thought, from Dee's instructions to us. I watched the shadows as Cossacks, ronin, and hatchet men scurried to find positions.

Dee turned to me and smiled. "You may employ the whistle whenever you can, now that they've locked themselves in. But take care for your own safety and that of our friends. Cartwright's devices and your companions' fighting skills—yes, and your own—will suffice to keep the conspirators at bay until you can make your way without peril to the door they came through."

With that, Dee vanished back into the smoke. I'd have

tried to follow, but zooming past me out of a cloud came Mei Qiang. I might have been the only one who'd heard Madam Wu's threat against the hound, and so I might also have been her only protector. "Come here, Mei Qiang!" I said, and she stopped but did not come to me. Instead, she froze into quivering attention. Her nose worked furiously, her ears stood sharp as she turned them left and right, searching through the smoke.

Feng appeared beside Mei Qiang at the same moment Madam Wu materialized ten feet before them both. The two women, once master and apprentice, patron and beneficiary, stared into each other's eyes.

I stared also, for Madam Wu had shed the cloak and stood majestically in a noonday-yellow Mandarin-collared blouse and long, flowing amethyst skirt. Through the miasma of Cartwright's weapons, the lady seemed to glow.

Mei Qiang, muscles rippling, waited.

Feng, with a gesture, gave a command.

The hound leapt high. Madam Wu waited until Mei Qiang was almost upon her; then she wheeled in the air and executed an outside crescent kick. The hound, struck squarely, yelped and twisted in the air; snarling, she landed on her feet. With blinding speed, Feng hurled four daggers. Madam Wu spun around, ensnaring the daggers in the lap of her skirt. She pulled the fabric taut, sending the weapons flying upwards. Snatching each out of the air in quick succession, she cast them all back at Feng. Feng somersaulted backward. As she rolled along the floor, she called to Mei Qiang, "Come!" The hound bounded toward her mistress's voice.

"Our movement could have used a woman with your skills," Madam Wu said into the smoke. "But then, perhaps not. Your compassionate heart makes you weak."

"And you have no heart at all!"

Her face lighting as Feng's furious reply gave away her location, Madam Wu leapt to the left and hurled two more daggers. Feng dodged them and threw three of her own. Madam Wu sidestepped and loosened a clip at her waist. She grasped a black leather handle and, spinning, unwound from about herself a three-sectional whip. Mei Qiang, growling and barking, launched herself again at Madam Wu.

"No!" I cried. I had been struck by a sudden fear when I saw Madam Wu's odd handling of the whip, for she took great care to touch only the handle and not the weapon's leather length. My shout was too late, though. The whip, whistling through the air, cut the hound along her flank. Mei Qiang yelped, but seemed undeterred; she growled, preparing to attack once more. Madam Wu spun again, wrapped the whip back about herself, and stepped into a ready stance.

Without thought, I dove across the room, landing behind the chair where Feng sheltered. "Poison!" I shouted. "The whip is poisoned!"

Feng's face drained of color. She called Mei Qiang, who ran to her after another bark at the sneering Madam Wu. The dog seemed to be prepared to ignore the slash on her side and rejoin the battle raging around us, but Feng, fear in her eyes, held her back.

A figure crab-walked out of the smoke to crouch on Feng's other side. Cartwright, grinning. "I heard your shout, Lao," he said. "I anticipated this, and I'm sorry to see I was correct. It'll be the venom of the black scorpion, concentrated and rubbed into the whip. They may have also used it on the hatchets and daggers." He shook his head. "Very unsporting. Here." He handed a vial to Feng. "This will neutralize it. Now, you'll have to excuse me. I was in the middle of something." With that, he vanished back into the clouds around us.

Maybe, I thought, it was time I made my way to the door,

where I could employ my whistle and perhaps bring an end to this melee.

Leaving Feng to treat the hound, I stepped from shadow to smoke cloud to overturned chair, attempting to avoid the fighters clashing on all sides. I had made progress when I found myself pushed aside by the large hand of Hoong. "What are—" I began, but when I heard a saber whistle past my ear, all my questions, as well as my quest for the platform door, were abandoned.

I ensconced myself behind an armchair and watched as Hoong crouched, the left section of his staff touching the ground, the right poised for the attack. Isaki stepped into a cross stance, twirling the double sabers he had stolen from me back to a center position. Both men stood briefly still, ready for combat.

Isaki initiated, spinning round like a whirlwind to cut at Hoong, but Hoong intercepted, matching him blow for blow. Hoong struck at Isaki's head and body, an attack the ronin blocked with crossed double sabers. Hoong stepped forward, striking at Isaki's head with the staff's free section. Isaki deflected with a saber and slashed diagonally downward. Hoong's staff repelled the blade. Isaki spun around and thrust out at Hoong, which caused Hoong to shift back, extending all three sections of the staff to block the stab with the center section. Smoothly, Hoong leapt behind Isaki and slammed both ends of the fighting sticks into the back of Isaki's head. Isaki, jarred, staggered and dropped both sabers to the floor. Reeling, the ronin jumped back, and then forward again to face Hoong barehanded.

Hoong swept the sabers aside with his foot. They slid along the floor to come to rest not far from me as Hoong attacked Isaki with the right section of his fighting sticks. Isaki intercepted with his forearm. Hoong struck with the left stick, and again, the ronin was able to intercept the strike and come around with his left hand to grab at the weapon. Seeing this as an opportunity, Hoong tried to crash squarely down on Isaki's head; but it had been a feint—Isaki caught both ends of the sticks, twisting them out of Hoong's hands. Hoong's momentary lack of balance gave Isaki time to sweep out his foot and send Hoong crashing to the floor.

I stretched for the sabers as Hoong rolled to his feet.

"Hoong!" I called.

He whipped his head around. Seeing what I held, he grinned. I tossed him one saber, then the other. He caught each and shouted back, "Thank you, little brother!" He whipped the right over his head to lie along his back and held the left in front.

Isaki examined Hoong's sectional staff. His eyes glittered. "These fighting sticks are similar to something we have. I am not unfamiliar with their usage."

"And these are Chinese fighting sabers," Hoong replied. "Now I'll show you what they're truly for."

Hoong opened his arms, sabers high, and the iron rings revealed themselves. Isaki was too skillful a fighter and too disciplined a man to show any sign of emotion at that moment, but looking back, I believe it was then that he appreciated his end.

Still, the fight continued. Hoong feinted a cut upward and used a double strike from under. Isaki dropped, blocking with the center stick. Hoong pounced forward and crashed down with a double chop that Isaki managed to deflect.

Isaki, using the right stick, brushed away the double sabers to strike out at Hoong's head. Hoong borrowed from this deflection, deftly spun, wrapped both blades around his body, and circled to block Isaki with his left saber. He slashed out at the ronin's leg, but Isaki skipped over the saber and struck downward. Hoong shifted into a deep back stance, blocking with the left saber and pulling back. "Lai gung ser jin!" Hoong shouted. "Pull the bow to shoot the arrow!" The right saber flew toward the samurai. Isaki managed to deflect the oncoming blow, but the deflection put him off balance. Hoong slashed with the left saber too fast for the ronin to respond.

Hoong recoiled with both sabers drawn to his right side. He looked at the sabers, at Isaki, and then back at the sabers in shock. "No, no," he murmured. "I didn't mean to do this."

I was confused; all I saw was a hairline cut through the samurai's robes. Then a gout of blood sprayed out, and Isaki collapsed.

"I die a good death," he breathed.

"A better one," Hoong responded, "than you deserved." By the time he bowed to his enemy, the ronin was dead.

CHAPTER FORTY-FIVE

Unnerved by Isaki's death, I determined to try again to find my way to the door and summon the constables. Again, though, I was thwarted, by a roar rising above the bedlam.

"Ah! I see you, proklyatiy Dee." Out of the smoke emerged Voronoff, bouncing like a boxer in the ring. He moved in like a pendulum, swinging from side to side at Dee, who had materialized a few feet away. "Come, we fight like men! No more silly Chinese tricks."

Voronoff threw a left jab. Dee parried it away with his right hand. The Russian followed up immediately with a wide right hook. Dee ducked under that. Now on Voronoff's right side, he pulled the bear-man in to three quick, hard knee strikes to the midsection. Voronoff, momentarily stunned, took two steps back. Sweeping out at Voronoff's ankle, unbalancing him, Dee executed a low stomping kick to his left knee, making the Russian buckle backward.

Voronoff stood and shook it off. "You want like that, all right. I watch you. I study you. I can play Chinese trick too." He charged in, circling his hands counterclockwise to thrust forward with a double punch, high and low. Dee jammed both, top and bottom, with right and left hand. The two met eye to eye.

Voronoff snickered. "Ha-ha. I know kung fu."

Dee laughed back. "Ha-ha. Let's see what you've learned."

The Russian rushed in with a series of punches, left, right, left. Dee slid back, slapping away each blow until the final one when he jammed Voronoff with a high and low double tiger claw trapping bridge hand. He enveloped both of Voronoff's fists, encircling them in a clockwise and counterclockwise pattern. His left hand tore toward the Russian's face, hiding the right reverse palm strike that slid in swiftly to crash into Voronoff's rib cage.

"Ha! Not fooling me!" The Russian parried the palm strike away.

But he had been fooled; the palm strike was also a ploy. Dee nailed him in the solar plexus with a roundhouse kick.

Staggering backward, Voronoff spat, "Pah, kung fu. Boxing still better." He charged forward with a huge, powerful right haymaker aimed at Dee's head.

Dee shifted his body, overlaying his hand on the Russian's blow, and coming in underneath, slightly crouched, in a kneeling position. His uppercut strike was squarely planted underneath the Russian's jaw, momentarily lifting him off the ground. Dee followed up with a swift left tiger claw strike to Voronoff's face, accompanied by a right thrusting punch that the Russian fended off with his left hand. This allowed Dee to come around and capture Voronoff's wrist and shoulder, dragging him forward. Dee spun his entire body around, executing a tiger tail hooking kick to the back of the Russian's head, clearly jarring him to the bone. Voronoff leaned heavily on a chair.

"Enough," said Dee. "I don't want to kill you. This fight is bigger than the two of us. We can—"

But whatever Dee thought they could, they didn't, and once again, the fault was partly mine.

Voronoff, shaking his big bear head to clear it, spotted me where I'd frozen near the platform door. In a lunge, he was upon me. I turned to run, but it was too late; he lifted me from behind and squeezed. My breath deserted me as I heard, "Hah, Chinaman! I squash your man like bug." As spots appeared in my vision, I flailed, feeling contact with the Russian's head, with his thigh, but knowing my blind kicks and punches affected Voronoff hardly at all—until suddenly and without ceremony, I was dumped to the floor. Hearing Voronoff moan, I twisted around to see him doubled over, both hands clutching his groin.

One of my kicks had landed.

I, Lao She, teacher and writer, had dropped the Russian bear.

I heard my own aching-rib wheeze. The moment seemed excellent for attempting to get my breath back. I crawled toward a chair, wondering if there was any furniture in this waiting room I hadn't yet hidden behind. My charge to summon the law, which I felt I'd been attempting to fulfill for quite some time now, depended on my ability to summon enough air to use my bobby's whistle. At this moment, that was beyond my capacity.

I peered out at the scene before me, all smoke and shouts, clanging and thumping. Dee called again to his Russian opponent. "Voronoff! No more."

"Hah! Chinese coward. Voronoff doesn't stop."

With a roar, Voronoff shot out a fast right cross at Dee's head. Dee met it with his left arm and followed through blindingly fast with a right hand strike. Dee's strike met Voronoff's jaw, but the Russian attempted to deflect, forcing Dee to drop down and attempt to use the tiger's paw fist formation to crack Voronoff's floating rib. It didn't land.

Dee tried again. "Enough."

"No, Chinaman! I crush your friend, I crush you too!"

Voronoff clenched Dee's right wrist in his massive left hand and shot out his right, grabbing Dee by the throat. As Voronoff pulled Dee's arm forward, Dee shifted his body back to dissipate the energy of the chokehold. He slapped his left hand on top of the giant's choking hand and wrenched it away from his neck, twisting the Russian's wrist left. Dee brought his right hand under, securing elbow and wrist in a lock. Maintaining the hold, Dee wheeled around, placing his left hand on Voronoff's jawline.

"Voronoff!"

"No! I kill you, Chinese rat!"

"Stop! You can't—"

Voronoff's own momentum as he tried to twist away broke his neck.

Dee stepped back and allowed the Russian's body to drop to the floor with a heavy thud. Dee shook his head. "This didn't have to be," he said.

But it did, I thought as I finally achieved the platform door. Voronoff and his bitterness, Isaki and his hauteur—neither could countenance stopping, and now both were dead.

I stepped onto the platform where the funeral train waited. Ignoring the complaints of my ribs, I blew my whistle.

CHAPTER FORTY-SIX

My police whistle was instantly answered with shouts of "Let's go, lads!" As he'd promised, Dee's constables were in place and came pouring through the platform doors. The waiting room was already in chaos, and now that bedlam multiplied. Above the shouts and cries and thunks of truncheons, I heard Dee call, "Lao! Feng! To the roof—some are escaping!"

He was nearby at an open door. Keeping to the wall to dodge bobbies and desperate Conspirators, I made my way to him.

"Take this," he said. He thrust a shrouded lantern into my hands. "When we burst through the door at the top, lift the shield. The light will dazzle them long enough for us to attack." He didn't start up immediately, however, but searched through the haze and the scrum. "Ah! There! Constable McCorkle! Come, lad! And bring another."

"Mr. Dee?" came McCorkle's voice.

"Yes! It's urgent! Come along!"

McCorkle turned to call behind him and then pushed his way through the battle—where the bobbies outnumbered the remaining Conspirators by three or four to each—followed by another helmeted constable. We six hurried up the winding staircase. As much faith as I had in the abilities of my three companions, I was hoping Hoong would join us. However, neither he, Jimmy, nor Cartwright were to be seen. Still caught up in the melee below, I imagined.

We achieved the top landing, and Dee put his hand on the roof door. I followed on his heels, holding the shrouded lantern. Feng and Mei Qiang crowded close, prepared to bound out after us. Dee threw the door wide, I flipped open the lantern's shield, and we exploded through, finding ourselves in one situation I had expected, one I hadn't, and one I never could have.

Two hatchet men awaited us on the tar-paper expanse. They lifted their hands to shield their eyes against the phosphorus glare. Without hesitation, Mei Qiang went for one and Feng for the other. McCorkle and the second bobby took quick glances around in case others were lurking. Seeing none, they set upon the men Feng and the hound were in the process of subduing.

That was anticipated; the rain crashing down upon us was not. We had emerged into the middle of a sudden wee-hour London rainstorm.

Also unanticipated, and unanticipatable, was the vision I caught as a slash of jagged lightning cut through the sky. Springheel Jack, cape billowing in the rain and wind, loomed against the parapet, away from the hatchet-men fight. "Dee Ren Jie!" he called. "Oi got yer now!"

I jerked about to look for Dee. There he was; and when I turned again, there was Jack. How was this possible? What was happening? Had the real Jack tired of Dee's simulations and finally appeared? But no real Jack existed—did he? As these thoughts tumbled through my mind, Jack and Dee tumbled about on the roof. Dee must have been more exhausted from the fighting than I'd realized, for Jack was getting the better of him. I had just determined to intervene when the situation went from the unimaginable to the unthinkable: Jack dragged a struggling Dee to the parapet, lifted him, and threw him off the roof.

"No!" I cried.

But too late. Jack cackled and ran across the roof to the staircase door. Pulling it open, he dashed inside and clattered down the stairs. I didn't follow, so concerned was I with staring down into the darkness and rain to see where my friend had gone. In another flash of lightning, I saw him—Dee, lying motionless on the top of a hearse carriage.

I looked wildly about me. The two hatchet men lay unconscious on the roof, their bowler hats and weapons scattered like toys. Feng and Mei Qiang had vanished, but McCorkle and the other constable came up beside me.

"Was that—?" McCorkle began. He looked down, paled, and made the sign of the cross. From below, I heard the screech of steel wheels. Peering desperately over the parapet once more, I saw a puff of steam dissipate in the rain as the train began to move.

CHAPTER FORTY-SEVEN

I exited slowly and with great care down the stairs we'd erupted up in such chaos. My mind churned furiously. I saw again the image of Dee, motionless on the roof of the hearse carriage as the funeral train made an early morning run to Surrey. Was the train's cemetery destination to be, ironically, my friend's final resting place? Had he been sent there, in a macabre and tragic twist, by the being he had pretended to be?

And Dee and Springheel Jack together—what could this mean? Had Dee never actually been—no, no, for I'd seen him put on the costume, the voice, the swagger . . . But then, who was this second creature? The real Springheel Jack? Not, as we had all surmised, a legend, but a man? A villain unhappy with another's impersonations, willing to help the Metropolitan Police but only as a corollary to eliminating his rival? It was a startling thought.

I reached the platform and peered into the waiting room, now a desolation of overturned chairs and smashed tables lit by the room's electric lamps. The acrid smell of explosives still lingered in the air as constables attempted to make order from the body-strewn chaos.

My only coherent thought was to find Sergeant Hoong.

Surely, he'd be able to shed light on this incomprehensible situation.

I made my way from the platform through the tiled corridor, avoiding the waiting rooms as seemed prudent. I might as well have been invisible for all the attention the bobbies paid me, and I was grateful for their distractedness. By the time I walked over the passageway cobbles to the Westminster Bridge Road, the rain had turned to the lightest of mists. Peer though I did, I found no sign of Sergeant Hoong.

I stood utterly alone in the pale light of the coming dawn, watching the last of the Black Marias pull away. I was exhausted and I was bewildered.

I heard Dee's voice in my head: *Pull yourself together, Lao.*

I straightened my shoulders. All right, then, I would make for Limehouse and wait at Hoong's shop. I was cheered by the knowledge that I had a plan and more cheered when I realized that, though no taxicabs were to be had on the Westminster Bridge Road, around two corners, I'd find Waterloo Station. There, I was sure to discover not only waiting taxicabs but, in the terminal, an open shop where I could purchase a cup of mind-clearing, muscle-soothing tea.

I turned my steps east in search of this bracing beverage. I did not achieve it, but the reason for that outcome dispelled the need.

"Mr. Lao!" I heard urgently whispered from an alley as I passed.

I stopped midstride. Taking two steps back, I peered within. "Jimmy?"

"In here."

I entered the alley, expecting to encounter the young man most probably crouching behind a barrel or a bin. Encounter him I did, but first, I myself was encountered by the wagging tail of Mei Qiang and the nod of Feng's head. Feng crouched next to Jimmy as he sat with his back against the bricks; his black-trousered legs were splayed out and the mask of Springheel Jack leered from the oily cobbles beside him.

"Jimmy!" I halted, unable to be sure what I was seeing. "What—it was you? Springheel Jack was *you*?"

"Aye, and 'tweren't easy, neither, playing this Spring'eel Jack wheeze. Can't say as I know 'ow Mr. Dee does it. The mask all 'eavy, and the bleedin' wings flapping round, and it's all jumping and leaping, and the rain bucketing down—'ere, wot's so funny to yer?" That was addressed to Feng, who was smothering a laugh. "I ain't made for this, I tell yer," Jimmy went on. "My fortune's in me fingers, not no ugly, grinning pantomime!"

"Jimmy, stop!" I said. "Stop! Tell me what's happened to Dee. You threw him off the roof, lad!"

"I never. 'E jumped, so 'e did, when I made like to throw 'im."

"But he landed on the train. He was motionless as the engine started up."

"Well o' course 'e was. It ain't likely 'e'd be taken for dead if 'e was dancing a jig." Jimmy gingerly tested his limbs.

"Taken for—"

But Jimmy, with a groan, clambered to his feet. "Come on, then, we're told to meet Mr. Dee and Sergeant 'Oong at the inn in West Byfleet for instructions. The Duck and Puddle."

"Sergeant Hoong?" I was still bewildered. "Sergeant Hoong is in West Byfleet?"

"Will be by the time we get there. Right now 'e's on 'is way to Brookwood Cemetery. Someone 'ad to drive the train."

"And what of Mr. Cartwright?" I asked weakly.

"It was 'is little bombs what got the train moving. Weren't no one to stoke the engine, but Mr. Cartwright said to Mr. Dee 'e could make the steam. Now you"—he pointed to Feng—"turn yerself around, lass. And yer little dog, too."

Feng, eyes sparkling, did as told. Jimmy stripped off the sodden Springheel Jack outfit, thrusting each piece into a burlap sack as he removed it. As he did so, he extracted from the sack clothing to replace the costume, until finally, wearing his customary trousers, shirt, corduroy jacket, and cloth cap, he laced up his boots, tied up the sack, and threw it over his shoulder. "Mr. Dee said we was to take the first train out. It leaves just after dawn," he said. "I just 'ope the Duck and Puddle lays on a proper breakfast."

CHAPTER FORTY-EIGHT

We easily found the Duck and Puddle near the West Byfleet station, and even more easily located Dee, Hoong, and Cartwright, for they occupied a table in an alcove immediately inside the door.

"Aye, then," the landlord called as we entered the place. "This would be the rest o' yer troupe! Don't say—I'll guess. The animal tamer"—pointing at Feng—"the high-wire walker"—Jimmy—"and the clown." As there was no one else remaining, that designation was clearly assigned to me.

"Indeed," boomed Dee. "Welcome, my friends! Landlord, more tea, if you will. Or bring something stronger if it's desired."

Jimmy's face lit up. "A pint o' yer finest ale, if I might."

I saw as we pulled out chairs to join them that Hoong and Cartwright were halfway through their own pints; in front of Hoong also sat the remains of a ploughman's lunch, and Cartwright was working on a plate of bangers and mash. Grinning, he had stood as we entered and remained on his feet until Feng sat down.

Dee had before him a pot of tea and nothing else, but waving an arm, said grandly, "If my troupe-mates wish victuals, let them eat! Circus is hungry work."

Jimmy brightened even more and requested a full breakfast, with eggs, sausage, tomato, black pudding, fried bread, and beans. Feng asked for toast and a boiled egg for herself, and a plate of sausages for Mei Qiang. I surprised myself by requesting the same meal as Jimmy; an enormous hunger had overtaken me. When the smiling landlord had left us I said, "Dee? Circus?"

Dee dropped his voice from its previous resounding level. "Rather an inspiration, don't you think? The invasion of a West Byfleet inn early in the morning by two Chinese merchants and a British gentleman, soon joined by another Chinese man, a Chinese woman, a British lad, and an exotic dog doesn't offer itself up to easy explanation. Therefore, we are a circus troupe scouting the area for villages likely to welcome our tent. Hoong is the strongman, and I'm the ringmaster. Cartwright is our man of business." The man of business tipped his now-dusty fedora. "We've experienced a warm reception here in West Byfleet."

"Indeed," I said, as the landlord set down Jimmy's ale and two capacious teapots with enough cups for the entire company. "And must I be the clown?"

"Not, of course, a perfect fit, but suspicions might have been aroused if no one took that role."

"My suspicions on that subject are already aroused. However, my elation in finding you thus up and about when last I saw you motionless upon the roof of a moving train—a funeral train at that—is such that I will disregard all doubts and enjoy this life-sustaining tea and the breakfast to come. On a single condition."

"Please, tell me. I will do my utmost to fulfill it, in order to allay any misgivings on your part."

"You must explain."

So Dee explained, as Jimmy and I worked our way through

fried eggs and black pudding, Hoong drained another ale, Cartwright sopped up his bangers and mash, Feng dipped the ends of her toast into her boiled egg, and Mei Qiang made short work of her plate of glistening sausages. Even Dee, who did not care for British food, joined in the drinking of the tea that continued to arrive in fat, round pots.

"The Railway Conspiracy, quite rightly, consider me their enemy," he told us. "For the most part, of course, my concern is with the disastrous consequences for China if Zhang Zuo Lin should gain real power. However, I can't help but consider also the unfortunate outcome that would result from the restoration of the Russian tsar.

"Dee! I took you for a staunch anti-Communist," I said.

"I am that," said Dee, pouring tea all round. Everyone tapped a finger on the table to thank him, a Chinese custom by now familiar to, and adopted with glee by, young Jimmy. Cartwright, I noticed, participated quite naturally. "But in practical terms, if one's ideal solution isn't available, one must look to the lesser of the remaining evils. A union of Russia and Japan, both ruled by ruthless autocrats, poses a great danger to China even without the threat of Zhang's rise." He paused to drink some tea. "The Chinese government agrees. I've been given a new brief by cable from Geneva. It's my responsibility to observe, report on, and do what I can to thwart the actions of the Conspiracy. This would be a demanding task in any case, but, as engineered by Madam Wu, the Metropolitan Police Force consider me a suspect in the Sailors' Palace bombing and the attempted burglary at Madam Wu's home. The incident at Mr. Cartwright's laboratory is sure to be added to that list, and my presence at the Necropolis Railroad terminal is undeniable. Therefore, this seems a useful time to disappear. As London has gotten used to the sudden appearance of Springheel Jack from time to time, I requested Jimmy's aid in enacting a scene—inspired by the execrable motion picture we saw—that seemed to result in my demise."

"Glad to 'elp, o' course," said Jimmy, through a mouthful of beans. "Though next time, if the fighting was less real-like, I can tell you, I'd be gladder."

"I'm sorry." Dee smiled. "But it was necessary for my decease to appear convincing."

"That's why you called for McCorkle and the other bobby. You needed more witnesses than just myself."

"I thought it prudent. Though if young Tim could not be quickly found, I'd have led you up the stairs in any case. I'd noticed the storm had started, and I didn't want to leave poor Jimmy standing in the rain."

"Obliged." The young thief touched his cap.

"Do you really think it will be believed, though?" I asked. "After all, there's no body."

"A body could tumble off the top of a moving train at any number of places, including various marshes and waterways, between London and Surrey," said Dee. "I think the Metropolitan Police, if they aren't bothered by me in the upcoming weeks, may be willing to tentatively assume me dead. Most Conspiracy members will, I'm sure, do the same."

"Most."

"Yes." His face darkened. "Not Madam Wu."

"That was my thought. Do you have any idea where she's gone?"

"I do not, and she must be found. She's the key to support flowing to Zhang Zuo Lin from outside China."

The landlord, smiling at the rock fall of plates, steins, cups, and pots on our table, which must necessarily mean a landslide of pounds and pence into his till, came to ask if there was anything else we required.

"There is not," Dee said, his frown instantly transforming to an answering smile. "I cannot imagine a better welcome than that which West Byfleet has given us! But we must be gone."

We gathered ourselves and rose to the scraping of chairs and the curious looks of locals who'd arrived for their own breakfasts without glancing into our alcove. Cartwright, Feng, Hoong, Jimmy, Mei Qiang, and I issued into the bright, breezy, bird-filled country morning. Dee settled our account and joined us.

"There's a train to Waterloo within the quarter-hour," he said. "Once we reach London, I'll disappear. Lao, if you'll send my possessions round to Russell's, he'll find a way to get them to me."

"But don't say yer really leaving," Jimmy said, sounding almost plaintive. "I mean to say, not going back to that Geneva place. Or China! London ain't the same without yer, Mr. Dee."

"No, Jimmy, have no fear. I have my brief. The Metropolitan Police Force must be set straight on my involvement in recent events, and Madam Wu must be found. I can best accomplish these objectives, or at least set in motion their accomplishment, from a clandestine position. At some point, though, I'll reemerge. I would prefer if you'd all"—he said this but kept his eyes on Jimmy—"stay out of trouble until I do. That way, you'll be available if I should need you."

"Why, sir, I'm the most innocent o' lambs, I am," Jimmy protested.

"No doubt," said Dee.

The gravity of Dee's agreement was undermined by Cartwright's "Ba-a-a-ah."

Cartwright, possibly taking his persona as our man of business too seriously, purchased first-class tickets for us all on the London-bound train. That generous action in effect provided us with our own compartment. Mei Qiang watched us each settle in against the plush seats (Jimmy: "Cor!") and then, as the train started up, the hound chose Dee's feet to lie across.

"You've made a friend," I said.

"More than one, I hope." Dee looked at Feng.

Feng nodded seriously. "I thank you," she said, "for giving me the opportunity to attempt to find justice. I'm sorry we were only partially successful."

"Partial success is success nevertheless," Dee replied. "We'll continue this effort."

"Then I wish you all a great victory."

"Wait," Jimmy broke in. "What yer just said, me lass, that sounds like goodbye if I ever 'eard the word."

Feng met Jimmy's eyes. "I've lost my patron. We must find our own way in the world now, Mei Qiang and I."

"You must no such thing! Are ye mad? I said already, we're yer pals. We ain't letting no pal wander off on 'er own, all alone in this world with no one to 'elp 'er out! Are we, gents?"

"Well," said Sergeant Hoong, "though of course, you must do as you feel right, Feng, I was hoping you'd come stay with me for a time at the shop. Your prowess in combat, and especially your skill with weapons, is such as I haven't seen in quite a while. My own abilities have rusted with the lack of a practice partner. Lao is learning—and, of course, as a street fighter, is more than adequate—but your training and talents would be very useful in honing my own."

"Oh, more than adequate, is that it?" I grumbled, but softly, for I was as interested as anyone in what Feng would say.

Feng said nothing, just regarded Hoong.

"And Mei Qiang, of course," Hoong said. "The back of the shop consists of a number of storerooms. One has been outfitted for my own use, and another could easily be made into yours. It will be small but comfortable. Jimmy, as he'll no doubt be on hand drinking my tea in any case, could help us with the rearrangement. Lao also drops in from time to time. I fancy we can entice Mr. Cartwright to come by on the rare occasions he's in London. That way, we will all be able to enjoy together the peace that the disappearance of Dee will provide."

"You mean, of course," Dee said, "you'll have the opportunity to console one another as you bemoan the dullness of your lives without me."

"Yes," said Hoong. "I mean just that."

Feng turned her look to Mei Qiang, who thumped her tail without otherwise moving. Lifting her eyes again to Hoong, the young woman said, "If you think I could be useful."

"Invaluable," said Hoong, and Jimmy gave Feng a playful punch on the arm.

"See?" he said. "Pals."

CHAPTER FORTY-NINE

At Waterloo Station, we said our goodbyes, Dee promising to remain in London and, as much as possible, in touch. Cartwright, Hoong, Jimmy, Feng, and Mei Qiang all walked together out of the station. Dee, who had emerged from our train car in a cloth cap not unlike Jimmy's and wearing, once again, the white fur eyebrows, stood with me to watch them go.

"Lao," he said in Chinese, as the crowd swallowed them up, "I feel I must apologize."

"If you're speaking on behalf of Hoong and his characterization of my martial skill—"

"I am not," he said. "If it means anything to you, I'm proud to have fought alongside you on numerous occasions." He smiled. "Despite your inability to master the one-inch punch."

My mouth seemed frozen but my chest began to swell.

Dee continued: "No, my apology is in another category entirely. I've often chided you for your attraction to British women. My disapproval is rooted in a certainty—which has not changed, by the way—that any fondness a British woman could feel toward a Chinese man is the same as she'd feel toward a dog or a parrot. True love is not possible in these cases, and thus, the man will end with his heart broken. I don't like to see my friends with their hearts broken.

"However," he continued before I could lodge a protest in support of the fair British sex, "I don't believe that, in any of your flirtations with British women, you've been as blind as I in my attraction to Madam Wu. You once said to me that British women are not alone in their ability to break men's hearts. I fear I must agree and commend you on your perspicacity." He stroked his chin ruefully. "And now, she has disappeared. I never imagined myself acting such a fool."

"Dee!"

"No, Lao, don't contradict me. She used my affection, and her escape is on my shoulders."

"No! Dee!"

"Yes. I—"

"Dee! Dee! Stop! She hasn't! Disappeared. Escaped. There. She's right there!"

He spun to see where I was pointing. On the platform waiting for the train to the Southampton ship terminal stood a familiar cloaked figure. Dee and I shared a glance—and we were off.

The Southampton train was due in three minutes. We were on the platform in two. Approaching Madam Wu through the crowd, we walked silently and slowly, until we stood behind her.

The timing of her spin indicated a clear awareness of our advance. "Dee!" she said with a sardonic smile, letting her cloak's hood fall. "You've come to see me off."

"I've come," he said, "to see that you stay."

"Then I must disappoint you."

With a lightning-fast lunge, he seized her arm. She twisted from his grip and swept a kick, which he bent backward to avoid. I, and others standing open-mouthed on the platform, watched them trade blows. Madam Wu's evident skills and the speed of the combat kept all but one large gentleman from attempting heroics on behalf of the lady. Dee dispatched this noble knight, flipping him so that he landed on his back with an "Oof." Madam Wu was an excellent fighter; but Dee, I knew, was better. Why, then, had he not managed to subdue her in one or two exchanges?

I saw the reason: Dee was holding back.

Wu Ze Tian had been his inamorata. He couldn't bring himself to use the kind of force that would be needed to defeat her.

I had no such warm feelings for the lady; in fact, her treatment of my friend filled me with the heat of righteous anger. It was up to me, then. As the Southampton train blew its approach whistle, I stepped forward. "Madam Wu!"

She whirled to face me. I rooted my soles, gathered the energy of my body from my feet to my forearm, and delivered onto her lovely chin a one-inch punch.

Clearly, I had, finally, mastered the thing. The force of it lifted Madam Wu off the platform and into the air. My warm glow of pride turned to cold ash, however, as Madam Wu executed a double somersault and disappeared over the arriving train.

I charged with Dee to the front of the track's bumper and around the engine to the far platform.

It was empty.

I peered up and down, along the tracks and platforms and into the crowded station. Madam Wu was nowhere to be seen.

Turning my abashed face to Dee, ready to accept a well-deserved reproach, I found him engulfed by hearty laughter. Catching his breath, he spoke. "Oh, Lao! That was splendid! If only Hoong had been here to witness it! You'll have to describe the scene to him."

"He won't believe me."

"No, probably not." Dee wiped his eyes. "I'll have to attest to your account when I reemerge."

"I'm sorry, though—"

"No, no. Finding Madam Wu will be no more difficult now than it would have been had you not spotted her here. I have already some thoughts on the subject. I'll alert people on the Continent, though I suspect if she heads there, her sojourn will be temporary."

"She'll return to China?"

"No. She will, I believe, return here. To England. Where we will await her."

Opening his fist, he gazed at the bat-carved bi on its thin gold chain.

"Dee!" I said. "You managed to retrieve your token in the struggle?"

He shook his head, still gazing at the jade. "Something even more wondrous, Lao. She put it in my hand." He slipped it on. "Farewell, Lao, for a time. I look forward to our reunion."

He grasped my hand, and then, in the swirling steam and churning crowds of Waterloo Station, Dee Ren Jie was gone.

ACKNOWLEDGMENTS

Both authors are grateful beyond measure to Josh Getzler, Jillian Schelzi, and Jon Cobb at HG Literary; to Taz Urnov, Juliet Grames, Lily DeTaeye, and Johnny Nguyen at Soho Crime; and to Sifu Paul Koh and Kristen Rosenfeld at Bo Law Kung Fu.

JOHN:

IT IS SURREAL that this book exists. So much of what has gone into this has taken place over many years, and a lot of fine folks have helped along in the process. Maryelizabeth Yturralde has been sent from heaven. (Note from SJ: I agree.) Cory Jones and Lorelei Bunjes for being so supportive of my author aspirations. Jake Thomas and Mason Rabinowitz.

SJ:

THANKS SO MUCH to:

Laurie King; Dana Cameron; the denizens of Rancho Obsesso; my fellow Sherlockians and especially the Tea Brokers of Mincing Lane; the New York Society Library, where so much of this book was written; and to Gary Siepser at the Saratoga Automobile Museum, who was so generous with his time and knowledge.